A Question

of Risk

Also by L.M. Shakespeare

UTMOST GOOD FAITH

A Question
of Risk

L. M. SHAKESPEARE

St. Martin's Press   **New York**

Library of Congress Cataloging-in-Publication Data

Shakespeare, L. M. (L. Marguerite)
    A question of risk / L.M. Shakespeare.
        p.   cm.
    "A Thomas Dunne book."
    ISBN 0-312-04407-0
    I. Title.
PR6069.H285Q47   1990
823'.914—dc20   89-78019
                                                  CIP

First published in Great Britain by Macdonald & Co., Ltd.

First U.S. Edition
10 9 8 7 6 5 4 3 2 1

for
DAVID

Fonti amoris,
sapientiae,
delectationis,
ingenii

Acknowledgments

I am particularly grateful to David Evers for his invaluable advice on background material. Also to Jeremy Norman for the interesting light he cast on certain aspects of the story and for the inspired phrase he used in another connection which resulted in my thinking of the title. My thanks are also due to Ian Posgate for intriguing discussions; and the poet whose name I cannot trace but who wrote the lines which I memorised fifteen or twenty years ago and quote on page 106; and, most especially, to my father, Dr John Ernest Thomas, for his help on the medical background.

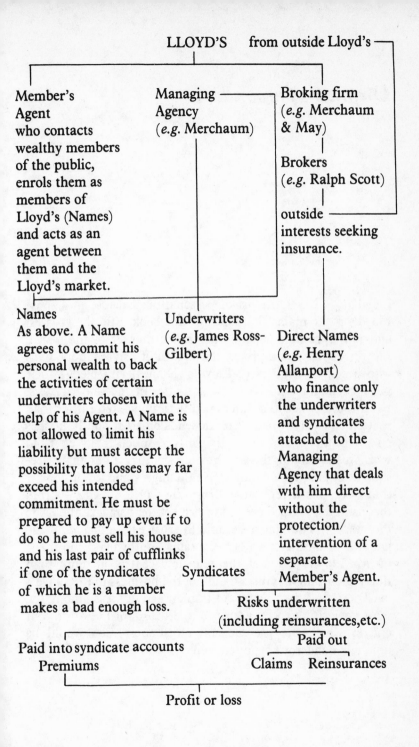

LLOYD'S   from outside Lloyd's

Member's Agent
who contacts wealthy members of the public, enrols them as members of Lloyd's (Names) and acts as an agent between them and the Lloyd's market.

Managing Agency
(*e.g.* Merchaum)

Broking firm
(*e.g.* Merchaum & May)

Brokers
(*e.g.* Ralph Scott)

outside interests seeking insurance.

Names
As above. A Name agrees to commit his personal wealth to back the activities of certain underwriters chosen with the help of his Agent. A Name is not allowed to limit his liability but must accept the possibility that losses may far exceed his intended commitment. He must be prepared to pay up even if to do so he must sell his house and his last pair of cufflinks if one of the syndicates of which he is a member makes a bad enough loss.

Underwriters
(*e.g.* James Ross-Gilbert)

Direct Names
(*e.g.* Henry Allanport)
who finance only the underwriters and syndicates attached to the Managing Agency that deals with him direct without the protection/intervention of a separate Member's Agent.

Syndicates

Risks underwritten (including reinsurances,etc.)

Paid into syndicate accounts   Paid out
          Premiums   Claims   Reinsurances

Profit or loss

Dramatis personae

Lloyd's . . . heads the list of personalities because in a sense Lloyd's is the main 'character' in this book. Still the greatest and most prestigious single insurance market in the world, Lloyd's depends entirely on the wealth of private individuals who become members of Lloyd's (Names) and pledge their personal fortunes to back the activities of the underwriters. Until recently Lloyd's functioned with unwritten rather than written rules. The institution depends on trust and flourishes on the reputation of its participants as much today as it did when it started in the seventeenth-century London coffee-shop belonging to Mr Lloyd. But the high standard of honour that won such a reputation from the world outside — from the insured — is also needed to protect the participants inside the market. They must be able to trust each other; and the handful of businessmen, sea-captains and owners who made up Mr Lloyd's original clientèle now centre on more than thirty thousand members handling the business in the Lloyd's market. Of all the theatres of human activity it is among the most powerful, expert, varied; a microcosm of the world, but one in which the presence of a dishonest man would be uniquely dangerous if undetected.

James Ross-Gilbert . . .	Leading underwriter of the syndicates managed by Merchaum Managing Agency. He is also Chairman of Merchaum itself.
Richard Trene (also known as Dick) . . .	His partner.
Ralph Scott . . .	Closely involved with James and Richard. Works as a broker for Merchaum & May, the brokers.
Sarah Scott . . .	His wife.
Nick Victor . . .	Broker with broking firm Cleave & Engels.
Marjorie Ross-Gilbert . . .	James's outgoing wife.
Philippa Oakes . . .	Mistress and new wife in line.
Mary Seymour . . .	Top-flight economist with Government and City influence who writes for *The Times* and lectures at London University.
George Seymour . . .	Her husband, and a well-known playwright.
Sir Kenneth Dunphy . . .	Minister for Trade and Industry; George's cousin.
Ann Dunphy . . .	Kenneth's sister.
Simon Laurie . . .	Currently a famous actor and also a Name on the James Ross-Gilbert (JRG) syndicates.
Lady Celia Merrin . . .	Simon's girlfriend, and Henry Allanport's cousin.
Henry Allanport . . .	Lord Allanport; a direct Name on the JRG syndicates.
Delia Allanport . . .	His wife.
Rupert Doone . . .	Delia's brother; a broker in the City and at Lloyd's.
Spencer Day . . .	Chairman of Managing Agency Day & Monitor, and also member of the Committee of Lloyd's.
Roger Collingham Tom Grates Roland Pierce } . . .	Other members of Lloyd's Committee.
Grace Derby . . .	A financial journalist.
Maldwyn (Mal) Harris . . .	Loss assessor/investigator with the organisation Shipping Investigation Securities.

Chapter 1

'ARE YOU REALLY the most successful underwriter and Chairman of the biggest Managing Agency in Lloyd's?'

'Yes.'

'Do you want to know who says you're not?'

'I'd be more interested,' he said imperturbably, 'to know how you managed to remember such a long sentence all in one, Pussy.'

It was a compliment. She smiled. From a man who believed that a woman's intelligence had to be in inverse ratio to her sexuality and physical beauty, Philippa Oakes knew how to take flattery. She lay in bed, her body voluptuous, damp, satisfied, flung out with probably unconscious grace half under the sheet. Outside, the afternoon London sky sailed indifferently past the window.

James Ross-Gilbert, dressed in his shirt and underpants, stood with his back to her, arranging his tie in the mirror. 'And who was that then, Pussy?'

'Laura.'

It was more of a pleasure to him to look distinguished than it once had been to look young, and these days mirrors gave him great satisfaction. 'Sour grapes!' he said, and winked at her unsmilingly in the glass.

'Come back to bed!'

He shook his head, looking at her reflexion past his own

without turning round. 'Wife time, Ducky. Plane to catch.'
He could see the hot dimples of desire denting the skin under
her eyes again, and turned round, still with one hand on his
tie, inflexible but pleased.

'Come here.'

He did, but only long enough to kiss her and feed, just for
an instant, the little flames that were beginning to burn again
under her skin.

'When will you be back?'

'Tuesday.'

'Oooh!'

He pushed back the sheet and stroked, very lightly, one
long line down the side of her body to the thigh. Her closed
eyelids began to sweat. 'You wouldn't like it anyway,' he said.
'It's going to be a business weekend.'

'Bloody Marjorie will be there.'

Surprisingly enough, she could even say that without
breaking her sexual continuity. He still gazed at her with the
solemn expression of age and status. She was exceptionally
beautiful. Her body showed no signs at all of the two children
she had had: wavy titian hair, skin of pure cream, five foot
eight inches, no distinguishing scars, thirty-three, born in
Manchester, and the new passport would have 'Mrs Ross-
Gilbert' on it and bloody Marjorie could take her alimony and
join the other three exes.

'Buy your wedding dress, Pussy,' he said. 'It will help pass
the time, and I'll take care of bloody Marjorie.'

He stood up and finished dressing. Shrugging on his jacket,
he stepped over to the window. It was a mews house, quite
small, and down below on the cobbles the Rolls had noiselessly arrived. He glanced at the time.

Philippa hadn't moved, but watched him through the crack
of her almost closed eyes. 'Say Hello to the Med for me.'

He gave one smile, and closed the door.

Chapter 2

'JAMES, WHO ON earth is Lady Celia Merrin? I thought you said . . .'

'One of our guests, Marjorie. She's Simon Laurie's friend of the moment and naturally we've asked them together.'

'Well, she needs a lift to the plane.'

'That's all right. Is she on her way?'

'But we're ready!'

This was Marjorie, standing just inside the open front door of the house in Chester Square. The afternoon had turned very grey, but it was getting glossed up in this corner of London by a consciously orchestrated scene of departure. A Ferrari loaded with luggage, a maid and a cook had just been driven off, and the Rolls was ready now to follow with Mr and Mrs Ross-Gilbert if only Celia Merrin would turn up.

'She's Lord Weeks's daughter.'

'Oh my God, not that one! Honestly, James!'

'No problem for us,' he said. 'We're going on the yacht, remember?'

She turned away, busy with her arrangements, and he watched her with cool detachment. He had nothing against Marjorie, but under the influence of her marriage to himself she had simply lost every shred of her charm.

A taxi had arrived, and an expensively scruffy-looking young girl stepped out. She looked up through a tangled mass of blond hair and said, 'Oh gosh! Don't say I've kept you.'

'Celia!'

James hurried down the steps with a delighted smile, kissed her, paid the cab and stopped himself just in time before taking her suitcase, and with a gesture drew one of the servants towards him at a run to snatch it up from the pavement and stow it in the Rolls.

'Marjorie, you haven't met, have you? My wife Marjorie, Celia Merrin.'

'My God, how grand!' Celia said, and carried on talking as they hustled her into the car. 'And Simon said we're being flown in your private jet. My Dad would adore this. He loves being posh, but Mummy won't let him because she says it's vulgar.' Neither James nor Marjorie was quite sure if they had heard what she said in the inevitable slight confusion of deciding where to sit, and she rattled on, smelling fairly strongly of gin, until they arrived at the runway.

Simon Laurie was already there, having come from the other direction where he was starring in a film in the west country. It was good timing. He could absorb the flak of Celia's doty conversation and slightly unsteady legs in his prestigious aura while the business side of the weekend assembled. By the time the ministerial car drew up and the Lloyd's contingent arrived, it had begun to rain. Nobody even noticed. Rain in England was already stale as last week's newspapers. It wouldn't be raining in the South of France. In a flurry of greetings and introductions, muted by that sense of being premature to the real action, they settled in the plane and flew immediately into the sunlight.

Mary Seymour, who had spent the afternoon in the newspaper office where some little tyke from Art had stolen the only comfortable chair out of her section, sank with real appreciation into the dark blue upholstered velvet. Her husband George, sitting beside her, smelt slightly of his bathless rush from the theatre to the airport. Sensing her attention but not knowing what it was about, he shifted his huge bony hand and wrapped it around her fingers while still lying back with his eyes closed.

14

She said, 'Gil's reviewing your play.'

'So is everyone else.'

She considered that. 'Yes. I suppose they are.'

He seemed to wake up suddenly, and said, 'Did you see it?'

'I sneaked a look.'

'What does he say?'

'Are you sure you don't want to wait and read it yourself?'

'Good or bad?'

She smiled at him with real affection. They were both as plain as two pikestaffs: dark blond hair, lumpy features, spectacles, forty-five and forty-three respectively. It was bad luck, as even genius needs a bit of presentation.

'Good,' Mary said. 'Something about masterly use of language up to your usual standard, moments which are deeply moving, but the direction lets you down at the end because of an over-quirky interpretation.'

George sighed. 'Thank God for a weekend away!'

'Away from what?'

'The theatre, of course. And the Press.'

She knew something. 'Did you hear that, Kenneth?' she said, talking over her shoulder to George's cousin.

Ann Dunphy, Kenneth's sister, sitting beside him, leaned forward and said, 'He's asleep, Mary.'

'Oh.'

'What do you mean?' George said, reclaiming Mary's attention. 'Is there something up?'

But she said only, 'Maybe. I notice Richard, James's partner, is with us this weekend. The combination of Sir Kenneth Dunphy and a bit of Lloyd's top brass and, if you'll forgive my mentioning it, myself, paves the way for some purposeful bargaining or at least discussion on current market issues. So when you talk of a weekend away from work, speak for yourself.' And she smiled at him.

Richard Trene, James Ross-Gilbert's partner, was sitting some distance behind, without his wife, drinking champagne. His wife had refused to come because Sarah Scott was included. Whether or not such an absence was an intelligent way of coping with a flirtation remained to be seen. James, who knew the story, speculated idly as he strolled down the plane towards his friend. It didn't matter to him either way. He sat down beside him.

'You've cooked up a really bloody working weekend, haven't you, James?'

'Don't be unfriendly,' Ross-Gilbert responded, cool and apparently unoffended.

'Well, I don't like having to field Sir Kenneth Dunphy, the Minister of Trade and Industry, at the same time as that blasted sister-in-law of his, Mary Seymour.'

'She's not his sister-in-law. She's his cousin's wife.' James sipped his champagne with the unhurried good humour of a hospital visitor who had set aside fifteen minutes, as needed.

'The *Sunday Times* described her last weekend as the greatest political commentator and wit of our century. Did you see it?' Richard asked the question indignantly, turning his head and adding the crucial point to his protest. 'She's as ugly as the back end of a bus!'

'What's that got to do with it?'

'Confounded woman!'

'Or that either?' James smiled, not because he disagreed. 'Look, Dick . . .' He spoke with charm, like a benign prince pointing out his own domain. 'Concentrate on the blue sea, the sparkling air, the sun. Talk to George Seymour about his plays, our actor friend about his, or flirt with Celia Merrin or Sarah, or both. You only have to give the impression that you back me up in everything I say about Lloyd's. The actual conversation you can leave to me and Ralph Scott.'

'And that's another thing,' Richard said, sullen again but quieter. 'If Sarah keeps on at me, there'll be trouble.'

'What do you mean?'

'I can hardly expect Ralph to like it.'

James considered. 'Don't rock the boat, then.'

'Aptly put. But what if she comes to my cabin, like she did last time, stark naked and saying she can't sleep?' In spite of himself, Richard had started to smile before he'd finished the sentence.

'My God, I don't know how you do it!' Ross-Gilbert flattered. 'But don't, for God's sake, let a row brew up with Ralph. We need a united front.' He got up, looking at his

16

watch. 'I'll get back to Marjorie. We'll be landing in five minutes.'

He went down the plane, invigorated by the almost ever-present sensation of powerful well-being that accumulated in the wake of his reputation. He smiled particularly at Mary Seymour as he passed her chair, and she smiled back. He said, 'Just arriving.'

She felt a little surge of electric attention as if she was a small child being primed for the seaside; or was there a more grown-up frequency there, a certain something else, quickly followed by distrust; and then was that just because, as a rather ugly woman, one didn't expect flirtation from desirable successful men only ten years older than oneself; or was it a tiny trace from a spark of something else, a flash of brimstone, a whiff of the devil, a warning flash of distant nasty lightning? Fortunately, having a brain like a human computer, she would be able to sort it all out in time.

Chapter
3

CELIA MERRIN, beautiful but with an awful hangover, lay with ankles, wrists, shoulders, arms strung like a fragile necklace over a deckchair at seven on'clock in the morning, Gossamer sunlight cast in an even mesh of gold and vanishing half an inch above the blue water gave her pale face the burnished outline of an old photograph. Apart from her, the deck was empty. The air, cool and delicate, smelt of peace and space and the final simple surprising unravelling of all human cares. Even later in the day, when one by one the guests began to circulate, the engine was started up and the crew passed to and fro on various errands, still that atmosphere of slightly dislocated contentment prevailed.

Simon Laurie, appearing on deck as on the margin of an already occupied stage, stood gazing at Celia. He was thinking to himself that she was like Wordsworth's description of the soul, 'remembering/how she felt but what she felt remembering not/retains an obscure sense of possible sublimity . . .' He looked around for someone else with whom he could share the joke of such a wittingly misapplied quotation, and, at once, there was George Seymour.

'I'll say one thing for you, James,' Marjorie privately declared later when George and Simon had been locked in conversation for about five hours. 'You are a brilliant host. I couldn't imagine why you'd invited our famous actor on your business weekend except as camouflage, and now look! He and your famous playwright are friends for life, leaving Mary Seymour free to pay attention to anything you say.'

But to return to something like midday on Saturday, Celia opened her eyes. The waiter had just snapped open a starched white cloth and laid it flapping on the table before her on the deck. In the wind of their passage its tethered corners rippled. She turned her head cautiously aside. Near by, Simon and George Seymour's conversation came to her with the intermittent soothing clarity of seaside voices. In beautiful stillness she watched the vast airy space of the blue sky and the open sea and the comfortable activity of the servants preparing lunch. It was a moment she would remember well for the rest of her life. Years later, when she no longer got drunk, it was one fragment of memory she could retrieve like an unbroken piece of beautiful china from a decade of shards.

Nothing in Ann Dunphy's experience had ever equalled that afternoon. James Ross-Gilbert deserved his wife's commendation of himself as a host for his treatment of Ann, if for nothing else. Sir Kenneth Dunphy, her brother, the Minister for Trade and Industry, had a reputation for both an acute and a discerning mind. In fact, he had neither. He simply had the face and figure of a man who should: tall, spare, handsome, with an aquiline nose and dark wavy hair. Men in the Commons called him brilliant in the same spirit as bread is generally cast upon the waters. But he was indeed an elegant man of very limited intelligence, who loved two things: power and his sister.

James judged that time spent being charming to Ann would stand him in good stead in the forthcoming discussion which he planned to orchestrate with his distinguished guests on the subject of the recommendations in the Fisher Report for the reorganisation and regulation of Lloyd's. He was right. What was less a matter of calculation and more of luck was that Mary Seymour should also be impressed. Ann Dunphy knew nothing about Lloyd's, and he had sat there patiently and seemed to put his whole heart into bringing her into the picture. He set the stage of the whole thing: Mr Lloyd's little coffee-shop in the City of London in the seventeenth century, with captains, owners and businessmen exchanging insurance deals on scraps of paper carried between the tables by the waiters along with the coffee. And the modern underwriting room in the new Lloyd's building operated in much the same way. As he talked, he was conscious at the same time of his wider audience listening to what he said, including his colleague Ralph Scott, with only half an ear, and Mary Seymour, who knew it all. But he kept his attention on Ann. She wondered if he had got some Irish blood in him to be turning it all into such a tale.

'Do tell me one thing,' Ann said. 'I've always wanted to know what they mean when they talk about an underwriter's Box. What's a Box?'

'Oh, it's a chair,' he said, and they all laughed. 'You see, in the original coffee-shop, the seating was a series of benches arranged in hollow squares each around a table, and that arrangement has been kept, and is what is called a Box. Each underwriter is alloted one in the Room at Lloyd's with a number, and he sits at it so that the brokers know where to find him.' He glanced up, and avoided Ralph's bitter eye.

'I'm such a fool. I should know all this already.' Ann said.

'Not at all. Not at all.' He gave her a rare smile, and although her plain face registered no reaction, she thought him absolutely charming. 'Very few people really understand how Lloyd's works, I can tell you,' He allowed a conspiratorial note of sarcasm to edge his voice. 'The way some newspapers report and I'm afraid some ill-informed Members of Parliament, Kenneth – ' he deferred to his important guest with a glance which the Minister acknowledged without rancour – 'you would never guess that Lloyd's is the most successful single insurance institution in the world with an unbroken record for honouring its debts.'

'Is it really? Is that a fact?' Ann said.

'Yes,' he said. 'Wouldn't you say, Mary? You don't deal in romantic fantasies.'

She nodded consideringly, and said, 'Yes, I think that's all true.'

If Sir Kenneth Dunphy knew that he was the actual focus

of a sales talk while this was going on, he didn't acknowledge it. He kept out of the conversation, sitting in his chair with his face tilted to the sun.

'And so the brokers go to the Room in Lloyd's,' Ann persisted, like a rather stolid middle-aged child, her face solemn and her plain grey hair hanging round it, 'and . . .'

'They carry leather folders full of slips of paper bearing the details of insurance orders and they go from Box to Box buying cover at the best rate they can get.' James was getting tired of it. 'All this is rather dry stuff, I'm afraid.'

'No, no. Fascinating.'

'Even so, you'd like a drink, I'm sure. Mary? Kenneth?' He beckoned to a servant who had kept his distance but with his eye on the alert. 'Bring us some champagne. And who would like something more strenuous? Whisky? Gin?' He sorted it all out, using the disturbance deftly to turn a page in the conversation. When they had settled down again, they were ready for business. James began by saying, 'I read your article on the Fisher Report in *The Times*, Mary.'

She said nothing, but merely looked an acknowledgement over the rim of her glass.

'I can't say that I entirely agreed with it, though.'

'Really?' said the Minister. 'I thought the general view was that it was time for a bit of formal regulation.'

'Some, perhaps,' was the grudging reply.

'Well,' Kenneth held his glass on the wooden arm of his chair and turned his head, 'functioning on unwritten rather than written rules can't go on for ever in such a growing market, you know.'

'With respect,' James said. He used that phrase now and then. There was a statesmanlike contradiction implicit in it. 'With respect, although of course Fisher has made some recommendations I agree with, I think that to start legislating over Lloyd's will be the death of it. It works very well as it is.' The fact was, he himself found it extremely convenient.

'I thought you were a witness,' Mary Seymour said.

'Not one Fisher listened to, it seems.'

When not in the company of other academics like Mary Seymour, James tended to have a thing or two to say on the whole subject of retired judges and academic luminaries being invited to interefere in commerce which they didn't understand.

'Then you think things should be left as they are?'

'Not entirely.'

Ralph smiled with cynical awareness into his glass. The yacht at anchor far out to sea rose and fell with a breathing motion on the water.

'I can see,' the Minister said, falling into line with the opinion of the moment with unconscious complaisance, 'that too much interference with the *status quo* could be dangerous.'

James kept silent, not reiterating his agreement. He let the Minister's remark stand a moment. He knew exactly how to create a climate of opinion among a small group of people.

'Where unwritten rules . . .' He got that far, facing to the sky like everyone else. Out of the corner of his eye he could see the Minister's short-sleeved linen shirt from Turnbull and Asser, and his grey flannel trousers. Ralph wore something similar. Dick Trene lurked somewhere out of sight in his weekend gear of short-cut shirt worn outside a pair of slacks. But James himself wore a long-sleeved shirt of very fine lawn, with cufflinks. The breeze blew the cloth with something like the debonair style of a Spanish matador, and he lay back at his ease with his legs stretched in the sun. This was only the beginning. He carried on not quite where he had left off, saying, 'As things are now, an underwriter may merely pencil his initial on a slip to indicate that he has accepted a commitment on some business, and that scrap of paper is honoured, no matter what it costs. My word is my bond. That's how the market operates. But let Parliament pave the way for rules and by-laws – but speak to Ralph. He doesn't agree with me, do you, Ralph?'

'There's no harm in introducing some of Fisher's recommendations.'

In actual fact, neither of them wanted any. An increase of formality in the market's structure and the imposition of new rules were something they both viewed with disfavour as promising to be intensely inconvenient. But it was a matter of tactics.

'Which ones?' put in Mary Seymour. 'Divestment? Brokers not being allowed to own Managing Agencies?'

Ralph was prepared to be open minded. This was stage one. He took up his cue, in his role of devil's advocate. James himself leaned back, the picture of a tolerant man prepared to listen. Sir Kenneth managed not to let his attention wander.

Looking from one to the other, Mary Seymour suddenly realised, without resentment, that in fact James and Ralph were working together. Before Sunday evening they would identify the better product. She already doubted whether 'divestment' would prove capable of removing grass-stains without prolonged soaking in boiling water.

'Simon!' yelled Celia, 'Everyone! Look, dolphins!'

It was while the assembled company was still hanging over the rail that the phone rang in Ross-Gilbert's day cabin, and the steward picked it up. Mentally reviewing progress so far, James made his way below deck with the steward following, and without bothering to close his cabin door picked up the phone. He was not expecting bad news.

Marjorie, trailing after him five minutes later to ask some stupid question, found him replacing the receiver, and was startled almost to tears by the look of absolute venom as he raised his face to hers. 'What is it?'

He decided to economise on trouble, and stepping past her to close the door, patted her on the shoulder, and said, 'Just business.'

'Something's wrong!'

'Nothing for you to worry about, Marge. Just some blasted fool in London.'

'Oh!' she said uncertainly. 'Well, I only came to fetch the camera. Have you got it?'

He gestured towards the bookcase without speaking and stood with his hand on the steward's bell, waiting for her to go. She bent carefully, anxious for her body to look good. She wore high heels and a backless sundress. The only thing she need really have worried about was being quick. When eventually she had gone, James pressed the bell and waited for the steward. In the time that it took for Ralph Scott and Richard

23

Trene to be fetched from the deck, he stood waiting like a man in a dream, surface anger burnt out in calculation. Predictably, when he arrived, Richard Trene was already in a panic. Ralph Scott, following close behind him, closed the door and said, 'Trouble?'

'Yes.' Ross-Gilbert's air of stern judicial calm both controlled and alarmed his partner, whose expression was already slightly soured with contradiction. James glanced at him, but with deliberate brevity. 'Trouble,' he continued, 'because some blasted journalist in London has written an investigative article for tomorrow's Press about Con-Re.'

'How do you mean "investigative"?' said Ralph slowly. 'Investigating what?'

'Roll-over funds, what happens to our quota shares, but mainly who . . .' He stopped short, then added, 'Who owns what.'

'Well, that's all right, isn't it?' Richard cut in with heavy aggression.

James just looked at him.

'How much have they got hold of?'

'A fair bit, Ralph. Someone seems to have poked his nose into bank accounts and share holdings.'

'Whose names have they got?'

'The three of us, and Peter, and a bit of misinformation about Nick Victor.'

There was a momentary silence. Finally, Richard said, 'Which paper?'

'*Sunday Times.*'

He came back at once. 'Well, it's valid business! Re-insurances passed on to registered companies. What's wrong with that?'

James turned, one hand in his pocket, the other resting on a sheaf of papers, of which he flicked the corners three or four times against the ball of his thumb. He said, 'Shut up, Dick!'

'Look here!'

James calmed him, smoothing the air between them with the flat of his hand. 'Sorry. Sorry.' He subsided. 'Let's have a drink, and I'll tell you both what's going on. Ralph?'

'Thanks.'

'Scotch for you, Dick?' He moved over to the drinks and took up the story once more. 'I forget the blasted hack's name; somebody new. Anyway, we will of course maintain, as we perfectly well can, that our methods are all accepted business practice. But I thought you should both be warned –' he handed a drink to Richard Trene and turned back – 'that an unflattering account of the layout will appear in the papers.'

'The public never does understand the convolutions of Lloyd's business.'

'That's it, Ralph. That's the line. And they don't.'

'I don't think we have anything to worry about,' Ralph continued in his bored drawl. 'But I could do with not being cooped up with Mary Seymour tomorrow. Can't you say the launch is broken down or the Sunday papers were sold out in Nice?'

Ross-Gilbert sighed. 'Well, such is fate. Now, Richard,' he said, turning to him, 'leave it to me. Ralph and I will do the footwork.'

The remark goaded instead of calming his partner. 'Don't treat me like some damn . . .' he searched for the word, 'wife!'

Ralph gave a short sharp bark of laughter. James tried to silence him with a look, but he carried on, 'James isn't giving you the heave-ho, Dick. That's Marjorie.'

'Enough. Enough.'

In the sudden silence, the throbbing of the yacht's internal workings emphasised the possibility of being overheard.

'It's all right,' James reminded them. 'The bathroom's on that side, my bedroom on the other. But appearances are important. We just happen to have people on board this weekend who won't miss it if we make mistakes.'

Richard stared glumly into the last of his whisky, swallowed it, and said, 'All right. Don't worry about me. I suppose it's all a mare's nest.'

Ralph, who rarely set eyes on Dick without developing a discreetly unpleasant curl to the corner of his lip, eyed him now without mockery. He watched him get up, the whisky-glass snap down with miscalculated force, the short-sleeved shirt and slacks, the pressed vowels, all of which would appear on the TV screen in time with their owner making a V-sign to

25

the Press from his multi-million-dollar estate in Spain. He had the sensation of his whole life passing before his eyes, but what the hell he was about to drown in was beyond his power to know.

Chapter
4

'I'M TOO OLD for that sort of thing.'

Mary looked at George with private regret because he was bound to take her down with him, being only two years her senior. She ventured to say, 'Well, I feel as fresh as a daisy!' but it didn't arouse any interest. 'How are you after last night, Celia?'

'Awful!'

There was a case in point. Young girl, just about able to stagger into the launch at two a.m. after dining and dancing in Monte Carlo, sitting with her eyes closed as they glided under the stars. How much of that magical pool of inky darkness and swimming glitter of lights had she noticed? Too tired (and too drunk) to care. And just because she was beautiful and young, everyone would assume that the evening had belonged to her. Mary observed this without bitterness; but no woman born really plain can ever be expected to get over it.

Breakfast was nearly finished. All the guests were on deck. Simon Laurie stretched in his chair, and said, 'Oh my! How perfectly wonderful!'

'Isn't it heaven? So beautiful.'

'And so peaceful. Isn't it, Kenneth?'

'I should say, my dear.'

'No builder's labourers moonlighting over the weekend with their trannies lashed to the scaffolding.'

Ann Dunphy looked bemused. She couldn't think what Sarah was talking about. Then she got it. 'Oh no,' she said. 'Of course not.'

'Think of something, Celia. Your turn.'

'Can't.'

They relapsed into silence, until Mary said, 'James really is amazing.'

Celia, still motionless with her eyes closed, murmered, 'I should say! Brilliant! He can dance, too.' Simon laughed, picked up her limp hand, and kissed it. She said, 'Well, I like all this luxury. I think he's jolly clever!'

'Here he is,' said Ralph, who was standing at the rail, looking out towards the land.

'I can't stand that Baie des Anges thing,' Sarah said, coming up beside him, 'What has he been ashore for?' She looked down at James as the launch came under the side of the yacht and he prepared to clamber out.

'The papers, I think.'

'Oh, good!' George exclaimed with sudden animation. 'Has James got the Sunday papers?'

Simon looked at him consideringly for a split second, and then said, 'Of course. They'll have your reviews.'

It was typical of Ross-Gilbert that he would actually go with the launch on this particular morning and get the papers himself. In the matter of his own fortunes and everything accruing to them, he allowed no one to come between himself and the event. In addition, his facility for impressing those around him with an awareness of his own presence was matched by the ease with which he could charm. It wasn't done by smiling. His behaviour was often almost severe. But, by contrast, when he did turn his attention on someone, he did so with a sort of concentrated composure that shut off all other claims and settled with a flattering intensity. He did this now to Mary Seymour. When he stepped on to the deck and had been charming in general for two minutes and praised his guests and the weather he distributed the papers, his cool eye checking the spontaneous warmth of their reactions like a prince who pushes away a handshake after half a second, he settled in a chair beside Mary with an air of confidential relief as if he had been waiting for hours for a chance to enjoy her company, and nothing else. His gaze became warm and confiding, and he simply said, 'Isn't this marvellous!'

Her heartfelt 'Yes' included, unawares, the additional pleasure of being flattered.

'I never tire of coming here, you know.'

'Oh, I'm not surprised, James.'

'Marvellous place! It seems to be like this all the time and almost all the year round.'

'It's the ideal weekend cottage, isn't it?' Mary said. She laughed. 'Only an hour from London.'

They were silent for a moment, and then James said, 'How's your university work these days? Are you still lecturing?'

'Yes, certainly.'

'And your column in the paper?'

'Yes.'

'And then you're on several advisory committees.'

'Not the Lloyd's bill, though.'

'No. Pity, that.'

'How do you mean?'

'We need all the help we can get.'

If someone had reminded Mary at that moment that she had known James Ross-Gilbert personally, as opposed to by repute, only for about two months, she would have been mildly taken aback. 'Well, Kenneth is your man,' she said.

'Oh yes, I'm glad to say.' He sighed. 'Bloody difficult, though.'

'Well, the Lloyd's market's not an easy one to understand. I suppose you've got to make a whole committee of outsiders actually grasp all these convoluted relationships.'

'Impossible.'

'Yes,' she said reflectively. 'I know what you mean.'

'You should just sit in on one of the parliamentary committees.' He had lowered his voice.

She laughed. 'I can imagine it must be hell!'

James was genuinely enjoying the conversation, the chair in

which he sat, the blue sky overhead and Mary herself. He was like a fisherman peacefully beside some other piece of water with some other fish just nibbling at the end of his line. He said, 'Describe it for me.'

'Well . . .' She glanced to one side, but Kenneth was talking to Ann, and the immensity of space seemed to make hearing at a distance difficult, like listening to a sound inside a bell. 'There will be at least one, and probably several, committee members who still have a basic misunderstanding of some of the essential working relationships in Lloyd's.'

'Yes.'

'They won't have straightened out the Managing Agencies who manage syndicates, as opposed to the Members' Agents who look after Names, for example. Or premium limits, or unlimited liability as it applies to Names, or any number of details. *But* they have to *pretend* they know, because they have been told once, and they are not going to admit they haven't grasped it.'

'Go on.' James was laughing, and her whole face and body were radiating the enjoyment of a performer with a special audience.

'Also, then, when it comes to arguing details of self-regulation, and divestment and the other Fisher recommendations, they are desperate. They can't bear to be insignificantly silent, but almost every foray into speech is fraught with potential disaster.'

'Have you sat in on one of the committees?'

'Yes, and I can tell you the footwork was hilarious.'

'But how on earth are they going to reach a sensible conclusion?'

'Oh, they will,' she said. 'There'll be four or five who really understand, and they'll end up recommending what the market wants them to recommend. And the others will agree like clever chaps who have too much sense of self-preservation to try to argue when they don't actually know what day of the week it is.'

He gave another little appreciative shout of laughter.

'And are you,' she suddenly said, 'pro or against Fisher, really?'

'Against.'

'Your Managing Agency is Merchaum, isn't it?'

'That's right.'

'So they are your employers. They manage the syndicate affairs and you do the underwriting for . . . how many syndicates?'

'About twenty syndicate numbers.'

'But aren't you also a controlling shareholder of Merchaum?'

'You have done your homework,' he said drily.

'So the fact that Merchaum also owns . . .'

'Merchaum & May?'

'Exactly. Merchaum & May, the brokers, means that you'd be in the front line if it came to divestment. The broking firm would have to divest itself of its interest in the Managing Agency, or *vice versa*.'

James looked bored. 'Pity Kenneth's not listening,' he said rather insultingly.

Mary looked at him. 'Regulation's always incredibly annoying,' she said sympathetically. 'But I think you're right about divestment, if that's really your opinion. How can a broker get his client a genuinely advantageous quote for a risk if he has an ulterior motive to accept the terms of a particular underwriter?'

'Oh, quite.'

'And, conversely, an underwriter decline bad business if he has an interest in the brokerage?'

'There is another side to it, you know.'

She remembered the state of play the day before, and said, 'How do you mean?', keeping the quizzical note almost out of her voice.

'With a secure business relationship, the brokers and underwriters can arrange more advantageous terms.'

'Who for?'

'Oh well, if you're going to take that tone, Mary.' He had let his eyelids droop as if to resist the glare of the sun. She stayed silent. Finally he opened his eyes, looked at his watch, and said, 'I would just love a Campari and fresh orange-juice, wouldn't you?'

31

'Oh yes,' she said. 'Marvellous!' As he rose, she reached forward and took up a copy of the *Sunday Times*. He knew that by the time he came back she would have come across the article on Con-Re.

For a while there was complete silence. Kenneth was reading the *Sunday Telegraph*. Mary turned first to the theatre reviews. George had walked to the back of the deck, and, returning, came over to her and said, 'Not bad, do you think, darling?'

'Very good,' she murmured, still reading. 'What about the others?'

'I'll fetch them.'

He stepped over to the table to take copies of the other papers, when Celia cut in, 'You're not the only one in the limelight today, George. Here's a whole feature about James in *The Times*.'

'Oh, really? Which section?'

'Business news.'

'What are you doing reading the business news?' Simon teased her indulgently.

'Oh, I'm just so tweeny-minded,' she said, 'I can't be bothered to look at what I'm reading before I start.'

'Oh, ouch!'

She stuck her tongue out at him. Mary extracted the business section and opened it.

'Pass me a spare copy of *The Times*, will you, George?' Kenneth called to his cousin, and George shuffled through the pile.

'Have this one,' said Celia. 'I'm going for a swim.'

By the time James returned, they had indeed read the article on Con-Re. The Minister would in all probability be too polite a guest to broach the subject, but James could see perfectly well what he was reading. 'I gather one of my firms is in the wars today. Here you are, Mary. Fresh oranges from Nice market, plenty of Campari, plenty of ice.'

'Oh, thank you!' She smiled broadly as she took it, her large solidly formed mouth curving pleasantly over robust white teeth, the sun or a reflection from the water momentarily reglazing the outer surface of her spectacles with a shield of light. She indicated the newspaper she was reading with her other hand, and said, 'Reinsurance is like the agro-chemical industry of the Lloyd's world, isn't it? The evil deeds department.'

He smiled back as if her amusing turn of phrase was all that mattered. 'Where's Ann?'

Kenneth said, 'Oh, I think she went off somewhere with Marjorie.'

'Will you have one of these, Minister?'

'Thank you.'

His elegant hand closed round the frosted glass and Ralph Scott, watching him, turned back to his book which he held open and unread before him, and directed his defensive and expectant gaze back on to the printed page.

'Have you read the article?'

'No,' James replied. 'What does it say?'

'A firm called Con-Re.'

He nodded as though that was as far as his interest went. Mary took up the conversation at the point where Kenneth would probably have let it drop. 'I dare say it's a lot of scurri-lous misinformed rubbish,' she said kindly. 'The writer is making out –' everyone listened to her, including of course Kenneth – 'that Con-Re received brokerage for reinsurance premiums which were virtually cosmetic arrangements set up between the broker and the underwriter to cream off money belonging to the Names.'

'Read it to us,' James said.

She heard perfectly the irony in his voice, and felt just slightly offended. She adjusted her glasses and read, 'Sums such as £40 million (My goodness! Is that a misprint? Anyway . . .) losses in excess of 130 per cent at the end of the third year . . .' She didn't look up for their reaction but remained, head bent, working it out. There was an uneasy silence.

Ralph Scott eventually put his book down and said in a quiet exasperated drawl, 'This time, James, we will have to sue. I insist.'

'Well, if these statements are not correct,' Sir Kenneth said, 'the newspaper will be in very hot water.'

'Con-Re is a perfectly valid business,' James announced. 'It is a genuine reinsurance company handled in a perfectly correct fashion. This is just some investigative journalist trying to be clever, and coming unstuck over the complexities of Lloyd's accounting.' He sat down heavily to emphasise his controlled exasperation.

'Well, on occasion it is somewhat convoluted, you must admit.'

'Mary!' George exclaimed. 'Hardly pleasant, you know, for James to be attacked in this way. And Richard and Ralph.'

'James knows what I mean,' Mary continued pleasantly. 'We were talking only just now about new regulations, and you can see they are needed if this is anything to go by.'

'What do you mean?' George asked.

'Well . . .' She hesitated over whether to launch into a full explanation for George's benefit of an issue which was so well known to James, Ralph and Richard, and – one hoped – Kenneth. 'If the brokers and underwriters belong to the same stable . . .' she paused, as if suddenly aware of potential embarrassment, 'it makes it tempting for them to cook up mutually beneficial arrangements; or as things stand, without specific by-laws, to have undeclared interests.'

'And is that what you're accused of, James?'

'Partly, yes.'

'I think we are being unnecessarily academic about it all,' Sir Kenneth said. 'After all . . .' He would have liked to say to Mary, 'One doesn't want to cause offence when one's a guest.'

Ralph Scott said, with some bitterness, 'I'm afraid we'll come across a considerable body of opinion which takes Mary's view.'

'But Mary's view is our view,' James burst out in apparent exasperation.

'Honestly, darling,' said George. 'I really don't think . . .'

'No, no!' James insisted.

'It's the penalty of fame.' This was Celia, who, back from her swim, had listened to the last ten minutes of the conversation. 'It's the penalty of fame! Look at what they say about Simon! Only last week they were trying to pin a scandal on him to do with some wretched creature, and he hadn't been seeing her at all. He told me so!' Her artless expression was so much a mixture of innocence and cunning that it was impossible to tell whether she dealt this blow intentionally or not.

Chapter
5

THE TRAIN UP TO Yorkshire was dirty and crowded; the chemical twentieth-century dirt of spilt sweet drinks made with noxious additives and manufactured snacks. Outside, it rained, and inside, the automatic door just behind Lady Celia Merrin was fixed permanently at open by a lounging youth whose foot was resting on the switch. Celia herself was drinking a double gin and tonic and smoking a cigarette in a non-smoking carriage. The ticket collector was at this moment on his way to ask her to put it out. She would not have responded well. The combination of youth, beauty, brains and a bad liver could make a person resistant to the voice of authority. The ticket collector would have found this out had not the train happened, at that moment, to draw into Ripon station. Throwing her cigarette on the floor and treading out the spark, she stepped out on to the platform. The rain that soaked the tracks and the surrounding buildings found its way in wet despondent patches on to the covered platform. Somewhere out there it was early summer. Two days ago in the south of France, no one would have thought otherwise.

At the exit, her face lit up at the sight of the battered but polished remains of the ancient Armstrong Siddeley belonging to her cousin, Lord Allanport, parked on the cobbles. 'Henry!' she said. 'I thought I'd have to catch the bus.'

'Well, you nearly did,' he said, throwing her case in the

boot, 'because William had to go to visit his mother in hospital so there was a general shortage of people to do things. At the last moment I though I wouldn't be able to drive over myself, but Delia said I'd got to.' He smiled at her. His eyes held a distinctive element of warm affection in the way he looked at people in general and not only, as just now, his cousin. He put his arm round her shoulder as they walked to the front of the car, and he opened the door.

Later, as they glided laboriously through the edges of town traffic, attracting occasional looks of astonishment or recognition, she asked, 'How's Delia?'

'Better.'

As he said that, however, a little dart of fear nicked the edge of his mind.

'A friend of mine's going to have a baby and she's having a ghastly time.'

'Really? I suppose it's not all that unusual, then.' Privately, from his point of view, nothing referring to his wife could be other than unique. 'She's so weak,' he added. 'I'm afraid she gets some pain, but she insists not.'

'Do you think so?'

'I'm not sure.'

'That's the trouble with angels like Delia,' she said. 'They're too gentle and unselfish to tell the truth.'

The open country now stretched in sodden acres of rolling greenery with, on the far distant shoulder of a hill, a cloud of blacker rain approaching and, under it, a radiant shaft of sunlight.

'You find out,' he said to Celia, 'and if she's worse than she admits, we must seek a second opinion.'

'Don't worry,' Celia said. 'If she's keeping anything back, I'll get it out of her.'

He glanced at her with a smile before turning in at a pair of white gates, and pressing the clutch for the semi-automatic preselect transmission to turn noiselessly down. 'You're a good friend, Celia.' She laughed. 'So's this car! And I love you both.'

They drove over two miles of pot-holes, the vast heavy frame of the car smoothing out the road like a tank. When they came within sight of the house, it started to rain hard once more. The gravel crunched wet under the wheels and the wipers started to go very slowly as if the wiper motor was wearing out. But if for the moment the climate and the countryside took the spirits of the observer on a downer, the house itself effectively reversed the process. Celia, shaking the rain out of her hair in the hall, felt immediately comforted.

Henry said, 'I'll go and find Delia. Go into the drawing-room and pour yourself a drink.'

As she walked over to the table where the glasses and bottles were stacked, she felt the proportions of the house and the familiar beauty of colours and objects as a palliative, more potent perhaps than the glassful she was preparing herself.

'She's in the conservatory,' Henry said a moment later, coming back. 'Bring your drink; we're having lunch in there.' She walked after him. 'I didn't ask you about your millionaire's yachting weekend,' he said over his shoulder. 'You must tell us all about it.'

In the conservatory, Delia was sitting in a basket chair with her feet resting on a stool. If she had been set there for a nostalgic film-shot of how life should really look, it could not have been better managed. She was wearing a blue sprigged dress that turned pregnant bulges into angelic folds of cloth, and her face, mild and smiling with a very short upper lip and almost no makeup, was framed in softly waving pale brown hair. The conservatory was large enough for two fully-grown palm trees, about fifteen feet high, and elsewhere in the lovely complexities of the entire glass structure, azaleas, geraniums and jasmine were in bloom, and walkways were framed with ferns.

'Oh my!' Celia said, reminding herself of Simon. 'Don't you look a dream!' She bent to kiss her, putting both arms round her and rubbing her cheek against her face. 'Thank you for making Henry come and fetch me. He's too lazy by half.'

'I like that! Where's your glass, you boozy little object? Lunch is ready. Are you going to have wine or finish your gin and tonic?'

'Can I have wine and leave the rest of this?'

The table was laid with a poached fish marvellously decorated with thin slices of cucumber, and bowls of sauce and salad.

'Come on. The weekend!' Delia said. 'We want to hear all about the millionaire's yacht and the famous film star.'

'Yes,' Henry said. 'What did you think of James Ross-Gilbert? He's got all our money. I want to know if he impressed you with his sagacity.'

'Oh, are you on his syndicates?' Celia said with surprise. 'I never knew that.'

'Why should you?'

'Well, I expect he's as clever as two sticks. He's certainly made a lot of money.'

'But what's he like?' Delia asked. 'Henry got his copy of syndicate accounts this morning, and there's an undetailed item down for two million pounds' expenses.'

'Peanuts to him, I should think,' Celia said.

'Whose peanuts? That's what I'd like to know,' Henry put in with half-joking sharpness.

'Oh!' Celia froze theatrically with her mouth full of grapes, chewed some, and then said, 'There was an awful row about something called Con-Re on Sunday morning.'

'What was that?'

She gave them a very clear account, which would have amazed those on board.

'You freeze my blood,' Henry said. 'I'm worried about that man.'

'Don't be,' Celia exclaimed, 'I've given you the wrong impression. He'd never worry himself.'

'That's not the issue,' Henry said with an ironic laugh, 'and I dare say you know it!' But he wasn't really worried. It hadn't yet reached that point.

'He exudes confidence,' Celia said. 'He's . . .' She paused, searching for words. 'He's rather flash, but not hideously so: a hyper-gent. He doesn't realise that himself, of course.'

'Don't be such a snob!'

'And he's so expensive and powerful.'

'Do you mean expansive?'

'I mean exactly what I say, Henry. Stop interrupting. He's

so expensive and powerful and generous, everyone is quite keen on him. You should have seen Sir Kenneth Dunphy! And Simon . . .'

'Oh, tell about Simon.'

They had had enough to eat. Delia, who had eaten very little, felt a wave of sudden dull pain and a certain sickness that should have gone by now. The sun broke through the glass with almost the same effect on her as if it had shattered it. Celia was not going to tell them about Simon, or at least not with the same unreserve. Henry, short sighted, thought that Delia suddenly looked pale and leaden. Concealed behind the leisurely way he took his glasses off and polished them on his napkin was a fear that bit his heart like a rat and made it jump.

'Excuse me, my lord.'

They all turned round to where the butler stood at the entrance to the conservatory. Henry said, 'Oh hello, William. Your mother's recovering, I hear.'

'Yes, thank you, my lord. She's cross, though.'

'I'm not surprised. Was that the phone I heard?'

He went off to answer it, and Delia said. 'I'm not feeling too well, Celia. Do you mind if I go and lie down?'

Chapter
6

'THINGS AREN'T GOING well, are they, Delia?'

It was surprising how, in the physical terms of objects supposedly made of dead matter such as chairs and curtains, books, tables, a small Chinese teapot on a nineteenth-century famille rose stand, a watercolour of sheep, the personality and temper of their owner should somehow get into circulation. This room of Delia's, where she spent much of her time, especially since her pregnancy made it necessary for her to rest, demonstrated that fact. It was peaceful: what a nineteenth-century writer might have described as grateful to the spirit.

'Not going well? I've never been pregnant before. How can I tell?'

'Well, I don't know much either,' Celia said, restlessly standing by the window, 'but I'm sure you're not meant to feel ill and sick after four months.'

The fact was that Delia, resting on the chaise-longue at the end of the bed, unaware of her danger and feeling better now that she was lying down, was being treated by her doctor under a wrong diagnosis. Because she was over thirty – five years older than Henry – she felt a certain unacknowledged guilt at any physical sign that might point to her age, as if the complications of a slightly later first pregnancy would be a fault on her part. Whether this attitude of hers had helped to cloud the issue or not, neither her specialist nor the local doctor had considered, with other than the complaisant reassurance of the old hand to the novice, her seemingly routine symptoms of sickness and malaise. In another month she would die unless something were done about it.

Celia said, 'You looked as pale as ice at lunch-time. You can't take risks, D.'

'In what way am I taking risks?' she answered in exasperation. 'I'm lying here, aren't I?'

'Well, you should see another doctor.'

'And get old Cobby all furious?'

'Dr Cobam's over ninety,' Celia muttered. 'And stop telling lies, Delia. You were in pain at the end of lunch, weren't you?'

'A bit.'

'Where?'

'Just my back; at the side.'

'You should get a specialist down from London or up from York or wherever they are. I'm going to tell Henry.' Celia looked really upset, or rather in the mood to upset someone else if she could lay her hands on an appropriate subject.

Delia closed her eyes. 'Stop bullying me, Celia.' It was intended jokingly, but exhaustion lent her remark a slight bitterness.

Celia came over and stood behind her. 'I'm sorry. But think how poor Henry would go mad if anything went wrong.'

'Well, it won't, as long as you don't scare me to death before the nine months are up,' Delia protested. 'For heaven's sake let me have a bit of rest now, before all that lot come over for dinner. We'll have a really good evening, I promise.'

Celia groaned, and said, 'Tom Crabthorne?'

'All right, but I've got some surprises as well.' She closed her eyes again and rested her head back on the cushion, saying, 'Sorry to be so boring.'

'You're not. Do you need a rug over you?'

In desperation, Delia let herself be covered up and Celia at last went downstairs.

It was not until the following morning that Celia relayed any of this conversation to Henry. At about eleven she appeared in the dining-room, where he was sitting over a cup of coffee and the newspaper, and said, 'Where's Delia?'

'Oh, you know she hardly ever comes down to breakfast. What are you going to have? There's kedgeree if you want it.'

'I might have some,' she said, going over to the sideboard and helping herself out of the hot dish.

'You'll be fat when you grow up.'

'I'll be more likely to be in prison for murdering Mrs Ellis,' she said. 'Would you like more coffee? That woman came barging into my room at dawn and drew the curtains.' Henry smiled. 'Delia must have told her to.'

He shook his head, still smiling. 'No, she didn't.'

'Not you?'

'No.'

'William, then. You wait, I'll make him sorry!'

'How are they going to get the house clean if guests stay in bed all day?'

'I'm not a guest. I'm family.'

'You're just a little fiend, that's what you are.'

'I'm twenty-five, Henry.'

'Blow me down!'

She looked at him and laughed. 'Either you feed me this delicious breakfast or you want to annoy me. Make your mind up.'

'Did you speak to Delia?'

'Yes,' she said. 'I suppose she's all right. I talked to her after lunch, but you'd gone out to the farm; and then in the evening she seemed fine, didn't she?'

'Yes, she did.'

'It was a lovely dinner party, actually. It was so sweet of Delia to get Rupert over.'

'Well, she wants you to marry him.'

'I might, if I had a decent job.'

He gave her a mocking startled look, and said, 'What has that got to do with it? And what about Simon?'

'Oh, Simon.' She pushed her plate away. 'Simon makes me miserable, nervous and hyperactive. But if I had a really good job, I could become nice enough to marry Rupert. As it is, my underused brains are turning on themselves all the time.'

'What's wrong with just enjoying yourself?'

'You're different from me, Henry. You're cool and elegant and light hearted. I'm not.'

He laughed. 'That's that, then!'

'You're brilliant, too, I know that,' she said. 'But you're also happy. Even when you're worried about Delia, or some acquaintance is spouting opinions that you can't possibly agree with or the papers run a scare on the man who's got all your money . . .'

'I don't know about that! Is there more this morning?'

'Yes. Look.'

He took it from her. 'It's Con-Re again,' she said, starting on the toast. 'I bet he did it.'

'Did what?'

'Paid insurance premiums into his own bank account.'

'Is that what he's accused of?' Henry looked shocked.

'They go round the houses, but that's where it's aimed at.'

Henry read intently, and for a moment there was silence.

'On reflection,' Celia said, 'although I thought old James was a whiz-bang, I don't think I'd like him to take care of all my money.' Henry continued reading, but he heard her. 'Or the promise of all my money, which is what you really mean, isn't it, Henry?'

'Yes. I'm a direct Name with Merchaum.'

'That's his Managing Agency that manages all his syndicates. Does "direct Name" mean you don't have a Member's Agent representing you?'

'That's it.'

'So you have no outside involvement to offset against his results if they were bad? All your money is on his syndicates?'

'Yes.'

'Unlimited liability: this house, the grounds, the farm, the furniture . . . If there was a slip-up and the cash was needed, instead of just the promise of it, they'd all have to go?'

Henry had put down the paper and was looking at her with an expression partly of familiar mocking indulgence and partly dry attention. 'Please don't stop,' he said.

'I'm not trying to tease you, Henry. This is serious. I'm just mentioning it, that's all.'

'Of course. Mention some more.'

'James Ross-Gilbert is also Chairman of Merchaum. Did you know that? And a main shareholder.'

Henry looked startled, and said, 'No, I didn't know that. I suppose the information was made available.'

'You've got unlimited liability and he's got unlimited licence.'

'God, Celia, don't put it like that. It sounds appalling!'

'Merchaum own Merchaum & May, the brokers, as well, so they broke to themselves. That's part of the Con-Re fuss.'

'I think I'd better go up to London and see him.'

'Well, take your tin hat!' she said. 'He can be very charming, as you know, and he's got them all wound round his little finger, even Mary Seymour. You know who she is, don't you? She writes learned articles on economic affairs in *The Times* and advises government.' She paused for quite a while, and in the silence the sound of distant farm machinery purred across the landscape. 'But I was looking at James Ross-Gilbert,' she said, meaning in her mind's eye, reassessing the images of the weekend, 'and I thought to myself that I wouldn't want to encounter him in a dark alley at night if he had any reason to think that one's existence was against his own best interests.'

'Really.' Henry was silent for a moment, and eventually said, 'Damn it all, he can't charge me two million pounds' expenses without a single explanation, even if he has returned me a profit for the last eight years. I have the right to ask him about that, at least. I'll go up to London.'

'Precisely,' Celia said. 'And at the same time you have the right to ask Delia's stupid specialist why she's still got backache.'

Chapter 7

'WILL YOU GO IN, please, sir?'

A quite exceptionally pretty girl held open the door to the Chairman's office. Moreover, she was new. In spite of the fact that at the moment he was too busy with Marjorie, Philippa and Con-Re to add to his preoccupations, James Ross-Gilbert did what he could to pave the way for a future possible encounter; that's to say he ignored her completely. He went past her utterly self-possessed in the manner that always tends to raise the question of how the possessor can be persuaded to parcel out a little fraction of himself to a new friend. When she had closed the door, he turned and looked at it.

Philip Carrington, the Chairman of Lloyd's, glanced at him with friendly impatience. 'You've got more serious things to think about this morning, James.'

'Yes, of course.'

'Come and sit down.'

'I hope you're not going to panic, Philip,' he said to his friend, putting his paper down on the desk and making a weary gesture, pressing the bridge of his nose with one finger.

'Certainly not. That would be to imply that I had no faith in you, James.' He repeated his gesture towards the chair, and after inspecting it as if it was in itself an option that he disdained, James sat down. 'I've got good news for you. The papers have dropped the story.'

'Oh? How come?'

'I had dinner last night with Faulkner. As you know, he's Jim Granger's brother-in-law.'

'Ah! The editor!'

'I told you the Lodge would be useful.'

'And I never argued about that. So our brother has persuaded his brother-in-law . . . what?'

'You're mocking, James.'

'Well – you should understand,' Ross-Gilbert said with a brief flash of real feeling, which stood out unexpectedly from his habitual manner as sharply as if he had suddenly thrown off all his clothes. His aura seemed briefly to shed a layer of fat light, and a thinner altogether more business-like dealer looked sharply up and said, 'Those types were getting on my back!'

'Yes. Well . . . Jim Granger's bought them off. And don't ask me what with, because I don't know. A private matter between them.'

'Some other blighter might get his nose into the trough,' James snapped.

'Come on, James, it's not like you to be pessimistic.' Philip regarded him in a very kindly way and walked over to where a miraculously silent coffee-machine had just boiled and filtered and switched itself off. 'I think we should wait a while until the memory of this little fracas has died down,' he said, pouring out two cups, 'and then you should make a declaration in next year's accounts about your shareholding in Con-Re.'

'And yours!'

Philips eyebrows went up as he handed James his coffee, but he said nothing.

'I'm sorry, Philip. Quite uncalled-for.'

'That's all right. These things get on one's nerves.'

'As you say – or rather imply – and quite correctly, it's I, as underwriter, who should have declared my shareholding in Con-Re, new regulations and all that . . . You're an outsider to this issue and your shareholding isn't the point.'

'I think that is true, you know.'

'No doubt about it. No doubt at all.'

The both tasted their coffee in silence. It was perfectly obvious to James that Philip was going to ruin everything. He waited with stoicism, almost counting Philip's cue, until he heard him say, 'How big is your shareholding, by the way?'

'Can't say.'

The flatness of his tone, the point-blank reply was a reproach – even an insult. Philip reddened. James stared at him over the rim of his cup. He wasn't offering any further contribution. But he gauged his aggression so exactly that as the moment of surprise faded and the Chairman paused, embarrassed and perhaps affronted, trying to choose a re-action, at that instant he allowed a slight smile to bend the corner of his mouth, and said, 'Leave that one out for the moment, there's a good chap. I'll see to it.'

Philip hesitated. 'All right.' He tried, but failed, to keep the relief out of his voice.

James stood up.

'Sorry I've got to go, Philip, but a Name is coming to see me at twelve. Many thanks.'

'Not at all. Not at all.'

'There's a quotation, isn't there? About relief and thanks.' Neither of them knew it.

James, as he hurried back down Lime Street, looked at his watch and reached the main door thirty seconds before Henry Allanport arrived and took the lift up to Merchaum. The opulence of Merchaum offices in general sometimes aroused an undercurrent of slight resentment as well as admiration. In Henry Allanport's case, the reaction was different. Although very observant, he had a habit of not drawing conclusions. In this case he noticed the prevailing luxury with a slightly different feeling than on other visits, on account of the two million pounds' expenses.

James had had time to recover from his interview with the Chairman, and, besides, it had turned out well. And then again, whether it had or not, nothing would have affected the smooth unrevealing charm with which he greeted the announcement of Lord Allanport. His aristocratic Names were the minor jewels in his crown, and he came forward now with both hands extended, saying, 'Henry, dear boy, how are you!' as if he had known him all his life.

Henry acknowledged the effusive welcome with just that oblique politeness with which a seasoned tennis-player would let a fast ground stroke go past him if he knew it was going to land behind the back line. Stylish, thin, younger and shorter than Ross-Gilbert, with his amiable manners and dry charm, he allowed himself to be swept into the padded atmosphere of James's office, smiling behind his glasses, reassuring his host on each new claim to a history of intimate friendship.

It was time for drinks instead of coffee, and James had standing ready a chilled bottle of white wine that had cost somebody forty pounds. The slightly humorous angle to Henry's habitual expression of dry friendliness was that he liked nice things. He took a sip from his glass and smiled at it, rather than at James, as if now he really had come across an old and valued friend.

'Were you up in London anyway, or is this a special visit, Henry?'

'I had a number of things to see to. Did you buy that Hockney from our gallery, by the way?'

'Ah yes.' James gave one of his rare smiles. 'Now, that reminds me.' But whatever it was, the phone rang, and he broke off to press a switch and say, 'I'm not taking any calls for the moment, Jane. I thought I made that clear. I'm sorry,' to Henry. 'Now, do you want a forecast on your results?'

'Yes, certainly. Have you a rough idea?'

James had the file out ready on his desk, and he opened it, and said, 'Eleven per cent.'

'That's very good.'

'Let me see, what are you writing now? Two hundred and fifty thousand pounds. Perhaps you should increase that; what do you think?'

'I could.'

'Would you like to go into it?'

Henry thought in silence for a moment, and then said, 'I really wanted to ask you about this figure on syndicate accounts.'

'Oh, really?' James let a small measure of surprise show.

'It's the item for two million pounds' expenses.' He took a folded sheet out of his breast-pocket, which turned out to be an item from the package mailed to him by Merchaum the previous week.

James took it across the desk and looked down on it in more than one sense. 'What about it?'

'Well, I hope I'm not speaking out of turn as a Name on the syndicates, but it is a very large figure, and there are no details given.'

'How do you mean, details?'

Just that brief question put in precisely that way conveyed the fact that the enquiry was resented, but more in sorrow than in anger, and was misplaced. But in fact his opponent, although taking the point with unruffled accuracy, was not disconcerted. 'I mean that if this figure comes off the top of premium income, surely the Names should have some notion of the items covered?'

'This office, do you mean? Or my car? No, no, Henry, don't apologise. No offence. But it's not practical, you know, for Names to attempt to participate as if they were on the Board.'

'Really?' Henry turned the stem of his glass between two thin fingers. 'I thought it was.' James laughed. 'I'm a direct Name, of course,' Henry continued, 'and of course you have a number of others; none of whom I know, as far as I'm aware, except Glyn Blacker.' He paused. 'I can't remember anyone else. But wouldn't it be a good and acceptable idea if there was an annual general meeting for Names?'

James spread his hands in a gesture of controlled horror. 'My dear Henry, not at all! We aren't enemies, you know. We're on the same side. A Name must trust his Agent. It's a very personal relationship between the underwriter, the Managing Agency and the Name; not a community of interests between the Names themselves.'

'I know that.'

'Well, then.' He came round to the side of the desk. 'Look. Lloyd's business is complex. You understand it, I know, but many Names ...' He made an expression that was self-explanatory. 'There is such a thing as world competition, even for Lloyd's. We couldn't operate if Names made the sorts of demands you're proposing, Henry.'

'Really?'

'No, we could not. Take my word for it.'

There was a momentary silence filled with calculation. James, the sensitive antennae of his instinct for supremacy testing the option of taking more offence; Henry with his powers of observation not cluttered by simultaneous attempts to manipulate or draw conclusions, waiting.

James decided against. 'Look here . . .' He went back behind his desk with the air of someone making a concession, and sat down. 'We do our best to control expenses.' He had made it completely impossible for his companion to demur, even though the potential absurdity of the statement remained unanswered. 'We are accountable, you know.' He looked across at Henry, taking in, and not without appreciation, the relaxed way he said there quite undisturbed. Normally such a questioner would have been reduced, by the treatment James meted out, to making an incoherent string of apologies. 'We are accountable,' James reiterated, 'to Lloyd's itself.'

'But not to your Names.'

'Now, Henry, this is not kind.'

And, thank God, the phone rang. James picked it up with a sharp sigh of relief that turned to another gesture, as if to say, 'We busy men . . .' Henry stood up. James said into the phone, 'Hold on a moment, will you?' He put it down on the desk and walked round into the room. 'Henry!' He held out his hand and gripped Henry's thin fingers. 'Confidence! That's the name of the game,' and he put his arm round Henry's shoulder who, watchful and unprotesting, walked with him to the door. 'We are here to answer your questions,' he continued unashamedly. 'Have no doubt about that. No problem. No problem at all.'

'Well . . .' There was a brief pause. James made a quarter glance toward the phone, calculated to speed his guest on his way. 'Thank you for the Domaine de Chevalier.'

'A pleasure, Henry. Goodbye.' He walked back and picked up the receiver, but before actually speaking into it, he turned the wine bottle and looked at the label.

Chapter
8

HAD JAMES ROSS-GILBERT known who was on the end of the phone he might have preferred the frying-pan he was in already. Only just over an hour earlier he had walked back from Lloyd's privately prepared to admit that he felt some relief. The disturbance about Con-Re had been very slight, attracting only the attention of the specialists, but had it gone on he would not have liked it. Now, he easily dismissed the subject from his mind. His suit was superbly cut. He kept his own counsel. He acknowledged those whom he chose as he passed them in the street crowded almost exclusively with men who worked in or around Lloyd's, and among whom he ranked as one of the most respected and admired. At any one time, if he turned his mind to the intricate maze of his own business involvements within the market, he was confronted inwardly with a mathematically developed structure of staggering extent and, to himself, satisfaction. He had reached the point at which he did exactly what he liked. The organisation that he and a few chosen partners imposed on their business, giving to their transactions the necessary format of Lloyd's legality, he would have defended to the last drop of even his own blood as above question. Anyone daring to question him – as from time to time a hapless Agent might raise some peripheral point or other, he would annihilate with all the pride and dignity of self-evident success.

The following day he was due to fly to the United States as an emissary of Lloyd's in connection with a negotiation with a major bank in Boston. At about the same time as other men were making their way around some kicked and painted filing cabinet to get a cup of mid-morning instant coffee, the preceding day had found him virtually enthroned in the ornate eighteenth-century Committee room at Lloyd's created by the brothers Adam and taken by the institution from site to site like a collapsible tent. Here it was set up again with all its splendour of gold plaster-work and vast rich oil paintings of ships in full sail smack on the top floor of the new block. The Committee in full session had met to acknowledge their unanimous approval of the appointment of James Ross-Gilbert to sort out a viable deal over reinsurances to cover unexpected developments in the States. He dictated his own terms to the following market for this service, his expression friendly but unsmiling: and men who knew perfectly well that they personally could not expect to emerge the winners from any negotiation with him were only too glad to agree all his conditions in order to have him negotiate on their behalf. James treated the appointment as a favour he was doing Lloyd's and they concurred.

With that once more uppermost in his mind, he had returned from his meeting with the Chairman this morning, and played the part of friendly tutor *cum* host to Lord Allanport. And he picked up the phone now with no expectation of having the newly re-established *status quo* disturbed.

'Yes?' he said.

'Is that Mr Ross-Gilbert?'

'Who am I speaking to, please?' It was not, as far as he was concerned, the moment for having total strangers put through to him, and he couldn't understand what Jane thought she was up to.

'My name is Grace Derby,' the caller replied. 'I'm a financial news writer doing a feature on aspects of Lloyd's for *The Times*.'

The contact between that information and his recent experience sent a spark into Ross-Gilbert's eye that could have given her a nasty shock if she hadn't been insulated with several miles of telephone cable. He expected her to say that she was enquiring about Con-Re, in which case John and his precious friend would have some explaining to do. For that reason only he waited, and then for the first time it just occurred to him that something might actually be wrong: that those first trickles of grit and dust might already have undermined a large boulder which even now toppled on its moorings. With the idea half formed in his mind, he said tersely, 'I'm waiting, Miss Derby.'

'Sorry. I'm calling in connection with Persian Arc's acquisition of Cleave & Engels.'

'Yes,' he said. 'The American firm that recently bought the well-known brokers and Managing Agency. That's not my concern, Miss Derby.'

'But I wonder if you could comment on the rumour that Merchaum have recently repaid the sum of nine million dollars into Cleave & Engels's account for an unexplained transaction?'

'What!'

'Oh, it's true, then?'

He recovered himself. 'On the contrary, Miss Derby. But obviously we do trade with Cleave & Engels.' He was loathing this conversation to the depths of his heart. He knew what she was getting at and he guessed that it was true. If it was true – and how else should it have been brought up – it meant that his advice had not been taken in a certain matter. Richard Trene had lost his nerve again. Contrary to their recent agreement, and rattled by the close scrutiny that Persian Arc were giving at this late date to their new acquisition, he had rushed over the nine million dollars which was one sum owed by Merchaum. It belonged to an arrangement which wouldn't exactly bear the light of unsympathetic scrutiny. A mutual involvement – and they had agreed that if Persian Arc suddenly decided to bring in some decent accountants, they should sit tight and not draw attention to themselves. If someone's nerve had snapped and a payment had been rushed in, he knew how and why and by whom without asking Miss Grace Derby. To be told by some journalist that Dick's shaky hand was rocking the boat again was more than he could bear.

She was carrying on all this time. Apparently Persian Arc accountants had discovered irregularities. He knew that. But now this little flicker of movement – nine million dollars – not a sum of money in itself to make a fuss about, but significant because it was, and so suddenly, there. Why was it there? It was not beyond him to sort this out, but he couldn't wait to get his hands on Dick Trene.

'Miss Derby,' he said. He had hit on a good temporary explanation. 'Do you know what a quota share is?'

'Yes, I do.'

'In that case you will perfectly well understand if I tell you that I have no doubt – although I can't myself be expected to know at any one moment the multiplicity of minor figures involved – that this is probably to do with a quota share due from Merchaum, the figure for which has not yet been processed through Cleave & Engels.' She sounded doubtful. 'I hope you'll forgive me, but I am just too busy at the moment to discuss it further,' he said. 'If you want to ring me again at a later date, please do.'

He put the phone down. He turned his head towards the window for a blazing second, then picked it up again and slammed it, with all his force, back into its cradle.

Chapter
9

GRACE DERBY, PUTTING the phone down at her end of the line, stood still and wondered. Her office was in the back of a building in Covent Garden, the window giving on to a small square with a tree. Here the financial magazine for which she mainly worked housed her, although she also contributed to other newspapers, and as she pondered, calculating her next move, the sound of other steps on the stairs and of distant and near clatter emphasised her actual stillness. A submerged message of something unexpected had brought her to a halt.

She was thirty-one. No one ever looked at her with the detached absent-minded gaze that she was now directing at the tree. Her presence upset people. They would say that that kind of disturbance was welcome any time, but in fact beauty and sexuality combined, as it was in Grace, is not always helpful. To describe her physically – a perfect figure but with a slight voluptuousness somehow combined with being thin, medium height, short wavy blond hair, large blue eyes, etc. – was a waste of time because it left out that indefinable aura of heart-breaking sexuality that was redolent in her every gesture no matter how indifferent she might feel and even if she was only picking up a biro to sign her name. She herself was unaware of all this, the only person in her own immediate vicinity interested in other things. From the point of view of her accidental victims, her own detachment was the last straw.

She was thinking of one of them now, although not as such. From her point of view, Spencer Day was a good friend. He was also on the committee of Lloyd's and would know James Ross-Gilbert. Eventually she turned back to the desk and dialled his number. She caught him just as he was leaving the office for lunch, and without letting her know that it was necessary, he cancelled someone else and arranged to take her out. The tree mentioned before had only just come into full leaf and now held over Grace's head, as she walked across the square, a canopy of fleshy green, still slightly crumpled like newly-emerged butterflies. The covert longing glances of men she passed (but not the ear-piercing whistles of navvies attached to the outside of the fifth floor of Dentons) to some extent resembled that walk earlier on in the day taken by James Ross-Gilbert down Lime Street. If he seemed to possess what men most admired in other men, she certainly possessed what they most admired in women. But her mind was on her job. She was a talented journalist, a good financial writer, and what had looked like an average story was giving out interesting signals of a lead to greater things.

Spencer Day, waiting for Grace at a table near, but not in, the window, controlled his nerves with a glass of white wine. For a journalist to come privately to him, a Committee member, for information about a possible scandal breaking in the market, was hardly proper. In fact you could say that it was completely offside for him to cooperate privately with the Press. The thought certainly went fleetingly through his mind. Went through his mind, but didn't stick there. He couldn't help himself. He'd do anything just to be allowed the opportunity to help her off with her coat.

As she came through the door, the casual checking glances of other lunchers changed frequency on impact with her arrival so that the rhythm and noise level inside was momentarily suspended on a different key. She didn't notice. She probably thought it was something to do with a door opening out of a confined space into the street.

Spencer got up and reached forward to kiss her cheek. Being happy was not his everyday state of mind. His pale thick skin, slack along the side of the cheekbones and under the jaw, showed a faint flush under the eyes. The hand that he managed to lay on her arm, in spite of the waiter's officious attention to her coat and her chair, was a caress of infinite tenderness. But he had no thought for the morrow. Somehow the knowledge that lunch could not possibly last for longer than an hour and a half had become an irretrievable non-fact. The same psychology or lack of it that makes a child break into heartrending sobs when it has swallowed the last mouthful of a really delicious ice-cream would seize and slay him when the moment came to leave. But for now he was happy.

'I don't know what to say about your news,' he said. 'Nothing's been mentioned in the shop.'

'Have a look at this.' She handed him a sheet of paper.

'Is this a sheet out of the accounts?' His voice was incredulous. His thin mouth that had been attractive when he was young and which his wife disliked, was caught characteristically in an interrogative tension as straight as a hairpin.

Grace bobbed her head on one side, and said 'Yes,' in a deliberately colourless voice. 'Why, what's wrong?'

'How did you come by it?'

'My business.' She smiled, looking straight into the very centre of his eyes.

Spencer said, 'A bit much, you know.' He couldn't help gasping, but not over the paper. He came back to it. 'You shouldn't really have this. It's private.'

'But that apart, what do you think of the figures?'

He looked at them, and frowned, but after a pause handed the paper back to her. 'I can't make a thing of it out of context. It's already known that some awful row is going to break over Cleave & Engels, but Merchaum is another matter.'

'Could they be involved?'

'How on earth would I know, darling?'

'Oh, Spencer!'

An expression for a moment comically glum shadowed his face. He knew that the reproof was to do with calling her 'darling'.

'Now tell me about James Ross-Gilbert.'

He put his napkin on the table and looked across at her. She was waiting for his answer. She was perfectly friendly, even slightly protective and affectionate. He said, 'Why do you want to know about James?'

'I'm not sure. Hack's instinct. He was dreadfully put out about Cleave & Engels.'

'Well, you won't find anything untoward there,' he said prophetically. 'I should think at the moment he's *the* most respected man in the market.'

'Why?'

'Because he's successful, that's why.' He thought for a moment, and then added, 'He's made such a lot of money.'

'Who for? Just himself?'

'The Names, the Agency . . .'

She nodded. 'It's odd, isn't it –' the waiter came to clear the plates – 'the way men react to the possession of money?'

Spencer was worried that she wouldn't want to have pudding, that she would say she had to get back to her office or to some appointment early, or in any one of a dozen ways cut short the lunch.

'Crême brulé,' she said, with a smile to the waiter.

Spencer breathed with relief and said almost euphorically, 'How about the Hayward after lunch? I want to see the Matisse.'

'I can't,' she said. 'But what do you think of Con-Re?'

He tried to concentrate. 'Was it in the papers at the weekend?'

'Yes.'

'Hmm.'

'The paper pulled its punches,' Grace said, 'because of libel. But the real suggestion is that Merchaum syndicates put reinsurance funds into a firm – namely Con-Re – in which James Ross-Gilbert had an undisclosed interest.'

'Oh ho!' Spencer looked deeply reflective rather in the same way as a person might who felt the first twinges of an attack of indigestion.

'Well, go on,' Grace said. 'You're not going to tell me that's all right?'

'It depends.' The trouble was that it sounded awfully like

an arrangement the poor chap had himself with a Bermudan roll-over fund.

'On what?'

He looked at her rather pathetically, having lost the thread.

'On what does it depend?'

'Well – whether or not he's declared the interest to his Names.'

'And has he?'

'Oh, I'm sure he has. I mean . . . He's a very successful underwriter. Highly thought of. He knows the rules.'

'I'm not suggesting he doesn't know them,' she said. He looked at her doubtfully. She was so beautiful. But he really did wish she'd shut up.

'And there's the subject of my phone call this morning.'

He gave her no encouragement in the hope she'd let it drop.

'This unexplained sum of money that's been pushed so hastily into the accounts of Cleave & Engels looks like an obvious attempt to regularise some figure the new auditors are looking at.'

'Oh, yes?'

'Nine million dollars,' she said. 'And I told you the explanation he gave me about quota shares. But I just have a feeling.'

'What of?'

'Oh . . .' She paused. 'A catastrophe?'

He was quite amused. 'Well, he's off to America tomorrow.'

'James Ross-Gilbert?'

Spencer explained the mission to do with negotiations on behalf of the Lloyd's market. 'And he doesn't like roughing it, I can tell you. He demanded return tickets on Concorde for himself, his mistress and her two daughters, two interconnecting suites of rooms at the most expensive hotel in New York, and a private plane to take him down to Boston and back.'

'And the Committee agreed?'

'His fellow underwriters paid. But, yes. They did.'

She laughed. When her chin came up there was a dimple just under it that he had once kissed; a stolen favour. 'Come on, Spencer, say you will.'

'Will what?' He hadn't been listening.

'Introduce me to him,' she said, apparently for the second time. Just at that moment the waiter offered her more coffee, and she refused with a very quick glance at her watch. It was nearly over.

'All right. I've got a lunch in the office next week that James is coming to. Agree to come to the Matisse exhibition with me afterwards, and I'll invite you to join us.'

'You're on.'

'I'll get Ann Paceman along from the *Economist* and *Register* as well to balance up.'

'He should be pleased,' she said, with about the same talent for prophecy as Spencer had shown in the conversation half an hour before. Laughing together, they went out into the street, and he parted from her quite cheerfully because there would be next Tuesday.

Chapter 10

RICHARD TRENE BENEFITED from one disadvantage: he had absolutely no charm. The absence of it made him, to some extent, in spite of all his efforts, straight forward. For example, walking into James Ross-Gilbert's office after lunch in response to his emergency phone call and finding Ralph Scott already there and Nick Victor, from Cleave & Engels, twitchy as always, standing by the window, he said straight away, 'You can count me out of this!'

Ralph gave him a look of absolute contempt, and Ross-Gilbert said, 'Perhaps you ought to find out what we're talking about before you opt out. After all, you're as keen to make your fifth million as the rest of us.'

That unsettled him. Nevertheless his first reaction had been right.

'Pour yourself some coffee,' James said, 'and come and sit down.'

'I don't want any coffee.' But he walked over to the same table, because that was where the drinks also were, and poured himself a slug of brandy without further comment. When he had taken a mouthful, he heard James say, 'Good. Now perhaps you'll tell us, Dick, exactly why you paid that sum of nine million dollars into the Cleave & Engels account, in spite of our agreement not to.'

Richard could recognise a really dangerous tone of voice

when he heard one. 'What do you mean by "agreement"?' he said. 'You dictated. I did not agree.'

'Call it what you like,' Ralph said with bitter contempt. 'But it's likely to land us all in a mess, you bloody fool.'

'James,' Richard said with quiet fury, 'get him off my back or there's no point in this discussion. I'm sick to death of being the butt of your poisonous upper-class venom, Scott. I'm warning you!'

For once Ross-Gilbert wasn't helping. Realising there wasn't much he could do about an enemy who was standing in the same room facing him, Dick capitulated, and said, 'All right. What the hell's going on?'

'Did you pay that nine million in?'

'Yes, I did.'

There was a bitter silence. Finally James continued, 'It may interest you to know that I had a telephone call this morning. From a journalist. Presumably she had some advance information, but what she hears today others will hear tomorrow. And she had heard of your precious nine-million-dollar cheque.'

Dick looked non plussed. 'Why?'

'Why?' James echoed him in a hardly audible tone that mocked his belligerent naïveté, at the same time looking at the other two while they silently stared back.

'What is this?' Dick's temper compensated for all his other reactions. 'It's like some bloody court-martial on telly! Is someone going to let me know what's gone wrong?'

James seemed to gather himself together, then said, 'That nine million dollars was part of a series of payments, wasn't it, Dick? Cleave & Engels had broked our reinsurances on long term business on a minus 40 per cent basis.'*

'Right.'

---

*Note: long term or long tail business is insurance for the sort of business for which the premium is paid on the day, but no claim can be expected to accrue until after a considerable lapse of time. Forty per cent basis is an agreement between an underwriter and a broker to allow an unusually high commission to the broker (in this case 40 per cent) on some particular bit of business. That amount is then paid into a firm in which the underwriter has a secret share. Not legal and not done; certainly not since the introduction of written rules.

'And Nick here and Tom with him bought shares in Con-Re.'

'Right.'

'With the proceeds of their 40 per cent cut of the reinsurances.'

'I know all this.'

'You know all this, Richard. But do we want Persian Arc to know all this? Or the Committee to know all this? Or *The Times* to know all this?'

The tone infuriated Richard Trene. He positively shouted, 'No we bloody don't. I'm no fool!'

Ralph, with a quiet sneer, half turning away as he did so, said, 'Out of the mouths of babes . . .'

'What did he say.'

'Never mind about that. The point is that on this and various other transactions the accounts of Cleave & Engels were . . .' He paused. It was a difficult moment. He picked unwillingly on the word 'short', and left it at that.

'That's why I paid in the nine million.'

'Exactly. You explained your line of reasoning before. And I explained to you as best I damn well could that if Persian Arc had bought Cleave & Engels without scrutinising the books all that carefully in the first place, well and good. But when they suddenly turned round and started really looking, that was not the moment to attract their attention to us by doing something foolish.'

Dick was silent, but then said, 'And has it attracted their attention?'

No one answered him. Eventually Nick Victor said, 'What are you going to do?'

'It depends,' James sat down at his desk. 'I think the Con-Re nonsense has been shut up.' Nobody asked how. 'But how much fuss are Persian Arc going to make? There's the Banque de Flors. Presumably they don't know yet, Nick, that you and the other three directors now own it?'

'I shouldn't bank on it,' he said, and made a fussy gesture with his hand to repudiate the pun.

'They'll uncover our share holding as well if they do find out. But the Swiss will never let them look inside.'

'Thank God for that!'

'So what do we do?'

'It's more a question,' Ralph said, 'of what do we say?'

'Whatever we do say – and do – we've got to have a consensus,' James insisted, looking at Dick.

'You must see that now, Richard,' Nick put in.

'All right.'

'Damn the Fisher Report!'

'Oh, save your breath, Ralph!' James said, exasperated. 'Disclosure's here to stay. We're stuck with it. My Names have made a killing, and we all agree that in the early sixties they knew their place and were grateful for what they got. But now it's different.'

'I think,' Richard said, 'that the premium that we've collected for reinsurances' – 'collected' being an extremely ingenious word to use – 'and the reinsurances that we have reinvested can all bear scrutiny perfectly well.'

The others looked at him.

'That depends.'

'And if not?'

'That's the other point of this meeting,' James said. 'I'd like you all to know that I'm going to retire.'

'Retire!' In all three of them the reaction was surprise mingled with suspicion.

'I've been quite open about it,' James said sincerely, as if there was credit in openness, which, forgone in one context, was all the more worth being given credit for in another. 'I've said before – haven't I Dick? – what's the point of retiring when you're too old to enjoy it?'

Ralph looked at him. 'You think we're for it, don't you?'

He didn't reply for some time. Then he said, 'There are some things it is never wise to say.' No one interrupted him. 'At least we can all agree that we've done well.'

Dick smiled unpleasantly at that one, but still was silent.

'All the little details, the regulations – we might have taken one or two short cuts. But my Names – as long as no one starts putting ideas into their heads – have done very well, thank you. They've got nothing to complain of.'

'What are we on about, then?' Ralph said unpleasantly.

'Questions.' James paused again. 'I think people are going to ask questions.'

'Maybe we can answer them.'

'Maybe we can. And it still is going to take a long time. And we should move some of our funds and rename the trusts, and a few details like that. Dick and I will take care of it once we have agreed the decisions. But I was planning to retire anyway, and as I like betting on certainties, I'm going earlier rather than later.'

'My God! You're really rattled, aren't you?'

'No. I'm not.' He was convincing. Of the four of them, he looked by far the least worried. 'So down to business. Bring up a chair, Nick.' He took a key out of his inner pocket and unlocked a drawer and took out of it another key, and with that key he unlocked an inner compartment of the safe and from the safe he took a file of papers, marked 'Location and Dispersal of Funds.' A cryptic heading.

'Think of them like a sort of removals firm,' somebody said many months later. 'They covered the globe.'

Chapter 11

'HOW DID YOU get on, then?'

It was seven o'clock, and Henry Allanport had arrived in the London flat of his brother-in-law, Rupert Doone, who lived in Knightsbridge and worked, incidentally, as a broker at Lloyd's. The flat was not large, but full of beautiful things. A person coming in from the street with their perception stripped down to charmless utility and the spirit lagging like a worn-out clutch could be revived in seconds. Henry breathed a sigh of relief, accepted a glass of wine, and said, 'Nowhere. I got absolutely nowhere.'

'Did you see him?'

Rupert was referring to the Chairman of Lloyd's. In fact Henry had had no difficulty in making an appointment following his meeting with James Ross-Gilbert. But when he arrived and tried asking the same questions he got absolutely nowhere, as he now said.

'Are you worried?'

'Well . . .' He was now sprawling in a large comfortable armchair upholstered in crimson velvet and having difficulty retrieving that fleeting unfamiliar experience of distrust. 'I got warned off.'

'No response to your request for information? No surprise about the two million pounds' expenses?'

'None at all. He told me that he couldn't interfere and did

his best to make me feel that my enquiry was bad form.' As he said this, he smiled in that characteristic way, bending the closed corners of his mouth in an ironic curve that somehow conveyed innocent enjoyment combined with irony.

Rupert – altogether a more straightforward, even obvious, type on every physical level, in spite of the beauty of his flat – looked solemnly back. 'They're a right Mafia, that lot,' he said. 'I may only be an investment broker who doesn't get to touch the hem of Ross-Gilbert's raiment' – his expression suggested that he probably had other reasons for not even wanting to try – 'But I've always been against the idea of being a direct Name on principle, and there's a row brewing. I know it. I feel it in my bones.'

'Do you really think he's no good?'

'That's putting it on the line. I couldn't say.'

'Well, then!'

'Ah, yes. But there have been a few rumours lately, and I happen to know he's been dealing in some long tail business which could turn out very badly.'

'Why? Why should he?'

'The figures look so good up front.' Rupert walked over to the window and looked down onto the square, one hand in his pocket, the other holding his glass, almost as if he expected to see someone there. His tone of voice was quite light hearted, slightly abrasive, like the tone of someone who spent much of their working life carrying out the orders of more stupid men. 'You get in all your premiums,' he continued, 'maybe for years, without claims. But God help you if the crunch comes!'

'He didn't get involved personally, where his underwriting was concerned, on computer leasing.'

'OK. But industrial disease?'

'Do you know something?'

'No, but I can speculate,' he said dismissively, 'and I don't want you blowing your brains out and my sister being left a beautiful widow living off social security in a flat in Hackney. By the way, she rang earlier.'

'Is she all right?'

Rupert frowned slightly, picking up the note of alarm. 'She is, isn't she?'

'Oh yes, I think so. The specialist says she's just a bit off colour; symptoms typical.' And yet . . . Henry did in fact feel about Delia's health as Rupert felt about James Ross-Gilbert. The consequence of Rupert's fears materalising would destroy Henry's material wealth and wellbeing, but the consequences of the former would destroy his soul.

He went out into the hall and rang her up. The floor out there was of broad polished elm boards with a narrow worn kelim and walls of old damask the colour of patchy blue Quink ink. He noticed this in the same spirit that Fagin noticed the rails of the dock, but the warning was of the obscure kind we are not trained to notice. Besides, Delia's voice, when she came on the line, was happy, calm, beautiful. He was immediately comforted, even triumphant. Before she had finished speaking, he had begun to plan to which restaurant to take Rupert for dinner.

Chapter
12

BEFORE SHE WROTE her article, Grace got Spencer twice on the telephone and wrung more information out of him. On Tuesday morning she handed in her copy before setting out for the offices of Day & Monitor. There was a logic in this. She couldn't expect to gain more confidential information over lunch from Ross-Gilbert himself, and it just so happened that her deadline didn't allow her the leeway to try. She also looked on it as a story that might continue for some time and the new insights she intended to glean would certainly not be wasted.

Day & Monitor occupied a modest old building in East-cheap, full of fine woodwork and good antique furniture. As James Ross-Gilbert made his way towards it, he was a prey to two totally contrary lines of thought. On the one hand his return from the States had been treated at Lloyd's in a style similar to Pompey's triumphal return to Rome. His reputation was at its height. He enjoyed it. He sipped the nectar of adulation from the golden chalice of wealth with a seigneurial calm that masked his other feelings – the other line of thought which occupied him now as he walked along the left-hand pavement of Eastcheap – which was a sense of being threatened. The obscure awareness poisoned the edges of his consciousness as he walked.

If he acknowledged it at all, he did so with a bitter repudiating calm. He would defend to the death his right to behave in exactly the way he had done and still intended to do. His somewhat second-rate education had provided plenty of dead ends and concealed corners in his mind, in which he could dump the inconvenient logic of honour. And yet, on his way to a convivial meeting of fellow operators in Lloyd's and a lunchtime conversational diet of market gossip and exchanges, the prospect of questions put him in a bad temper. He disliked these sorts of events. In which case, why was he going? He stared discontentedly to one side and caught a view of himself reflected in the plate glass of a shop window. He couldn't say. In his conscious mind he was unaware of and unwilling to admit the advance of the hour of reckoning, and this partly explained his ability to maintain such a convincing bearing as he still acknowledged – as it were – the cheers of the crowd. But deep inside him was another awareness altogether more instinctive and elemental; and the hand of this shadow of the reigning prince already clutched the poisoned dagger of the assassin.

Henry Allanport might have to sell his estates and, with them, lose his livelihood. His wife would be literally worried to death. Faith Contay, a widow living in Devon whose husband died two months before, would commit suicide when she found herself penniless with three children to support.

But the man whose actions threatened all this never hesitated. Arriving at his destination, Ross-Gilbert walked proudly in. His handmade shoes gleamed against the carpet as one by one he mounted the narrow stairs. And when he got to the top and had allowed himself to be ushered into the board room, which was also the dining-room on these occasions, he found the other guests already waiting. He had not got over his deep-seated ill humour, and the consciousness of being the guest of honour failed to sweeten him.

But he saw at once where his own focus of attention could settle with at least some satisfaction to himself. This decision was made seconds in advance of his hearing her name, and his outer shell of inflexible calm concealed an inner sensual response as effectively as Grace's own physical makeup normally achieved the reverse. The announcement of her name following on this reaction for once brought a touch of colour to his cheek, so slight that no one would have noticed it. He remembered the telephone call. It took him a moment to recover. When they were seated he was, thank God, next to her. The Grace Derby who had telephoned his office was a dangerous potential enemy. He would see to it that the one who got up from the lunch table was only hours – or perhaps a day or two – from becoming his mistress. For the whole of the first course and half the second he took no notice of her at all. He responded with much more complaisance than he had intended to the inevitably adultory attentions of the other guests. When he wished, he could be very charming. He led the conversation and made them laugh. Grace was rather cut out. But then he turned. At first matter of fact, then with growing intimacy, he settled his whole attention on her. He kept his expression somewhat grave. And then he smiled at her.

Later, after the luncheon party was over, Grace walked through the Matisse exhibition with Spencer Day as promised, but the pleasure he had been anticipating eluded him. She had just said, casually, that she had thought James Ross-Gilbert 'rather fantastic'. Although her tone was light hearted, he could see that a certain component part of her normal manner had left her. Indifference. He had not gauged the depth of her indifference to himself until he saw the change wrought by its absence when she was talking about someone else.

'I didn't introduce you for you to fall in love with him,' he growled.

She said, 'Don't be stupid, Spencer.' But she was so happy for some reason or other that she put her hand through his arm and hugged it. He didn't even wince. His case was so hopeless there was no point. 'He exudes such an atmosphere of power,' she carried on. 'I can't help finding it interesting. Other men wobble like jellies when you're talking to them, but he's like a rock.'

Unlike Celia, who dressed with great chic combined with the romantic overtones of an old photograph, Grace favoured very well tailored, rather conventional, even boring clothes.

Inside this comparatively stuffy casing her body moved with blood-curdling allure as she progressed through the gallery on Spencer's arm. From time to time an envious glance directed at him changed as his miserable expression gave the game away.

'I handed in my article, by the way,' she now added thoughtfully. 'I don't think it will please him much.' Spencer cheered up a fraction. She continued, 'It did look as if he had been cheating.'

'My God!' He absolutely came to a halt. 'Is that what you've said?'

Matter of fact but slightly ill at ease, she bit her lip, assessing the point. He dropped his eyes to the narrow wooden boards of the gallery floor and her conventional high-heeled shoes poised with classic feminine delicacy against them.

'Based on that information you gave me and, of course, my own background and researches,' she told him, 'yes.'

'You don't quote me, do you?'

'Of course not,' she said, and added, 'But now that I've met him, I'm not sure that I'm so pleased.'

When the article appeared the next day, very few people were. Restricted as it was to financial minutiae and unsensational in tone, it was nevertheless immediately and totally obvious to leading members of the market that a real problem had arisen. It was seen to be possible that there had been a misuse of Names' money by means of diverting premium income into reinsurance companies secretly owned by underwriters and brokers involved, and from which funds were forwarded into bank accounts and used for personal purposes.

As soon as he saw the article, Spencer knew that there would be serious trouble, and a phone call from the Chairman's office giving notice of an emergency Committee meeting in the afternoon alarmed but didn't surprise him. It wasn't only his part in giving information to Grace that upset him. It was the fact that they could handle these things very well among themselves as long as no outsiders were included in the proceedings. Take his own Bermudan reinsurance company, for example.

He walked through Leadenhall Market on his way to the meeting at Lloyd's, directing at the lobsters and fresh bread and bottles of wine and cheeses and exotic vegetables and flowers for people's wives and lovers after work the unseeing eye of one who was calculating how easily he could sell certain investments and reimburse the funds in plenty of time for any call above and beyond outstanding claims liabilities. If the syndicate needed those reinsurances they could have them. And yet some interfering outsider, quibbling about the way he chose to arrange the money, could make him look dishonest. If the same explanation was all that was needed to get James Ross-Gilbert off the hook he should damn well have it, and Grace would just have to get a flea in that delectable ear if she invited Spencer to whisper into it again.

The atmosphere in the Committee room was anything but pleasant. Spencer kept his eyes averted and his thin mouth turned right down at the corners. When the meeting got under way, an almost comic battle took place among those present between the posture of righteous enquiry into the rumours, and speculation on the identity of the mole responsible for informing the Press of certain details. Spencer's mental and moral confusion mounted with every second. He was not afraid that Grace would let him down. He could look everyone in the eye and enquire with the best of them who it was who had supplied the information. But apart from that, judging by the grave expressions of anxious rectitude on every side, any practice outside the strictest rule-book was abhorred by each and every man there. And yet, for example, not to mention the undermining awareness of his own arrangements (which he couldn't help assuming were duplicated by other members present) Spencer could see around him at least eight men who to his certain knowledge creamed off the best business that came to them on the Box, and siphoned it into Baby Syndicates. With such an arrangement the underwriter, with two or three friends and relations, could make up to 100 per cent more from the proceeds of the Baby than all the other Names who supported him on other syndicate numbers. He sighed heavily, fed up with the whole thing. He himself did not have a Baby Syndicate.

The meeting around him had gradually converged on the problem of how to evolve an acceptable public presentation of these facts, if they were true. But nevertheless it did appear that a small hard core – Tom Grates, Roger Collingham, Roland Pierce among others – were pushing for an immediate enquiry into Con-Re. Spencer eyed them with bitter and weary cynicism. He half hoped that their concern was genuine; that they really were men whose own transactions could bear a similar scrutiny. That Philip Carrington himself was such a close associate of James Ross-Gilbert and had worked with him for so many years would, you might have thought, have disqualified him from nomination to carry out this particular enquiry. And yet viewed the other way – which was the way it did get viewed – perhaps he was the obvious candidate. It was agreed that he would report back to the Committee. The meeting ended. The members dispersed slowly, delayed as always by exchanges of information and gossip. Spencer, disaffected, depressed, and with a bad conscience, implied that his wife was waiting for him to go to the theatre. He went down in the lift with Ralph Scott.

'Bad business,' Ralph said as they stood there, his words not really breaking the oppressive silence. 'I wonder who's been talking to Grace Derby. She's too good looking, that's the trouble.'

Spencer managed to produce a wan smile. 'We'll be able to look after it,' he said. 'Rome wasn't destroyed in a day.'

Chapter
13

AT ABOUT THE same time as Spencer was not going to the
theatre with his wife, Grace opened the door of her flat to
James Ross-Gilbert and welcomed him in. Earlier in the day
he had telephoned her office. She had been about to leave,
but turned back from the door to answer the phone. The floor
of her office was covered with ancient green lino, pitted with
the old indentations of stiletto heels. When the sun shone, as
it did then, the room smelled of warm newsprint and stale but
comfortable chemicals used by the cleaners.

Hearing James's voice at the other end, she felt her heart
miss a beat, from guilt or excitement or both. 'I know what
you're calling for,' she said. 'You didn't like my article.'

'You're right,' he said grimly. 'I did not. Will you have
dinner with me tonight?'

'What do you mean?'

'Dinner. Eat. Restaurant. I want to have an opportunity to
tell you the real story.'

'Oh!' she said. 'I see.'

There was an awkward silence. At his end of the phone he
also was alone in his office, although there the resemblance
ended. Lying back in the William and Mary armchair behind
his desk, he fixed a hard gaze on the Gainsborough drawing
that hung in the corner between the bookcase and the wall,
and said, 'Well, what's the answer?'

'Yes,' she said. 'All right.' She tried to make the journalist speak and not the woman, but he was an old fox and he could hear the difference.

'I'll pick you up at seven-thirty?' So she gave him the address of her flat, and here he was.

Now that he was here, he seemed to have dropped the hard tone of the inquisitor and walked over the threshold unmistakably with the air of a man who had come to take her out to dinner purely for pleasure. Grace, who was accustomed to knowing exactly where she stood with her own rather prosaic reactions to the enthusiasm she aroused, for once found herself in the same boat as she habitually put others. She was both pleased and disoriented as if by a powerful magnet placed at an angle to her normal course. He stood there looking aggressively handsome and too tall, not trying for one minute to simulate the more nervous charm of a younger man. Unaccustomed to feeling nervous herself, she cast him a look almost of resentment, waiting for him to reply to her offer of a drink, but his momentary air of affability had disappeared and he was looking round the room as if she wasn't in it.

'I'm sorry,' he said, bringing his attention back as if it bored him. 'I'll have some whisky.'

It was almost as if James had been taught seduction by a man trained in hostile interrogation. First he deprived his victim of her accustomed reassurance. His behaviour was again rather distracted and solemn. He would not smile when a friend expected him to smile, or talk when a friend would normally talk, neglect a hand or turn away from an upturned cheek. Give her in fact a hard time, in a very subtle way. And then, when the effect began to tell and she had lost her assurance, her sense of superiority, he would let the concentrated focus of his intimate attention return, and the first smile would be like the offer of a cigarette or a warm blanket. Now he took the whisky from Grace's hand without meeting her eye. As if drawn to balance his indifference, she felt her attention riveted to his distracted cool examination of her flat.

'The domain of a hard-hearted business journalist,' he commented at last with a smile of sorts, but not the one he was planning to make her wait for. She felt slightly hurt, although normally it was an interpretation of herself she clung to. She walked back across the room without replying and picked up her own glass. While her back was turned, he watched her move and she caught, when she swung round, the tail end of a look so sexual in a predatory, not the familiar admiring, way, that it had a physical impact on her skin.

She spoke quickly. 'You don't have to take me out for dinner.'

'You mean we can just stay here?'

'No. I mean, you don't have to bribe me to listen to your point of view.'

'Don't I?' He took a sip of his whisky without coming any nearer.

'I'm not emotionally involved,' she said. 'I'm a professional journalist.' She bit her tongue. Stating the obvious was a classic way to draw someone's attention to the fact that it wasn't true. And was it not true? She ploughed on. 'Are you saying that I've been unfair?'

'I haven't said anything yet.'

'Your presence here implies it.'

'Does it?'

She could just stop herself from exclaiming 'Oh!' but her body felt as if she were having to repel waves of conflicting magnetic pressure, as if the air inside the room was charged.

Without actually smiling, he said, with a very much softened look, 'Don't let's quarrel.'

'The trouble about Lloyd's,' she said desperately, 'is that it really is quite complicated.'

He nodded. 'Good.'

'Thank you, but you don't have to behave as if I've just passed an exam.'

He said nothing. She had just settled in a chair some distance from him. She wore a plain shortish skirt which, when she sat, became tight. He stared at her for a moment, ruthlessly. He made no effort to disguise his expression but instead of arousing her opposition, it seemed to draw from her a helpless response.

'I want to be friends,' he said. 'You're very well known and respected in your field as I am in mine. We should understand each other.'

She nodded and looked at him. Her short hair swung out in a gold mass as she held her head consideringly at an angle and looked back at him. Or tried to. 'Are we having a conversation about business, or not?' she said.

He didn't answer, but put his glass down slowly, not taking his gaze away from her. She looked straight back into his eyes, but this time with a result not dissimilar to that when a small child puts two fingers in the holes of an electric wall socket. His unsmiling return stare went straight through her body and nearly caused a serious shock to her heart; or to some part of her anatomy. She couldn't speak. The biter bit, as Spencer might have said.

James Ross-Gilbert walked towards her, his eye fixed with a hard greedy stare on the fevered glaze that had come over her skin. He said quietly, 'Say that again.'

'Are we having a conversation about business, or not?' she repeated, looking up at him.

'No,' he said, smiling. 'Not any more. We're going out to dinner, and we'll talk about business if you like, but then we're coming back here and I'm going to make love to you.'

Before he was even half-way through the sentence, he had her complete agreement.

Chapter
14

WHEN GRACE ARRIVED in her office the next morning, she was late. She picked up a message from the switchboard asking her to phone Mary Seymour.

Tim Nesbrit, coming down the passage, said, 'Ah, Grace! Editor wants you.' He was on his way somewhere else, holding a small stack of papers in one hand. He had thin straight black hair which separated like a torn crow's feather, and tall thin suits crumpled but mildly romantic like a clever undergraduate – of forty.

Grace said 'Thank you' with one quick glance, which he fielded on the outside rim of his spectacles and hurried off unscathed.

She held the piece of paper with Mary Seymour's name on it in front of her as she walked to Keith's office, as if it needed reading more than once. 'Look what I've got here,' she said, when she got to his desk.

He raised his eyebrows, pushed some papers aside, and leaned back in his chair. 'Just wanted to say it was good, that coup of yours.'

'Thank you, Keith.'

'Will there be any follow-up?'

'Yes, I suppose so.'

He put his head slightly on one side. 'Now why are we depressed?' For once, Grace looked past him. Everyone on the paper knew that Keith was a B.F. He must have picked up the nuance of her reaction, because he went on to say, 'Get us sued by Lloyd's, Grace, and even you'll be out on your ear.'

She rested the fingers of her right hand on his desk, and shifted her weight on to one leg. 'Although it may make you feel grand to say that, Keith,' she said, 'we both know that if you lost your job nobody else would want you as editor, whereas if I lost mine, there'd be a queue outside the door.'

He couldn't think what to say to that. He would have given his eye teeth to come up with a quick response. In another forty-eight hours, if he was lucky, he would.

'Well, thank you for your congratulations,' she said. 'I had better go now and ring Mary Seymour.'

She walked away, not depressed at all but tired, and trust a fool like that not to know the difference. She came down very hard on the poor idiot not because he had no sensitivity and very little brain but because notwithstanding both these disabilities he had managed to get himself made editor. But the new mistress of James Ross-Gilbert should, by her own criteria, have been the first to realise that the ability to get a job and the ability to do it were not just different abilities, but sometimes appeared to be actually mutually exclusive. Take Ross-Gilbert; the Lloyd's market was founded on trust. And she herself knew perfectly well that he could not be trusted. Yet just the thought of him, a rapid mental collage of a look, a part of his body, and her entrails dive-bombed with a small orgasmic leap as she walked along the passage, leaving the question of his suitability for work in Lloyd's entirely behind.

When she got to her office, she immediately dialled Mary Seymour's number. At the sound of Mary's voice she swivelled her chair round to look out of the window at the same time as holding the phone, and replied that, yes, she was interested in following up some information in connection with her recent article. In effect it put her in a very awkward position, and she had lost her enthusiasm for it. She frowned on a scene below her in the street. A girl walking past with her friend went over on her ankle, not enough to twist it; but she stopped. The friend looked back. She wore a turquoise skirt. The girl bent sideways and hitched her shoe on to her foot and rubbed the ankle, tottering on the other leg. The bird's-eye view gave her a foreshortened spider-like pattern for a moment before she set off again. Now Grace said into the phone, turning from the window, 'No, I've never heard of ROSE. What is it?'

'It stands for Research Overseas for Secure Enterprise: R.O.S.E. I have been making some enquiries into it for other reasons. Basically it was set up to provide confidential political and financial information to British and American businesses thinking of setting up in less stable countries: Africa, South America, Third World . . .'

'Sounds a good idea.'

'Yes. Exactly. But expensive to set up and politically sensitive.'

'Yes, indeed. What happened?'

'It failed. Many millions down the drain. It could have been different, and that's partly my interest. But I came across certain information in the meantime that might be relevant for you. To do with James Ross-Gilbert and Dick Trene.' Grace just nodded. 'They backed it.'

It was a pity that, whereas you could declare an interest if you were on a jury, there was no such let-out for a woman journalist who had just fallen in love with the target of her investigation. 'With Names money?' she said.

'It must have been,' Mary answered. 'Five million pounds' worth of investment. But that's not necessarily the most surprising part of my information.'

Hearing the pleased edge to Mary Seymour's voice, Grace struggled to suppress her irritation. It was hardly appropriate that she, a quite well known young financial journalist, should be annoyed at attracting the help and attention of someone as eminent as Mary Seymour. Working in related fields of journalism made them acquaintances, but there the semblance of equality ended. Ministers in government consulted Mary Seymour.

'Did you get that?'

'I'm sorry,' Grace said. 'The line was bad. Can you repeat it?'

'I said that the really important point is that it appears that

James Ross-Gilbert had made over a sizeable number of shares in ROSE to a certain very senior politician. This same politician has all his personal and family insurance handled through James Ross-Gilbert, and I doubt that he has ever paid premiums. But that's immaterial compared with his involvement with ROSE.'

Grace said, 'Can you give me the politician's name?'

Mary hesitated, then said, 'Do you mind if I just check on that?'

'He must be very high up.'

'He is.'

Before she could stop herself, Grace sighed.

'Do I take it that you want to follow this up?'

'I'm sorry.' Grace felt at her wit's end. 'There's a problem.'

'Oh?'

'Can I ask how you got this information? I mean, is it reliable?'

'That's all right. I can reassure you about that. A firm called Shipping Investigation Securities.'

'Shipping?'

'They started in shipping fraud, but like most successful firms they've diversified. A friend of mine – a leading underwriter in Lloyd's – knew about them.'

'And are they investigating JRG syndicates?'

Eventually Mary said, 'Yes. But I can't say who has commissioned the investigation, I'm afraid. It's not official.'

Grace's temper boiled over. She seemed to have blown the whistle and summoned a pack of wolves. One chance, one smell of blood, and they came scampering from every corner with eyes aglitter for the prey. 'I'm sorry,' she said. 'I don't think I can follow this up.'

'Oh?' Mary's voice reflected the unexpectedness of this response. She paused.

Grace said, 'Can't you use it?'

'Complicated. I'm involved over ROSE purely in the light of its potential as a business aid if re-established. The JRG angle is really a separate issue. I thought you had taken his story on and would want to pursue it.' Grace made no response, and so, after an instant's pause, Mary, her voice colder, added, 'You're sure about this?'

'I appreciate your ringing me. Thank you very much.'

Putting down the phone, Mary could not have been more dissatisfied than Grace at the other end of it. By the time she got home in the evening, the problem had crystallised in her mind as a personal one. She suspected Grace of having been corrupted, and she wasn't far wrong.

It so happened that she and George were alone for dinner.

'Why don't you just leave it?' George said about something else. 'The Department of Trade enquiry is enough extra work at the moment.'

'You think so?'

She looked down, projecting the crisis of her uncertainty on to the knives and forks she was holding over the table, finally putting them out in the wrong order and having to pick them up again.

'Well, what's the other problem, darling?'

There was a shabby armchair in the kitchen especially for George to sit in while others were doing the work, and this was precisely what he was doing. There was a pint on the table beside him and he was reading *Middlemarch* as a preliminary to possibly writing a screen play for TV. But he was very interested in these conversations with his wife. He liked knowing what was afoot.

'Shall I tell you?'

'Yes. Go on.'

'Wait a minute.' She opened and then shortly closed the oven door. A surprisingly ferocious billow of steam came out of it, and she straightened up, taking her glasses off and wiping them on her skirt. 'Where's that gin and tonic?'

'You put it on the fridge.'

The kitchen being in the basement on the garden side of the house, the view was up over sloping turf. The birds had quietened down. The soft evening light and still sporadic twittering from outside encroached, in intervals of the conversation.

Mary now described ROSE to George, as she had to Grace; the viability of the idea, the size of the enterprise.

'I've heard of that,' George said. 'I'm sure that was the

organisation that commissioned John Jorrick to do a pre-liminary recce in Africa.'

'Did they!' she said. 'Of course, he'd be just the sort of person they'd look for. Did he get paid?'

'I can't remember. But it's folded up?'

'In spades. It lost millions before it was even ready to do business, and the project was abandoned.'

He looked at her sitting there on the kitchen stool, her feet tucked up on the bar, her apron, the wholesome solid animated contours of her face, the thick glasses, the unexpectedly attractive hair, wavy bobbed and golden. The white hairs were on the top left-hand side. He shifted his arms and accidently knocked *Middlemarch* on the floor. 'Is that the end of the story, then?' he said, picking it up.

'It would have been, only Roger Collingham rang me in college yesterday.'

'Oh. Haven't seen him for some time.'

'I know. He said he was sending someone to see me from Shipping Investigation Securities that he had hired to check out James Ross-Gilbert's underwriting.'

'My God! Really? You mean on behalf of Lloyd's?'

'No. It's confidential, George. You won't mention it, will you?' He never did. 'Roger and two other members of the Committee commissioned SIS privately.'

'Why, what for?'

His expression was just guardedly experimental as she put her glass down and said, 'Fraud.' But he still looked quite uninvolved, like any man just having an interesting gossip. 'Where syndicate funds are going, in whose name, whose pocket, etc.'

'But I don't see why you should be involved, darling,' he said. 'Isn't it a bit reminiscent of the ghastly yacht row?'

'It wasn't a row.' She looked at her watch and switched off the oven. Outside, the light had faded, and through the uncurtained windows the air in patches was a brilliant dark enamel blue.

'I liked James,' said George. 'He seemed to admire you very much. I think it's a pity the way men like him suddenly attract the unsympathetic attention of the Press and from then on they can do nothing right.'

'Don't be absurd, darling!' his wife said, and it was the one thing that could make him feel annoyed. Her factual two-hundred-kilowatt mind didn't always cut through to the one and only version of the truth. 'We're not interested in gossip.'

'Who's we?' he said. 'Surely you don't come into it if Roger feels the need to check out a Lloyd's matter?'

'We do,' said Mary, 'when his investigation stumbles on the fact that Ross-Gilbert was a main backer of ROSE with stolen funds. And . . .?'

'Hold on.' The phone rang. It was outside the kitchen in an adjoining small study, and George could only just hear it. He got up.

'Don't be long, darling,' she called after him. 'Everything's ready.'

In fact, he was out of the room for some time. When he came back, he said at once, 'That was Kenneth.'

Evidently Mary had no need to ask what Kenneth had had to say. She already knew, and she could see from George's expression that he was not pleased.

'He's extremely angry, Mary. He says he gave you a brief to investigate ROSE as part of a DTI exercise into the future commercial usefulness of the idea, and you are allowing outside influences to add on to your lines of enquiry.'

'Really?'

'You seem to have some kind of fixation over this business. What on earth has James Ross-Gilbert ever done to you to make you so interested in giving him a hard time?'

She ignored that.

'Look . . .' He looked around the room himself, as if that was what he meant for a moment. He saw that dinner was ready and went over to the window and started to draw the curtains with a sort of controlled anger that did not become him at all, but he went on. 'If James Ross-Gilbert was involved as an investor in ROSE, using money that was not his, that's a Lloyd's matter. It's not for you . . .'

'But . . .'

'Wait!' He actually held his short-fingered rather meaty hand spread out in the air.

She took off her glasses and rubbed one eye patiently. 'Go on then,' she said.

'Now you seem to have got hold of the idea that he passed on shares acquired with these ill-gotten gains to *Hugh*.' He brought out the name 'Hugh' as if it was almost unpronounceable. His wife tried to get a word in edgeways, but again he forestalled her. 'You ring up Kenneth – Sir Kenneth Dunphy – and calmly tell him that his master is involved in a criminal piece of financial lunacy!'

'Yes, George, that is so.'

'What do you mean – *that is so*?'

'Exactly what I say. All right, it would have been none of my business and I'm sure Roger Collingham would not have rung me up to tell me about it if their man had not come up with this entirely unexpected angle on ROSE. But he did come up with it. While investigating the JRG syndicates' financial arrangements behind the scenes, this investigator discovered – a fact – that Ross-Gilbert invested in and acquired shares in ROSE, using Names' money, and that these shares, or some of them, have been passed on to his important friend.'

'What if this so-called Shipping Investigator has got it wrong?'

'He hasn't. I've seen some of the paper work.'

That seemed to give him pause, but he soon began again with, 'Kenneth is absolutely furious.'

'With you?'

'Yes. You're my wife!' His tone was unflattering. 'He says he saw you today. Why didn't you tell me?'

She said, 'I was in the middle of doing so when the phone rang, remember?'

'He wants you to retract the article you're writing.'

She shook her head with two short definite jerks.

'Well, give the job to someone else.'

'I tried, but Grace Derby wouldn't do it.'

'It could be the end of your career. You won't be given any more government work if they see you can't be trusted.'

She looked at him with fury. Her complexion went blotchy with anger.

'Let them sort it out,' he pleaded. 'Don't be so absolute about every damn thing. They'll see to it without your help.'

'And keep their credit, I suppose, intact under a sham surface!' she shouted. She slammed her glass down on the table. 'Do you mean to say that even you come down to this if the protagonists are rich and important enough? You want to help form a square while the two head men get their trousers back on. No!'

'Why not!' He came right up close to her just to make bloody sure she heard, and shouted it. 'Why not? What is it to you?'

She turned sharply away in order not to hit him. 'What it is to me,' she said when she could speak, 'is just fairness and an honest response to information received. And perhaps because I'm a woman and don't wholly go along with the aggressive time-serving aspects of the little world you men have cooked up for yourselves in the last two thousand years, but would prefer to see things change, albeit not overnight, towards giving credit where credit's due and the recognition of real ability and value instead of beefy little politicos with sharper elbows and more aggressive hunger for pre-eminence hacking their way to the top of their stupid little hierarchical machines while the good and the brilliant are ignored or starved out on low pay!'

'I never heard such rubbish in my life! Surely you're not trying to make some idiotic feminist point?'

'No, I'm not, you fool. I'm making a point about true values, lack of which certainly has been one of the prime causes of the subjection of women.'

'I give up! Can't you forget all that and realise that in this instance people must act together?'

'Yes,' she said with undiminished fury. 'I heard that the other day – someone called them the "Gentlemen's Mafia". Too true. But can't any of you understand the difference between team spirit and collusion?'

'Bigoted rubbish! People make mistakes.'

'Call it what the hell you like. This time I call it fraud.'

He was making for the door. He wanted to stop this appalling row, but on turning back saw, as plain as a building on fire, dislike burning in her eyes as they were directed at himself. Aghast, he felt the sting of tears. He said, 'You'll get your newspaper into a colossal libel action if you don't watch out!'

And she said, with unexpected quiet ferocity, 'Watch me!'

Chapter
15

HE WALKED PAST a Member's Agent whom he knew, whom he had been introduced to, without a flicker of acknowledgment. It was James Ross-Gilbert's own building, his own office, and he walked down the passage in his shirt-sleeves, knowing that the Agent had an appointment with him, knowing that he was being kept waiting, knowing that Dick Trene behind closed doors had been beavering away at relocation of funds and trusts since seven a.m. like a frantic nanny packing for a family of refugees; knowing that the Chairman's waiter had telephoned to request his presence at eleven thirty. And yet, even in the most private moments of his own secret thoughts, his inflexible dominance maintained guard over the untarnished fantasy of his professional standing. As he sustained his opinion of himself with such mastery, his office staff, involuntarily following his lead, found the traces of recent rumour and disquiet wiped off their conscious minds like recycled tapes. The Agent, an intelligent and highly educated man with a pertinent question to ask, was made to feel it was impertinent and sent off with a flea in his ear. And James, when he was good and ready, put his coat on and walked over to Lime Street.

Fred, the Chairman's waiter, sat all day outside the Chairman's office organising the appointments in his master's diary. Although James was in no mood to feel sentimental about Lloyd's, he felt the usual complaisant satisfaction on seeing Fred. In the beginning when Lloyd's was a coffee-shop frequented by sea-captains and other customers who invented among themselves the idea of insurance, the waiters carried messages from table to table offering prices from man to man for this cargo, that journey, that vessel. The waiters who still circulated in the Room downstairs, in their old red coats, and who still carried messages but no longer coffee, were of a different breed from Fred, who was the grandest of them all. He knew everyone and had become unconsciously adept at those small marks of special notice – the trusted old retainer's touch – which reinforced the gentlemanly pretensions of those who needed it most.

James, for example, as a long-standing personal friend of the Chairman, could arrive and say, 'Morning, Fred' and expect an especially respectful smile and a warm, 'Good morning, sir.' It was just coincidence that on this particular day a miscalculation of bookings had landed the Chairman's diary with a double date that needed embarrassing replanning, and Fred's preoccupation with it detracted from his attention. James's manner froze slightly. Just as the plague in Egypt was attributed to God's disfavour, this coolness of Fred's he attributed to recent articles about himself in the Press. For the first time a chip was taken off his sang-froid. Impervious as he was determined to be to comments from his peers, from this unexpected direction a small barb actually penetrated his self-esteem.

He was about to sit down and wait when the door of the Chairman's suite was opened from the inside by the beautiful Penelope. He followed her in, forgetful this time of any consideration beyond the immediate horizon. She held open the inner door, and James, with his quick instinct to retain the upper hand, cut short the warmth of what would have been his greeting at the sight of an official from the membership department seated slightly to the side, with a spiral notebook open ready to receive the records of page one.

Philip Carrington had risen, preparatory to giving James a warm welcome, but noticing the direction of his gaze, cut himself short and said, 'Do you know Nigel Dunlop?'

James restricted his response to a cool nod in the official's direction, and said, 'I had no idea this was to be a formal meeting.'

'No more than what is customary, James.'

'I have been "accustomed" to meeting you as a friend, Philip.'

The Chairman looked embarrassed on his own and on the recorder's account. Whether James was being disingenuous or not, he had his old friend at a disadvantage. Nigel Dunlop, on the other hand, seemed completely unconcerned. He didn't even have the imagination to enjoy the encounter, and when he went down to the Club room for lunch it didn't occur to him to mention it.

'I should have perhaps warned you that this is to some extent a formal meeting,' the Chairman replied. 'The Committee have appointed me to make some enquiries of you in connection with Con-Re.' James knew perfectly well what the meeting was about. 'In such circumstances, we must have a recorder present, James. You know that.' James remained standing nevertheless, letting an expression of extreme dudgeon darken his face like a rebellious schoolboy. His friend cast about for a solution. 'Would it satisfy you if we had a preliminary discussion in private?'

'That would certainly be something.'

Nigel Dunlop got up.

'If you wouldn't mind, Nigel.' He made an unresponsive gesture of acceptance, acknowledged Ross-Gilbert in his farewells and departed, leaving the two of them alone.

'I gather,' James said as soon as the door was closed, 'that this is some sort of a disciplinary proceeding.'

'Not exactly,' Philip said. 'But this Con-Re business won't go away by itself. The Committee wanted to appoint someone. So I thought, James, it had better be me.'

For a significant moment the two men looked directly at each other. James sat with his legs crossed and all the outward appearance of elegant, if slightly ill-humoured, relaxation which didn't alter when Philip said, 'If I am to continue in confidence with you, however, I must know more about the extent of these share holdings, and other matters.' It was not so long since the previous interview that either of them had forgotten it. James now said 'Certainly' in a prosaic tone that cut short all the reference to his former response. In fact he intended to be anything but candid. Even Philip would not stomach the unedited scenario from which Dick Trene, Ralph Scott and himself, to name the main participants, had derived their wealth.

'To begin with, what is your holding in Con-Re? I presume you have one.'

James replied, 'Twenty-five per cent.'

'Richard Trene?'

'Twenty-five per cent.'

What they had actually done, to put it very bluntly, was to reinsure at minus 40 or even 60 per cent, paying those inflated commissions into Con-Re, the shares of which were wholly owned by them. These amounts were later transferred to personal accounts in a Swiss bank (the Banque de Flors), which they had also acquired. None of these acquisitions was disclosed. They operated, in theory at least, on the understanding that any unexpected claims could be met by recovery of the various monies from among these accounts. But with long tail business covering ten or fifteen years, such an unlikely eventuality seemed negligible.

Philip continued, 'Others?'

'Ralph Scott, 20 per cent. Nick Victor, 15 per cent. Do I have to mention the remainder?'

'Yes, please.'

'Peter Anlack has 8 per cent. That twit Bunny Yiles, 7. Well – you've done the same yourself, Philip, before the Fisher Report. Before disclosure became all the rage. Changing with the times is more easily said than done.'

Philip looked up with a considering stare, which his companion finally turned off with a look of mild apology.

'I may point out to you, James,' he said, 'that I have never transgressed any obligation of disclosure. Moreover I would not have consented to be involved with you on such a matter had I known how you were handling it.'

'Of course not. I'm sorry.'

'Thank you.' There was a longish pause before Philip continued, 'Quota share reinsurances.'

'What about them?'

'Lloyd's is concerned, James, about quota share reinsurances written by Cleave & Engels as reinsurers of certain JRG syndicates, Merchaum & May being the brokers.'

'And?'

'I'm referring to a loss ratio of 30 per cent.'

'Pretty good, I'd say.' Ross-Gilbert kept his eye on the toe of his shoe poised so nicely, in the Elizabethan sense of the word, a marker for his own attitude.

Philip gave a sharp sigh and sat back in his chair, pushing the file out of reach with a gesture of irritated dismissal. 'Too good. Don't be disingenuous, James. Not now. Not here and now: and to me.' He got no answer, so eventually he carried on, 'That's 70 per cent profit. And where does that profit end up?'

The true answer would have been Con-Re. A whole chain of companies was concerned with reinsurances of the JRG syndicates, and the chain ended up in Con-Re. But James didn't want to say this. He got up suddenly. He seemed to have moved under the lash of an inner frustration that left him stranded with nothing to do but walk across the room.

Philip followed him with his gaze locked in silence, waiting for his reply. If the reply was along certain lines and if other questions turned out to be equally . . . He fumbled for a word, and gave up. Leave a blank for that one, like place-names in nineteenth-century novels. In the geography of moral depravity, one would as soon not be too specific. And he winced, having accidentally cut himself with his own unspoken choice of words.

'You don't need to look as if you're in such pain, Philip.'

'Don't I?'

'You're the Chairman. You run this lot.'

'And so?'

'Now who's being deliberately obtuse?'

'If you mean, James, that I can whitewash what you've done, whatever you've done, you're wrong.'

'I'm not asking you to. But you most certainly could.' He stopped as if in mid-sentence, and then added, 'And you might have to.'

'Are you trying to imply that my reputation is also at risk in some way?'

'No, of course not.'

'Because I come now to a quota share reinsurance that was run five years ago between my own agency and one of your syndicates. No doubt you recall. Long tail professional indemnity risk.'

'Ralph Scott broked that, too, if you remember.'

'No, I don't remember.'

'At minus 40 per cent. And you got a share.'

A sharp faint spot of carmine, like old-fashioned rouge, appeared low down on Philip's otherwise papery-coloured skin. Ross-Gilbert, watching him, let an expression of premature satisfaction just tinge the overall bitterness of his face. 'We're in this together, Philip, I'm afraid.'

But he wasn't having that. 'On the contrary,' he said with grim determination, 'other members of the market who have been involved with you may have done so on a false basis, not knowing, since you seem to have taken the trouble to conceal your dealings, what the true commitment was. If you now tell me that I have been involved where, unknown to me, certain factors of the arrangement were incorrect . . .'

'You know damn well it was "incorrect", as you put it!'

'I did so unknowingly,' he finished as if there had been no interruption, 'unaware of the scope of your activities. I hope I make myself clear.'

'Splitting hairs, Philip. Splitting bloody hairs!'

'Well, you make your mind up.' He was a harder opponent than James would ever have expected. His face had none of the bloom of satisfied exploitation and good living that his own had. He was thinner, older, dryer. But if in the past he had allowed himself to be bullied, that was history. Matters had reached the end of a line.

'Can I pour myself a drink?'

'Please do.'

'You?'

'Whisky, then.'

James poured it. Nevertheless he hadn't succeeded, by the interruption, in reducing the impact of Philip's challenge to himself. When he said, 'You make your mind up', he was referring to a choice which James could make between an outside throw at blackmailing or at least embarrassing the Chairman, or accepting his help.

'So what is it to be?'

James shrugged, drank some of his whisky and looked his old friend in the eye.

'Then I'll have an answer to my question, James.'

'The quota reinsurances?' Philip nodded. 'Con-Re.'

'All of it?'

'In the end. A whole chain of companies was involved, but that's the one they ended up with.'

'And are those funds still in Con-re?'

'No.' He said it short and clipped, like one who chopped off a hope with satisfaction.

'Where are they?'

'Wherever the various participants have chosen to put them,' he said unpleasantly.

'But those premiums are Names' money which may be needed to set against losses. Are you saying that they have been removed to private bank accounts?'

'Say what the hell you like.'

'In the case of losses, what then?'

'You know very well. It's all recoverable. If there's a bad loss, Ralph, Nick, Dick, myself – he paused spitefully – '*et cetera* – we can all pay back in.'

'You mean the funds are invested?'

'Not exactly.'

'Not invested.'

James refused to answer for a full two minutes. He dropped his tone of bitter raillery, and, if anything his expression hardened. The truth, if the word was appropriate in the circumstances, was that he minded bitterly the appalled and obvious distress of his friend, with whom he had worked almost all his life. Look at him! He said it. 'For God's sake, Philip, pull yourself together! What on earth do you think I've been living on? Nobody seriously thinks, do they, that all the plodding little by-laws, especially the new ones, of the Lloyd's market really help the enterprise to be brilliant or allow anyone – anyone – to make the sort of empire I've managed to cut out without a bit of bending?'

Philip said wearily, 'You've got it wrong. What about Collingham Ward Kaye and the TSR3 group of syndicates? Or Ben English?'

James said, considering a moment, 'I'm still way ahead.'

'Is that what you call it?'

'Certainly I do.'

'Well, I've got news for you, my dear fellow.' He used the erstwhile familiar term of affection without sarcasm, and James's eyes snapped warily to attention. 'Your days of being "ahead", as you call it, have come to an end.'

'What do you mean?'

'I mean that, at the very least, what you have described is a serious misappropriation of syndicate funds.'

'No, it is not.'

'What is it, then?'

James paused. 'I don't know what it is, for Christ's sake!' He paused again. 'Come on Philip! Let's drop this charade.' His bearing carried such conviction! He turned round in the middle of the room as if to find somewhere to deposit his glass in order to leave enough space for the rational sincerity that gripped him. 'I agree it could – would – look bad in the papers. But nobody need come to any harm.'

Philip said drily, 'I'm sorry, James, I can't do it. Even if I wanted to.'

'Can't do what?'

'Whitewash this affair.'

'Nobody's asking you to. Just don't go round like some damned officious Nanny looking in other people's drawers.'

'I'm afraid, as Chairman, I have no choice.'

'You have! You're asked to enquire, aren't you. Well, do so.'

'I've got to ask the right questions, James.'

'You ask whatever questions you like, but get this clear. Either, when the recorder comes back, I give the answers we both agree, or, if you're determined to tell all to your precious Committee, you can expect to have to include the details about Combe.'

'But that is just a personal matter. Nothing to do with Lloyd's!'

'Have it your own way. If Jane won't mind . . .'

It was no more than Philip should have expected. He was sitting sideways in his chair and glanced with one distracted sightless stare out of the window and back again, as if measuring it.

'I mean that,' James repeated quietly. 'I'm sorry, Philip. One good turn deserves another.'

In the silence that followed, Philip neither hated James nor expected to be able to persuade him. Finally he said, 'I must have your resignation from Lloyd's forthwith.'

'All right!'

He couldn't miss the tone of light-hearted contempt. The fact that this solution accorded for some reason with a convenience of James's own making he did miss. He was slow to produce an answer, and James had already cut him off again.

'All right, you shall have it now!'

James pulled his chair to the other side of the desk with the bullying joviality of one man who knows he is injuring another. The Chairman, after a moment's pause, lifted the phone and asked for the recorder to be sent back.

Chapter 16

'CELIA, RAVISHING, LOVELY creature! What can I do for you?'

'How clever of you, Ossie, to guess I wouldn't ring unless I wanted something!'

She was not alone. Hovering over the bath in which she was immersed up to her neck was her Nanny, Babs, old now and no longer the dark-haired girl who had held Celia's mother between her soft bosom and starched white apron, but with the same expression of doting censure, torn between listening to the conversation and remonstrating about the overflow. Except for the two of them, the large London house was empty.

'At last! You want my body.'

'If I wanted that, Ossie, would I use the telephone?'

'You might,' he said doubtfully, 'as a preliminary.'

'It's your mind I want.' She leaned back and a pint of water shot over the rim on to the floor. With a silent gasp of remonstrance, Babs snatched a towel.

'I've heard some gossip and I need some authentication.'

'About what, Flower of my Life?'

'Lloyd's.' There was a short pause, and then she added, 'How much?'

'Dinner at the Caprice?' he said.

Celia put one wet hand over the mouthpiece and said, 'Can you lend me seventy quid, Babs? I'll go to the bank and pay you back tomorrow.'

Ossie, at the other end, closely though he resembled someone who need never eat again, waited with an anxious expression fixed on the photograph of a nude boy propped on the mantelpiece between a bound edition of copies of the Stock Exchange daily *Official List* and an almost powdered leatherbound volume of the records of eighteenth-century tea- and silver-dealing in China before the beginning of the Opium War.

Babs nodded her agreement to the loan of seventy pounds. When she had first gone to work for Celia's grandparents, she had earned ten shillings a week, and now she pointed to the carpet and said, 'Don't spill any more water.'

'All right,' Celia said to Ossie. 'Come and fetch me at eight.'

'What does he want, then?' Babs asked as soon as Celia had put down the phone.

'It's me,' Celia said, leaning back again in the water. 'I'm getting him to check out some information for Henry.'

'Oh.'

'To do with Henry's underwriting at Lloyd's.'

'Uh.' There was a second or two of silence. 'If you spill the water,' she said after this pause, 'Mummy won't let you use her bathroom whilst she's away.' Celia took no notice. Babs reverted to the subject of Ossie. 'Why do you have to take him out for dinner? Doesn't he have any money?'

'You know Ossie, Babs. He spends it all on what he calls the pleasures of the flesh. And, besides, I want information from him, and it's only fair to pay. I'll get Henry to give me the money back.'

'What does he know about Henry's business, then?'

Babs was still leaning against the edge of the bath, which, being large and old fashioned while she was short, came up to what had once been her waist.

'Why don't you sit down, Babs?' Celia said. 'Throw my clothes on the floor and sit on the chair.'

Babs looked deprecatingly at the arrangement referred to. 'They are on the floor, anyhow.'

'Not all. But I must admit you're standing on my best skirt, Babs.'

100

She obediently moved her feet and then bent down and started to retrieve the clothes and fold them, saying again, 'Does he know about Henry's business, then?'

'There's nothing about Lloyd's and the City generally that Ossie doesn't know,' Celia said. 'He's famous for it.'

'I thought he was one of your tutors at Oxford.'

'He was – is. But he's an authority on the whole history of financial institutions: money in ancient Egypt, investment banking, the stock exchange, Lloyd's. Whenever he's not at Oxford, he's foraging around the City for information. I used to see him there when I was broking for Wayne & Stanley, after I came down. He helped get me the job. Pass me that bath essence will you, Babs?'

'Which one? This?'

'No. The small blue one.'

'That's Mummy's best.'

'Then she'd want me to have it.'

'No, she wouldn't.'

Celia decided not to argue. She got up abruptly and caused a tidal wave of bath water while reaching for the bottle.

'Oh, you naughty girl!' Babs put a towel down on the floor. 'It's gone on your own skirt, so serve you right.'

'No! Babs, can't you lift it up? Give it a shake. I've got to wear that tonight.'

'All right.' She shook it out and laid it over a towel rail. 'It's all right.'

A lovely smell of carnations spread from the bath, and Babs leaned on the edge again. She looked at her watch and said, 'I'm missing my show.'

'Oooh!' Celia mocked her. 'You're a martyr to television.'

'It's all I've got to live for,' she said vindictively, but smiling. 'Stop it now, don't be silly. You're making me wet. I can see it again on Sunday.' She sat down again and watched Celia beginning to shampoo her hair. 'Does he work in the City as well, then, or what?'

'Ossie? No, he goes there to pick up information.' She had the shampoo suds piled on her head and reached for a towel. 'He knows everybody, from the Chairman of the Bank of England to the boy who sorts Lloyd's mail. He's very grand, you know, Babs. Just because his clothes and his morals are filthy, it doesn't mean he's not important.' Babs gave her a repressive and at the same time conspiratorial look. 'He's got a daft way of talking, anyhow,' she said.

'Daft or not, they think the world of him in the City, I can tell you. The sight of his coat-tails disappearing up a flight of stairs is enough to change the share index.'

'Oh.'

'He talks to everybody, you see. He doesn't limit himself to the important ones who are the managers. He's very popular; a legend, almost. He picks people up all over the place and takes them off for coffee, lunch, tea, drinks, dinner.'

'He's fat, isn't he? Good Lord!'

'No wonder! But you'd be amazed at the information he puts together out of it all. It's getting so that top people will cancel a lunch appointment if they meet Ossie in the street.'

'You haven't got the soap out.'

'Oh.' She plunged her head under the water again.

Babs said, 'Why do you want him to talk to you about Henry, then?'

Celia leaned back, wiping her face, her hair sleek and dark with the water. 'Because there's a rumour that the underwriter who handles all Henry's Lloyd's business is crooked.'

'Does Henry know?'

'Yes.'

'What does he say? Could he lose money?'

'Lots.'

'And there's Delia. Is she better?'

'Well, they say she's all right. But she shouldn't still be having backache and indigestion and all that, should she, Babs?'

'Perhaps it's the worry.'

'Exactly.'

'She's not so young, mind.'

'Don't say that.' And then she couldn't hear any more because of the noise of the hairdryer.

Later, when Ossie rang the bell, Babs let him in before Celia could get to the door. Confronted by the overblown dishevelled figure of Ossie bending kindly to kiss Babs in the hall, she said, 'Look what I've got! A nice bottle of Krug.'

'Vision of Delight!' He exclaimed at the sight of Celia standing like a ray of sunlight in the shadows of the hall holding a bottle of champagne.

'Then come up to the drawing-room and drink it.'

'Where did you get it from?' remonstrated Babs. 'Celia, come down this minute. Is that Daddy's?'

Ossie hovered undecided between them, his foot on the bottom step, his very large but above all soft body, swathed as it was in various odd garments of antique design, making him canny about climbing stairs if champagne was not going to be at the top of them.

Celia, prancing ahead, said, 'Mind your own business, Babs', but Babs had gone already to check if the key was on its hook in the kitchen, and back again, protesting in the full flow of an obviously familiar tirade. Celia paused, felt in her pocket, and threw her the key – a single Yale that fell on the patterned stone floor of the hall with a light bounce.

Ossie said half-heartedly as he started to climb, 'If you've stolen it, Dear Heart, perhaps we oughtn't to drink it.'

'I haven't,' she said resentfully. 'Simon bought us a caseful, and I keep it in Dad's lock-up because it's cool, that's all. You open it, Ossie. I'll be back.'

He took the bottle with pleasure and set it gently down. The sound of Celia's shoes clattering down the stone stairs, and her voice calling 'Babs!', combined with the distant barking of a dog in the gardens and the green light filtering through the windows on this side of the house, reminded him of days long before Celia was born when he was a young man with a reasonable amount of money and an untarnished expectation that a world so full of inventiveness and eccentricity would appreciate his. Now that he was over fifty and he had spent more than he should of his inheritance, and the world had persisted in its determination not to pay him much for his work, he dabbled in melancholia as well as his other preoccupations. An ageing voluptuary of doubtful habits, he drew the cork of the champagne, in spite of his apparent physical clumsiness, with the sublime grace of a clown not falling off a ladder.

'Thank God for that!' said Celia, reappearing in the doorway. 'You're a genius, Ossie.'

'Generous creature!' he exclaimed. 'Have you placated darling old Babs?'

'More or less,' Celia said.

'She only loves you. Like I do.'

'You describe her by implication as a lascivious old sybarite?'

'Nonsense!' The calm concentration he was giving to each detail of his physical surroundings, but most of all to the champagne, was undisturbed.

Celia said, 'At which part of my description do you cavil?'

'Old, of course.' He considered two chairs carefully and chose, on the grounds of its colour, an armchair upholstered in dark green. 'I am not old.'

She didn't know quite how to respond to this dignified announcement. He was well over fifty. Someone thirty years older than oneself usually does seem to be on the brink of all-round obsolescence. And yet a man as indiscriminately lecherous as Ossie, combined with his extraordinary powers of observation and memory and his legendary greed, clearly was not.

'In my youth,' he said now, 'I was a rich man. Now I am no longer rich, I refuse to be old as well.'

'That's logical.'

'It is not. But it is a superior mode of thought to logic.' He drank some of his champagne and smiled with pure − or at least unmitigated − pleasure. 'I can tell that this is to be a memorable evening. Shall I recount to you some stories of my young days?'

'No, Ossie, you shan't.'

'Of your young days, then?'

'I beg your pardon, Ossie, but I *am* young.'

'We all feel that, Dearest One,' he said mournfully. 'Always. But only a little time is needed to introduce a frisson of doubt. The voluptuary who feeds on the hearts of fifteen-year-old girls would not accept one of twenty-five, and you know it. From this knowledge comes that breath of unease which you deny.'

104

'Don't be so revolting.'

He held out his glass with a forgiven smile, and watched in silence as she filled it. 'Ah, how well I remember,' he said, holding it up to the light as if the colour reminded him of something, 'that morning in early summer two years ago when picking my way home from an exceptionally protracted evening encounter at our venerable university – of which you are now a graduate and I a don of legendary reputation – we met by the river and talked.'

'Magdalen Bridge.'

'The light of a new day as pale as white wine just beginning to spill over the water.'

'About broking,' she said, with an actual shudder. 'Why didn't you tell me that the City was a boring claustrophobic dumping-ground for 90 per cent materialistic bone-heads and 10 per cent geniuses like yourself, and I'd be expected to spend all my time with the former?'

'You flatter my powers of perception; something not easy to achieve, but you have just done it, Miracle of Prettiness.'

'I loathed it.' She took a gulp of champagne as if washing her mouth out. 'Standing in queues on the floor of Lloyd's having one's knickers pinched by goofy males with pin-striped brains. How can you bear it, Ossie?'

'They don't pinch mine, more's the pity.'

A sudden uproar of gunfire from downstairs indicated that Babs had turned on the television in the small sitting-room.

'Have some more champagne, Ossie, to make up for the disappointment.'

He smiled up at her, a childlike pleasure illuminating his large and dishevelled features, as he held out his glass.

Sometime later they went out into the street together to get a taxi. Ossie, in consequence of some of his worst excesses, walked slowly and with a shuffling panache. 'When we get to the restaurant,' he said, 'you will tell me what it is that poor Ossie can do for you, other than those things that he has already mentioned that he would like to do and you won't let him.' He climbed into the cab without drawing breath. 'But until then, Dearest One, let us talk about amusing things. Much as I like to be useful, it is an indulgence. There are

105

some things that one really must not overdo.'

In profile, his enormous nose and bulging eyes swept unforgettably past the speeding backdrop of the park. The light had faded to a moth-like dimness, with a touch warmly soft in the air as the brush of such a wing. 'I will now tell you a poem,' he said. 'It is called "The Sea".' He took her hand. His fingers were puffy and huge, and held hers like a giant inspecting a small flower. 'It's not my poem.'

'Whose?'

He made no answer, but intoned:

You eat ships,
You taste wrong.
You isolate and desolate.
You are no friend
    to man.
Yours is the
    subtlest beauty.

'Who wrote that?'

'I don't know. I read it once in the *Spectator* when I was about your age.'

'Maybe I will marry you, Ossie.'

'Sweet Child! You have all the generous impulses of a pure heart. First champagne and now marriage.'

'And dinner.'

'That is yet to come. Ah, life! Always one more thing to enjoy before being absolutely swallowed by the abyss!'

'What abyss?'

But they had arrived, and there, shimmering on the pavement like an oasis in the desert, was the Caprice.

Chapter 17

AS A YOUNG MAN, Ossie had been both handsome and brilliant. He had inherited money, and with a gargantuan appetite for all the pleasures of the intellect and the flesh he had gone up to Oxford and achieved a double first in history and, in a sense, a double first in love, since his affairs were wonderful, passionate and with both sexes. Offered a fellowship, he specialised in the history of financial institutions. His fellowship became a lectureship, but there he had to acknowledge that he had entered something of an academic cul-de-sac. His speciality had become an obsession. His expertise engulfed all the modern, in addition to the ancient, institutions and his love of conversation and philandering being equally extreme, he added to his scholarship that quintessence of real life: a talent for gossip. The City institutions that depend so much on the exchange of information that underpins the exchange of money witnessed the arrival of the younger Ossie with hospitable detachment. He would lunch with this underwriter, discuss an academic point for a paper with that dealer. He would have tea and cakes with an old acquaintance in the records department of this institution, a cocktail with a retiring Managing Agent from Lloyd's. The next day, a chance encounter with a former student in the street would lead to a confidential chat over coffee, discussing his reasons for deciding to leave in six months. Ossie would depart only in time for lunch – perhaps an appointment that happened to be with an old friend in senior management in the same firm. And then tea with another, and cocktails with another. His body, mirroring the repository of his mind, grew huge. He now earned virtually nothing besides his university pittance. He dealt in the sort of information that it is illegal to pay for. He was reduced, by the objects of his passions in the field of art and sex, to a small flat in London in addition to his rooms at Oxford, and between these places and the City, his comings and goings were observed, as time went by, with increasing veneration and astonishment.

Now, with his eye fixed on a dish of *Nage de poisson au beurre de homard,* he said, 'Your cousin Henry is in an undeniably unfortunate situation.'

'We want to know how unfortunate, Ossie.'

She rested her elbows on the table and stared at him. Her own face – so delicate and beautiful but, it must be said, slightly clichéd, like the ideal type of the photographer's model used to advertise cigarettes in the sixties – was misleading, implying a predictability that she totally lacked. 'How unfortunate, would you say?'

Ossie reflected on both her question and what she had said before. He savoured, between mouthfuls of steamed turbot, salmon and scallops in their lobster sauce, the familiar and equally delicious sensation of the coming together of information with the insatiable appetite for it that he also possessed. For example, to add a dimension to Celia's description of the weekend on the yacht, he knew about the quarrel below decks between James and his partners. Shipping Investigation Securities, whom the three Committee members under the private leadership of Roger Collingham had hired, had flown their investigator Maldwyn Harris out to question the yacht's crew; and Mal Harris was another of Ossie's unlikely friends. He had not disclosed the names of those who had commissioned the enquiry, but Ossie already knew, having been told by Mary Seymour.

'I will tell you what I know,' he said, 'and you can judge for yourself.' He paused while the waiter came to the table and poured more wine. He appeared to be concentrating on the filling of his glass, but in his thoughts he was assembling all the details of his recent researches. Eventually he settled himself in his chair and began, 'We are discussing the rumour that our friend James Ross-Gilbert may have made fraudulent use of the monies entrusted to him on behalf of his Names – the investors on his syndicates. So far, Con-Re, a reinsurance company taking JRG business, is said to have been treated like a private property – which it was, incidentally – since its shares are secretly owned by JRG and his associates. The premiums sent to it were passed on to a Swiss bank called Banque de Flors. It has been suggested to me that this bank may have been bought secretly by directors of Cleave & Engels and also James Ross-Gilbert, Dick Trene and Ralph Scott. Now, the syndicates in question are many and various, since our hero managed to secure new syndicate numbers to the value of twenty-one.'

'Good God!' she said. 'Twenty-one syndicates? How on earth did he manage that?'

'Flower of my Life, we will be here all night unless I skate lightly over the details. Now, into this magic bank whose doors must, according to Swiss law, forever remained closed to the impertinent enquiries of honest men, vast sums of money have flowed. As you, Exquisite Mélange of Beauty and Intelligence, know, I do not use extravagant terms in my conversation lightly.' He leaned forward without a smile. 'But when I say large sums of money . . .' He spread his hands. 'And what does the market think of him? They think he is the very model of the perfect gentleman, although, between you and me, whereas a snob might be overwhelmed by his wealth, a discerning person could not make that mistake.'

She remembered James on his yacht, and laughed.

'But . . .' and Ossie paused dramatically, 'they called him "brilliant", which was a far worse mistake, and one which I'm sorry to say men often do in the hope that the same may be said one day of themselves. Cunning, yes. Ingenious in the intricacies of his web of finance.' He froze his gestures in an eloquent tableau of discreet admiration. 'But no more. However, such a proliferation of syndicates allowed scope for unprecedented sums of money to be dealt with, varying proportions from 10 to 60 per cent of which ended up in his own hands and those of his friends. But now . . .' he quelled an incipient interruption, 'if the underwriting that he did was itself fundamentally sound, all could yet be well, in a manner of speaking.'

'And is it?'

He looked at her. 'Alas.'

'Oh hell!' A shadow crossed her face as if a filter was slotted over the lens of that old camera. 'How bad will the losses be?'

'Terrible.'

'That's brief for you, Ossie. Are you trying to be discreet again? Because my cousin Henry stands to lose every penny he's got, and his wife is pregnant and not doing well, and the worry is going to kill her. When I say I want to know, I mean I want to know.'

'Spare me, Vengeful Child!' He flung a hand over his eyes. 'To destroy Ossie's digestion by glaring at him like that will help no one.'

'Carry on, then. I'm sorry.'

The wary eye that observed so accurately from behind the stalking-horse of all his badinage softened. 'Very well, Dear Heart, it's like this.' He reached into an inside pocket and took out a folded slip of paper, but didn't read it at first. 'As you know, marine syndicates do incidental non-marine underwriting. In the past – the future, I can tell you, is very different – incidental non-marine business escaped much scrutiny. And, as we know, our friend James was adept at non-communication when it suited him. He underwrote long tail American liability business.'

'Oh no!'

'You understand what that means. The market didn't generally know what he was underwriting and, of course, with long tail business the profits look *very* good – until you get your delayed loss. And all these silly American judges, Sweet Creature, award outrageous compensation nowadays for trifling setbacks suffered by employees or sick people!' His expression was so aggrieved that her sense of humour started to come back like a revived blood-supply. 'Mark my word, they won't be able to buy insurance at any price soon, unless they come to their senses.'

'What liability did he write, exactly?'

Ossie unfolded, with deliberate drama, the piece of paper he held in his hand. 'Medical malpractice; director and officers' liability business, products liability, professional indemnity.' He raised his face like a priest at the end of a funeral service and slowly lowered his glasses. 'He wrote them on an excess loss basis, and by my own rapid calculations based on a trifling detail mentioned by Mr Scarfy Matthews over tea yesterday, losses could easily be £200,000 per £20,000 share. I'm sorry, Vision of Loveliness, but this is what you get when you ask for plain speaking.'

'Surely the auditors will have set reserves? And the premiums paid for that long tail business? He's been paid for those reinsurances. The money will have been invested and will be there to meet the losses ... Oh!' They shared a mournful silence. '*Not* there. He's spent it. I forgot. Banque de Flors. Con-Re ...' Her voice held back tears of suppressed rage that glittered in her eye. 'Henry wrote half a million. As a direct Name.'

'I know.'

'Oh, do you? I suppose you would.'

The waiter had brought the summer pudding and Ossie, with the happily renewable optimism of pure greed, transferred his attention to it. She watched him in silence.

Eventually she said, 'I suppose the complete picture hasn't emerged yet. You're the only one who knows all the people who each know their little bit.' He cast her a grateful glance of agreement. 'But surely he can be arrested on criminal charges? Or did somebody say he is resigning and going to live abroad?' Ossie nodded, waiting for her to follow her line of thought to its bitter conclusion. 'If somebody served a writ on him now, would it fail because the facts aren't out? I suppose it would. But once he's gone abroad, the DPP would have to prosecute to get him extradited.'

'I am not saying his crimes are not serious enough to warrant that, Angel Heart, but they won't do it.'

'Why not? You know something else?'

'I do.' He looked once regretfully at his empty plate. 'I am a man of honour.'

'Of course you are,' she said. 'What's that got to do with it?'

But he decided to let it pass. 'I am party to some knowledge of an exceptionally sensitive nature that has direct bearing on your hopes in connection with Mr Ross-Gilbert and the public prosecutor's office. They will not bring a case.'

'Why?'

'Thereby hangs an embarrassing little tale.'

'Embarrassing for whom?'

'I will tell you. Approximately six years ago a clever gentleman conceived a plan for an international company giving business to cover for new enterprises opening up abroad. Where a country's government was somewhat of an unknown quantity for European companies considering expansion, their investigative team would research and keep up to date a detailed assessment of local hazards in personnel, ideologies, corruption, state financial controls, etc. Rather like a network of commercial embassies independent of the Foreign Office.'

'Brilliant idea.'

'Indeed, Dearest One. And *very* expensive. It was called R.O.S.E. – Research Overseas for Secure Enterprise. James Ross-Gilbert was one of the major backers of the scheme.'

'Wow!'

'You can imagine, Dearest One, whose money he used.'

'Bloody well Henry's.'

'Among others.'

'It failed, of course.'

'Yes.'

'So?'

'While the project was still in its hopeful phase, the shares that James Ross-Gilbert received in return for his investment he gave to a *very important person in government.*'

'Do you mean the Prime Minister?'

He shook his head, either in denial or regret at her indiscretion, and said, 'We need not name the gentleman in question.'

'Named or not, he was a receiver of stolen goods, then.'

'Indeed.'

'He would be named all right if the DPP prosecuted Ross-Gilbert, and the ROSE episode came out.'

'So they will not, take it from me. For that very reason.'

She said, 'Lloyd's then! *They* can prosecute.'

He had hunched himself up and pored, now, over the table like a chess player anticipating the last moves of the game. Fixing upon her his bulging and baleful eye, he moved from check to checkmate. 'Unfortunately . . .'

'Oh no, Ossie!' The sharp indignation of her voice drew for a moment, the attention of the nearest table.

'A little bird has told me that he has resigned from Lloyd's'

'But he'll have to give six months' notice.'

'It's been waived.'

'Whose idea was that?'

'The Chairman. He obviously sees it as an honourable solution to the impending Con-Re disclosures. But, alas, there is another angle to it.'

'Won't that mean Lloyd's can't prosecute either, if he's not a member?'

'Exactly.' And he leaned back. The game was over. Checkmate.

Celia sat for a moment in silence. The lively buzz of the restaurant and the flashes of dark reflection from the shiny black surfaces moved into the silence between the two of them like elements in a film set. Finally she said, 'Well, thank you, Ossie. You have given me a very complete picture. I knew you would.' He smiled apologetically and said nothing. 'You are probably the only person who knows all this at the moment, except Ross-Gilbert and his cronies.'

'I think so.'

'And Shipping Investigation Securities?'

'Perhaps.'

'Maybe, if the DPP and Lloyd's are no use, they might help. If it comes to it . . .' She called the waiter over without finishing the sentence, and asked for the bill. 'I hope you don't mind,' she said. 'I must get back to ring Henry.'

His expression was desolate. As they walked out between the tables he saw beside someone else's plate a small dish of petit fours. He stopped, and for fully five seconds gazed down at them like a starving man until Celia, firmly pulling his coat-sleeve, dragged him away.

Outside, the softness of a summer night enveloped them. Up in Yorkshire only a slightly sharper wind ruffled the edges of the sky. Waiting for her call, Henry, alone downstairs while Delia already slept, stared across the garden towards the park. He saw the luminous shadows of tall pale delphiniums in the borders. In the glass of the uncurtained window the gilded reflections of the drawing-room were superimposed on the darkened world outside. He held a glass in his hand and stood gazing in silence until, behind him, the phone began to ring.

Chapter 18

DURING THE NIGHT it came on to rain, but stopped before the sun rose. Here in the country there was a smell of morning, of water evaporating off lush grass, of sunlight liquid and shimmering and not yet hot; a smell of England. It was going to be a lovely day than which no day can be more lovely when the landscape finally gets down to it.

Delia said to Henry, 'Don't go. It's far too nice.'

He looked as if he wasn't going to argue. They were still in bed. The room had filled with sunlight since the curtains were drawn, and the gentle twittering sounds of a new day fell softly as shadows into the unguarded peace. It was quite unlike him to be lured away from such pleasures by any officious call of duty. He preferred not to interfere with a Fate in which he had such confidence. Normally, the light-hearted optimism that disarmed trouble before it happened resulted in a self-fulfilling prophecy about everything being all right. Add to that a disposition to be happy and the opportunity to be lazy whenever possible, plus an attitude of affectionate ironic laisser-faire towards the bad, and he might indeed have stayed with his cheek against Delia's bare shoulder basking undisturbed in happiness and serenity.

Now he smiled, not answering at once. The trouble was that he thought that this time he had no choice. He could not in fact qualify as a genuinely lazy man who would let something spoil rather than be obliged to move. And he thought that the news Celia had given him the night before made it more or less essential that he should be at the Merchaum Agency annual reception in the evening. In London. The irony lay in the fact that when Fate is determined to tear a man's heart out, she has double rows of teeth.

'I'll come back tonight,' he said. 'Agency receptions don't go on late. I'll leave London without even stopping for dinner.'

'I'll come with you.'

'No, don't. You rest. I won't even go up until after lunch.'

In this way, he spent the morning with Delia and said goodbye to her just as the afternoon began to be drowsy. She sat down in a covered chair near one of the borders holding a book, whose white pages he could still see from quite a long way off. She was wearing a blue dress of a more faded colour than the sky, and she just leaned back as he reached the corner and shaded her eyes from the sun. He knew she would be smiling.

When he arrived in the City at the end of the afternoon, he walked into the room in which the reception was being held, noticing that everything seemed unchanged from the previous years, except his own frame of mind. The Names, many of them up from their country estates, the women smartly decked out, the men discreetly proud of themselves, in the circumstances. In theory, this party was given by Merchaum in their role as Member's Agency, to the Names whose allocations, as members of Lloyd's, they managed. But since Merchaum, in its other role as Managing Agency, also managed the twenty-one JRG syndicates and virtually restricted the Names' allocations to these syndicate numbers, almost every guest was a direct Name. James Ross-Gilbert himself, as Chairman of Merchaum and lead underwriter on the syndicates, was the unrivalled star of the occasion. And he seemed to occupy that role with the same assurance as in previous years, his popularity undiminished. As he moved through the room, his Names courted his attention and laughed at his jokes with the same admiring and confident enthusiasm.

Henry looked for one trace, one fleeting oblique glance, one sign of any disturbance, and saw none. Catching sight of him, Ralph Scott found an opportunity to break off a conversation and came over. Momentarily his habitual expression of distaste for some unspecified local annoyance gave place to one of pleasure as he greeted Henry. The fact that he afforded himself the luxury of continuing to care for someone who embodied the virtues he himself had given up perhaps pointed to one explanation for the sourness of this habitual frame of mind. In response to a question as to who would take over as lead underwriter when James retired, Ralph mentioned the name of one of the longest-standing deputies and also a new acquisition from another firm.

They had been joined by a tall magisterial figure whom Ralph introduced as Giles Anderson, so that they were no longer alone when Henry asked, 'Will a number of the syndicates continue to write a large amount of long tail American liability business?'

Ralph said, with barely a pause. 'You'll have to ask Dick that. I'm only a broker, you know.'

But Giles Anderson was frowning as if he'd noticed a cockroach in his champagne. 'What is that you said?'

'Long tail American liability business.'

'That's what I thought you said.' He looked like the sort of man who had the knack of letting people know if he wasn't pleased. He was searching his memory now, holding his head up rather like a dangerous animal smelling the wind. 'I remember I made enquiries last year,' he said 'About the time Crabbe Acheson caught such a cold along those lines. I was given to understand that we weren't involved in that type of business.'

'Apparently we are.' Henry turned relentlessly back to Ralph, although he appeared physically relaxed and he smiled and said, 'Surely Merchaum & May have been broking quite a lot of it?'

'Oh everybody does some.' Now that the encounter was turning sour, Ralph's own feelings had returned to normal. Henry didn't press the point.

But Giles Anderson, who would have carried the question

117

forward on the spot, and anyway would not forget it, had seen another friend. At the same time, James Ross-Gilbert was just mounting the small platform at one end of the room with his deputy, Nigel Waterhouse. They seemed to be looking round for somebody. Dick Trene was missing. After a few minutes, the senior partner of Merchaum called for silence.

There followed a presentation and a retirement speech and some emotional tributes to James, who bore it all with the conscious dignity of a school hero leaving for the outside world. Henry, looking at him in the light of his accumulated researches of the recent weeks, and of Celia's revelations and the rumblings of the Press, could hardly understand how the *status quo* of previous times could survive intact. Ross-Gilbert's surface shine, which had always been there even to the oblique and tolerant glance of a man like Henry Allanport, now seemed overtly flash, compromised by unwholesome suspicion like water on a shark's fin. Although his clothes were immaculate, his thick white hair shining above a healthy and quite youthful face, the eye was drawn to his hands, which, even at this distance, looked puffy and useful only for rather unpleasant tasks; and the large signet ring that flashed too brightly in the exploding lights of the Press cameras.

Because there were some members of the Press there. They had been invited reluctantly from one point of view, willingly from another. Setting aside for the moment their recent scandalous business allegations, not to mention unseemly titbits to do with his divorce from Marjorie, it was right that the farewell of such a notable City figure as James Ross-Gilbert should be recorded in the nation's Press. James, who looked over the heads of his flock trustingly gathered around him, their confidence and admiration as yet unaffected by rumour, orchestrated his own gestures and their responses with assurance. But, at the same time, part of his mind speculated with restless annoyance on the absence of Richard Trene. In it, he sensed the relentless acceleration of disaster. But his heart beat no more quickly. No trace of sweat showed on his temples. He was only conscious of an unusual intensity as his instinct monitored the exact climate of this triumph. He felt it like a cold restriction laid across his nerves. He put his left hand in his pocket and smiled slightly at the end of a joke. The skirt of his jacket pushed back over the long elegant line of his legs, he stood and received the affectionate laughter of his friends. It gave him time to look once more over their heads for bloody Richard Trene, but he was nowhere in view.

Henry, watching him minutely, saw the look. Now the last words of farewell were spoken. He said something like, 'Without you, the business of Lloyd's itself could not carry on. Without your backing I could not have had this interesting and rewarding career. Thank you.' And they began to clap.

Almost simultaneously one of the two reporters took a step forward. He was an older man. His well-worn suit was pulled out of line by the camera straps. His voice sounded uncommonly loud as he called out, 'Are you aware, Mr Ross-Gilbert, that Richard Trene has left the country?'

At first a variety of reactions filled the space in which he expected an answer to his question, and he asked it again. His voice shook as if he was nervous, and the other camera flashed to record the indomitable froideur of Ross-Gilbert's reaction. Nigel Waterhouse had jumped up and was pointing one of the waiters in the direction of the door, presumably to show the newsman out of it.

'I'm sorry,' Ross-Gilbert now said with venomous contempt. 'Did I not mention it? My partner Richard Trene is on holiday.'

One or two Names laughed. He made as if to step down from the platform, but the newsman, with extraordinary courage, stood his ground and asked another question. 'Are you also aware,' he now said, 'that your partner is thought to have absconded with funds embezzled from syndicate resources?'

The pull between the wish to dismiss this contentious interruption of an important and moving event and the wish to hear more could be seen at work among the Names like conflicting tides in water. Ross-Gilbert was caught in mid-step. He remembered in time not to answer, but even for him a complete grip on this event was not possible, and into his eyes and on his face there appeared an expression which, although it was directed at the newsmen and not his audience, appeared in the papers the next day for all the world as if, like a wolf, he was unmasked above the cowering flock of Names gathered around him.

Henry looked for Ralph Scott in the crowd. He saw him near the door with two waiters. Nick Graham, the Chairman of Master's, whom Henry hadn't noticed before, approached the microphone. The newsman was now being hustled to the door, not unduly protesting. After all, he had got his story.

'Please!' Nick Graham's voice rose above the fairly well mannered confusion. 'Richard Trene *is* on holiday. This extraordinary allegation is most ill-timed and has no bearing on our farewell to our friend and colleague today. James . . .' he turned to him, 'we all wish you a very happy retirement. Farewell. And thank you,'

They did their best. There was some clapping, and James was back on form. But some of the air of privilege had gone, the sanctity of a protected enclave. The Names felt it, although good manners restrained them. The skilful vigour of a well-fed not uneducated élite coped with the conflicting needs to leave promptly or to flesh out the planned farewells. The fact was that Richard Trene was indeed absent. His presence had never been noted by anyone with much enthusiasm. Now his absence lay over this vital celebration like a smell that all concerned tried hard not to acknowledge.

James Ross-Gilbert's demeanour, as he circulated in the dwindling atmosphere, denied the murderous hatred he felt in his heart. He had no doubt at all that England had seen the last of his treacherous partner who had turned tail and run, his craven lack of nerve exposing the unprotected flank of his master. But at least he, James, had the power of personality to uphold his supporters' illusions of himself to the bitter end. To look at him now, as Henry was doing, was to see a great and good man, confident in his own integrity, upheld by the unfailing good opinion of his peers, bidding farewell to humble friends who were reluctant to see him go and who mistrusted the harsh treatment they might get once he was no longer there to protect them. At the end of one such speech,

James glanced up and caught the eye of Henry watching him. There was a cool sparkle in his ironic gaze of which James was suddenly intensely aware. While listening to some woman's artless speculations on the joy of retirement, a part of his mind digested that look. He recognised an adversary who, assuming he had arrived earlier on the scene, would have been a problem to contend with. Now, he thought, a strategic departure would solve that problem along with all the others. Even so, he just lacked the nerve, when the moment came, to shake Henry by the hand without the most extraordinarily unpleasant frisson of disquiet running through him. It made him turn his mouth down at the corners at the same time as attempting to smile, uniquely disconcerting him.

'I hope you are not going to leave the country too soon,' Henry said.

'So do we all, Lord Allanport,' struck up an admirer. 'It's too bad of him.'

But James knew what was meant, and would have had to reply had Henry's attention not been claimed at that moment by two people who came towards him across the now half-empty room. As they approached, Henry, with a gesture of apology, detached himself from the conversation and took a few steps to meet them. James kept a half-wary eye on the group. The young man was a stranger to him, but the girl he recognised as Celia Merrin. At one moment he thought he saw Henry stumble, and the young man seized his arm as if to steady him. There was something going on. Another guest, catching the direction of James's eye, turned, but observed nothing unusual. He could not know that he was witnessing the moment when Henry Allanport was told of the death of his wife; of a sudden collapse, no 'will she, won't she', no intensive care. She was dead. Dead. Henry stood quite still as if, until he moved, the last traces of a life of which she was a part surrounded him. From across a now unbridgeable chasm the distant figure in the faded blue dress smiled her last farewell. He could not take his eyes off her.

Celia said, 'Henry?'

Somebody was trying to say Hello to him, a woman in a royal blue silk dress who had blundered up in the general goodbyes, marginally disoriented with drama and champagne, saying, 'I saw you earlier, Henry, and couldn't get across. How are you? How's Delia?'

He smiled at the woman politely, and kissed her on the cheek.

'Oh, good heavens!' she said, catching sight of her husband. 'Paul's always in such a frightful hurry. I'll have to go or I'll never hear the end of it. Love to you both,' she called over her shoulder.

When she had gone, an infinite poisoned space closed in around him.

'Henry darling,' Celia whispered, 'Shall we go? Rupert's got a taxi.'

He nodded, but first he turned quite slowly, as if drawn by a look behind him. James Ross-Gilbert, still besieged with old friends but still observant, met his eye. The party was almost over in more senses than one.

But he, James, was still one step ahead. He had chosen a prosperous future out of England. It was his own independent wish. In fact, everything was all right except for that one look – that instant in which, by what trick this inflexible master of chicanery would never know, his perception was turned on himself. He caught Henry Allanport's eye and it was like looking into the funnel of a volcano. An anger reached out to seize him and a despair so black that he could almost have cried out, 'What have I done to you?' Eventually he could recognise that to squander and steal another man's entire estate, to harass the last week's existence out of his wife and possibly to be responsible for overloading her husband's attention at a moment when he crucially missed warning signs of her ill-health – all this was in that look. And, what was worse, he understood it. Afterwards he forgot. But for that instant he saw what he had done. It was not that he cared; but it was the first time the idea presented itself that there might be a price to pay. Celia said again, 'Henry!' and he turned away. But for a fraction of a second after he had released his gaze, James's own eye bore the impact of the look that had been exchanged. The injury he rapidly forgot. But he had read another message that was not so easily brushed aside: and that was vengeance.

Chapter
19

'HOW DID SHE DIE?'

Misery made the inhabitants of the half-lit drawing-room gauche and awkward like bad actors on a stage at the rise of the curtain: the heartbroken young husband, Celia the beautiful cousin, Dr Cobam the old doctor, uneasily assessing his own professional discomfiture, and the faithful servant.

William said, 'It was just after five o'clock, m'lord.'

Henry bit his lower lip and continued to gaze fixedly at him as he stood, almost like a man accused. Celia turned away to hide her face. The room was like a wilderness. Nothing was different but nothing was the same. Doors were left open, lights not lit. Outside, from the uncurtained park, a fiendish night wind was blowing from the trees.

'M'lady came in from the garden with a bad headache, and said she would like a cup of tea brought up to her room, and could Ellen fetch some aspirin.'

As he continued his account, William's face changed colour. He had gone to the kitchen, but by the time he came back he found Lady Allanport half-way up the stairs, hanging on to the banisters, having some sort of a fit. Her lips were blue and her face was very pale. She seemed about to say something, when her body was seized with convulsions which made it impossible for him even to stop her falling. He tried to catch her, but her limbs jerked uncontrollably, knocking him aside. He shouted for Ellen, who was already half-way across the hall, and when she saw what was happening she dropped the tea and held her spread hands rigid over her face. He shouted at her again to ring the doctor.

'My lady breathed very fast,' he said, unable to stop the tears running down his face. 'The the blueness went from her lips and I thought she was coming round, m'lord. But she suddenly went as stiff as a board. And died, sir.'

Henry stared still at him as if waiting for more. The poor man failed to stifle a sob, and spread his big hands once in an eloquent gesture of desperation, but stood his ground.

'Did she say anything?'

'No, m'lord. I don't think she could, m'lord.'

'Nothing at all?' Unwittingly Henry's voice held a slight note of pleading as he asked the question 'Nothing at all?' and received no answer.

Old Cobam muttered 'Eclampsia', shaking his head and mumbling over it.

Henry said, 'Thank you, William.' He didn't – perhaps couldn't, in spite of his almost dreamlike composure – say more. But his talent for friendship made his look and his tone of voice the opposite of a formal dismissal.

William wanted to say something. He could just manage to say, 'I'm so sorry, m'lord.'

Henry met his eye and said nothing, but smiled a brief bleak smile of mutual understanding.

When William had gone, the burden of enquiry was obviously going to fall on Dr Cobam, and he shuffled uneasily, longing for his bed.

Henry, who felt that he would never forget one single detail of these horrific hours, saw exactly how he felt, and braced himself against his own anger. Let him make no excuses. He had withstood all the enquiries about Delia's headaches, her nausea, her backache, with the indulgent overconfidence of an old campaigner. And not he alone. Sir Gerald Carhampton in London and Cobby and his young assistant here. In spite of all his care, they had missed something vital, and he cursed them. He turned and leant his elbow briefly on the mantelshelf with his fingers pressing between his eyes. After a moment he said, 'What went wrong?'

Dr Cobam said, 'There's no doubt about it at all; eclampsia.' He raised his eyes in a pathetically defiant attempt to lend himself the dignity of making a pronouncement, and he did it as if addressing a Board. 'It's rare.' It sounded like a justification. He could hear it himself. He said again, in a slightly firmer voice, 'I must say, it's rare.' He looked very distressed. It was a miserable way for things to turn out, by which he meant his reputation in old age.

Henry nodded. 'You said that. You said that it occurs in first pregnancies. But can't it be detected?'

Dr Cobam was about to reply, but Henry went on, 'My wife had all the tests and check-ups. More.'

The doctor shook his head. 'The problem is,' he said, 'that she appeared to be in good health.'

Celia, although keeping silent, looked at the old man in frank fury.

Henry, seeing her expression, let a wave of tiredness or despair soften his tone. He said, 'She didn't, you know. We were all worried about it; all asking questions.'

'I meant,' Dr Cobam corrected himself, or not quite – he wasn't making a concession, 'not good health exactly; but those symptoms are often consistent with a perfectly normal pregnancy.'

'But in this case consistent with the onset of eclampsia?'

There was a pause.

'Yes.'

The monosyllable, just that one inexcusable word, seemed to kill her again. The atmosphere of the room absorbed it only slowly, like a poison. The sound of it seemed to linger.

Henry looked up. He saw the doctor standing there, looking tired but not daring to sit down, and Celia. He said, 'Sit down, Dr Cobam. I'm sorry . . . Please do sit down. Would you like a drink? Celia, how about you? I'll have something myself.' He turned to where William was accustomed to leave whisky and other drinks prepared with glasses and ice for the evening. It was all there. It made a diversion.

It was not, after all, recrimination that he was after. He only wanted to know and to know. The whisky made Dr

Cobam more communicative. He explained the symptoms of eclampsia – the nausea, and the pain in the back which was really from the kidneys and not the usual inconvenience of pregnancy. A simple urine test would have shown albumin in the blood, indicating a state of toxaemia leading to eclampsia. He sought to imply that all the other modern tests and scans could cloud the issue of a simple precaution like this one, and there was even some justice in what he said. Her specialist in London had even missed it. The last statistic he had read showed six hundred women a year dying of eclampsia. It was an occasional hazard, usually of a first pregnancy. It was simply something you could miss.

Something you could miss. When Cobam was gone, and Celia, Henry made no attempt to go to bed. He stood looking out into the park, as he had done the night before. But instead of seeing the reflections in the glass and the painted shadows of flowers, it was just all darkness that seemed to draw in the soul. He drank, but misery forestalled the fumes rising. He merely knew that in the morning the arrangements of death would take over, and until that time he would watch the day break.

Mary Seymour, at breakfast with George not many hours later in London, said, 'Have you seen this picture of James Ross-Gilbert in *The Times*?'

They had made up their quarrel in a fashion that marked the subject out as one phase in a celebration. For this reason she was able to flaunt the paper around without stirring more than a trace of lingering reserve in George, who glanced up from his own paper with a polite interest that changed on looking more closely.

'Poor fellow,' he said, with the slightly annoying sympathy that had marked his attitude from the first. 'They've certainly made him look a right villain.'

Mary twisted round on the kitchen stool to reach toast out of the toaster. 'Looks terrible, doesn't he?'

'Pretty threatening, I must say.' He started to laugh. 'Look at that woman's face! And that one next to her!'

Mary leaned over and giggled, holding her corn-coloured

hair back with her hand. The women in question gazed up at the platform with sheep-like faces, caught in as accidental a moment of wide-eyed innocence and admiration as he, James Ross-Gilbert, showed the wolf.

'*James Ross-Gilbert denied that his partner Richard Trene had absconded abroad with funds belonging to members of the syndicate.* Good Lord!' He looked up at his wife.

'Exactly.'

'Do you think he has?'

'You're a fine one, George!' But she smiled as she said it. 'You're appalled at aspersions being cast by informed enquiry, but as soon as you see something in the Press . . .'

'That's different,' he said. 'And, besides, you got some of your information from that ass Gordon Hollander.'

'That's hardly reprehensible,' she retorted. 'You might as well pick a quarrel with someone for quoting the Bible.'

'If you mean the unedifying squalor of ancient Israeli history, I would.'

'Don't be nasty about the Old Testament, George.'

He laughed. 'It's such a stupid name.'

'Ossie, you mean? Well, it's a nickname. For obvious reasons.'

'I've got to go.' He stood behind her and put one hand over her breast while he kissed the inside of her neck. She loved it.

'Don't drink too much at lunch time.'

'What did you say that for?' he said, turning in the door.

She kept her back to him, smiling. 'I know whom you're meeting.' She turned. 'That drunken Irish writer friend of yours.'

He poked his chins forward and scratched the side of one cheek, as the light glanced off his spectacles. 'Just see you're here when I get back!' he said threateningly, in a bad American accent.

Ten minutes later, Mary walked to her car. No one turned to look at her in the street; a nice, wholesome, ugly, middle-aged woman going, some might assume, to do her shopping. On her way to LSE, the telephone rang in her car.

Liz Hatch's voice said, 'Dr Seymour? This is Sir Kenneth

Dunphy's secretary. I have the Minister here. Could you hold on, please.'

People always asked that at the junction of Hyde Park Corner. Not being a particularly good driver, and having been taught in that school that says that unless you turn a corner by feeding the steering wheel through both hands like a piece of string you'll go to hell, this sort of situation taxed Mary's ability to the utmost.

'Sorry, Kenneth,' she said. 'I'm on my way to college.'

'So I gather,' he replied drily. 'Now listen to what I have to say. There has been a frightful row here, thanks largely to you; but it seems your information was not entirely without foundation.'

If that had been George speaking, she would have said, 'Of course not.' She kept quiet.

'I'd like you to come and see me today,' he continued. 'Could you manage about five this afternoon?'

'Yes, I think so.' It was more than other people's lives were worth to try to sneak a look at her diary while she was driving. As it was, a motor-cyclist roared in front of her wheels and gave her a finger-sign for something she hadn't even been aware of. 'I'd better call you back to confirm from my office, but I think that's all right.'

'Thank you, Mary,' he said, and rang off.

She drove thoughtfully the rest of the way up the Mall, along the Strand and up Kingsway. She had time before her lecture to make a phone call not only to Kenneth's office, but also to Roger Collingham. Fortunately, he had not yet left for Lloyd's, and she was able to reach him without any delay.

He sounded glad to hear her. 'I'm expecting a grim day,' he said, 'and if the Minister for Trade and Industry is ready to take an interest, then at least we have a chance of getting Ross-Gilbert before he leaves the country.'

'Well . . .' Mary was now sitting on the wooden table which constituted the desk in her private room. 'I shouldn't bank on it. He wants to see me – about ROSE, of course.'

'How do you mean, not bank on it?'

'I've a feeling that Kenneth only wants to see me to apologise for being rude at the same time as bargaining against any more disclosures.'

'Mmm.'

'That's why I wanted to ask you if there was any chance that that man from Shipping Investigation Securities could be available this afternoon. I'd like to take him with me. They have all the hard evidence available so far.'

Roger looked at his watch. 'I've got to be at a Committee meeting at Lloyd's in quarter of an hour. But I'll ring you back. Will you be at LSE? Until when? I'll make it before twelve thirty then. Goodbye.'

He walked out hurriedly after putting down the phone, not wanting to be late. This meeting being held at Lloyd's was for the purpose of hearing the Chairman's report on his enquiries in connection with Con-Re. A propos that conversation at the beginning with the delectable Philippa, if there had been a rival to the title of most successful underwriter and Chairman of the biggest Managing Agency in Lloyd's, it would most likely have been Roger Collingham. In different areas of the market they were both leading underwriters, although Collingham did not share James's flamboyant style or for that matter the inexplicable magnetism of his charm. But, in this matter of the personal and to some extent unorthodox attention he was giving to Ross-Gilbert's affairs, he was motivated purely by his impersonal devotion to the principles of honour upheld by Lloyd's. To discover that a man who embodied the absolute antithesis of these principles had, for years, been courted and looked up to by member of Lloyd's, was a bitter blow to the reputation of the institution he loved. He did not intend to let him get away with it. He was afraid, however, that for the Chairman – ignorant as he was of the private steps taken by some members of the Committee to acquaint themselves with the real facts – there might be personal reasons to overlook misdemeanours on the part of James Ross-Gilbert.

In this he underestimated him. For what there was of heroism in the rather desiccated and ordinary character of the Chairman had risen out of the ashes of his friendship with James, and he had decided to tell the whole truth. He would certainly begin with the edited version of their conversation recorded after the re-entry of Nigel Dunlop. But then Philip Carrington had decided to tell the Committee of the interview that preceded it, including his reason for having only his own written notes in verification.

When all the members of the Committee were assembled, Fred informed the Chairman that they were ready, and he went down. Across the open marble floor and skirting the glass-walled drop down into the atrium, he hesitated on the threshold of the great Committee room. He could never rid himself of the impression of an element of pantomime, of childhood theatre implicit in this anachronistic structure of gilded plaster-work, ceilings and real windows erected like a giant doll's house inside the aggressively twentieth-century framework of a modern building. In today's case the element of theatre was almost unbearably heightened. Since the decision to request an enquiry, James Ross-Gilbert's retirement from Lloyd's had become known, and today's papers contained another undignified and worrying hint of scandal and disruption in connection with the reports of the Agency meeting. Philip also had seen the photograph in *The Times*. All this was reflected in the taut and apprehensive atmosphere as he lookd round the table and opened the meeting.

He got through the first steps of his report in the dull grey magisterial tone he sometimes set himself. But then he wavered. Once again a flush, this time of fear, marred the usually bloodless pallor of his complexion. The story he now had to tell was potentially damaging to the self-respect of each one of them here, and he wondered if he could bring himself to recount it. He opened the written notes he had made for form's sake, and kept himself going for one more moment with the gesture of returning his fountain-pen to his inside pocket. With the heightened sensitivity of a man standing on the edge of a cliff, he was aware of Roger Collingham's intense scrutiny, impatience from others, a certain restless apprehension from Spencer Day. Ranged between these attitudes, the other members of the Committee waited for what he had to say. He had no choice but to say it.

Concealed share ownership, the astonishing purchase of the Swiss Bank, the private bank accounts receiving payments, by however devious a route, from syndicate premium income, the 'investments' – he recounted it all. Some members were not as shocked as he would have expected. And again, although he would forget it once this moment was over, at the time he was almost supernaturally intuitive of their reasons. Roger Collingham, Roland Pierce and Tom Grates, he realised with a little shock of fear, already knew. They would not have swallowed the edited version if he had tried to limit his report. Others communicated to him an undercurrent of something he could only describe as embarrassment. He preferred not to wonder why. In him, Mary would have recognised the ultimate in that gentlemanly tradition of always helping another to get his trousers back on in private. The next time, it might be you. This time, it very nearly had been.

Spencer Day himself, listening to the evidence against Ross-Gilbert from his own vantage-point of perpetrator of several slightly similar schemes, struggled not to believe in the disgust and condemnation he read in the expressions of those around him whom he respected most. He longed for them also to have undeclared shareholdings in the main reinsurance company to whom they gave business. How many of them had used syndicate funds as personal collateral? The possibility that perhaps they had not, struck him to the very heart. Collingham? Potter? Tom Grates? The questions wore him out. This struggle, that had haunted him since that meeting with Grace and stalked the dark corners of his mind, was destroying him. In continuation of that perpetual inquisition he held against himself he asked again now, had his own business practices been, in fact, intrinsically dishonest? He broke the rules, or at least the new rules. How was he to know that other people were sincere when they said they did what they did? He pulled his mind back to the question at issue. These annals of the JRG syndicates were, he realised only too clearly, appalling. And those around him were appalled. And he, Spencer, was tarred with the same brush. He inwardly turned away from his catechism in despair. Outwardly he only looked slightly thoughtful – perhaps inattentive to the immediate debate, but his heart was broken.

Ultimately, all he felt he wanted was for Grace Derby to have lunch with him again: to lay his head against her shoulder and find a bit of peace. Throughout the debate Ross-Gilbert was to him not only a dishonourable member of a trusted society, he was also a triumphant lover; the better man. The pain of the acknowledgement was so excruciating that it cut his heart like a rusty razor, and his heart bled acid. Was he to be on a par with James Ross-Gilbert in this unforeseen dimension of dishonour and treachery in business, but in that other role pushed totally aside? To have what he could not bear to have, and not to have what he couldn't face life without? Whether James resigned or not from Lloyd's, as apparently the Chairman in a mistaken impulse of protectiveness had allowed him to do, seemed immaterial. What if that did mean that Lloyd's could not prosecute him? What if Collingham there, with his large solid blond face so set with an oblique inner knowledge of something or other, insisted that the DPP would not prosecute either? It would not make any difference to Grace.

But it made a difference to that other matter. A sharp charge of fatal despair went through him like an electric current, earthing to the boardroom floor. For an instant he hoped that he was having a heart attack. But his mind continued to go round and round, checking and rechecking, with gruesome intensity, his own position in this mess, and he was still alone.

When the meeting was over, he left with everyone else. As he got out of the lift with Roger Collingham, Roger gave him an odd tap on the arm and said, 'Just as well that chap did spill the beans to the journalist, whoever he was, and set the ball rolling.'

So he knew. And he would get to know other things.

This impulse on Collingham's part that was kindly, that was meant to reassure Spencer in case he was feeling the strain of the witch-hunt for the member who had informed the Press, was in fact the last straw. Spencer walked out of the building, but returned after five minutes as if he had forgotten something. The waiters had left. The building was closing. He went up on one of the outside lifts. He never had been shy of heights. He stood against the rail and watched the roof of St Peter's Cornhill sinking under him as the lift climbed the high building wall. On a fine evening, the City still caught the heart. Not quite 'earth hath not anything to show more fair'; but something yet. Although he observed this he did not, after all, question whether or not to kill himself. He was a man whose last moment had come. His consciousness coasted in a state not dissimilar to bliss. When the lift reached the top, and the door opened, he took off a shoe and jammed it. After a moment's pause, listening for footsteps, he walked back out on to the platform.

The only difficulty lay in leaving Grace, who inhabited this world. With his eyes fixed on the panorama around and beneath him, he assessed once more with poignant longing what chance he might have with her. This time the answer pained him less, as if the roots of his human feelings were already numb. He felt the rail under his hand. He would have to smash the glass to make a wider opening. It needed strength. Or ingenuity. He was already too hypnotised by death to do it. And then the thought of the impending scandal over the JRG affair at Lloyd's, and the hue and cry that it would cause, lashed past his deadened senses. Without pausing to realise how he'd done it, he swung his shoulders out over the abyss. His body caught at the irrepressible reflex of balance, but only with the waning attention of a kitten bored with a ball of wool. His hand slipped against a bolt. His remaining shoe smashed another panel from the outside. His mind did not function again until it hit the pavement.

If his body had been a bomb, it could hardly have caused more carnage on the street. A man who happened to look up at the crucial moment shouted or screamed so loudly that his voice could be heard just outside the Monument station, where Roger Collingham was buying a copy of the *Evening Standard*.

'What's that?' he asked, as a woman's distinct screams were added to the echo. The newspaper man's eye was on the next customer and counting out the change.

Spencer lay quietly, in spite of the chaos going on around him, in a pool of his own blood. Someone spoke to him, but his mouth had become confused with other parts of his body. He couldn't remember where it was or how it worked. He wanted to say something. His eyes were open, but what they saw muddled him. For a moment there was nothing, and he thought he'd gone to sleep, but he woke and suddenly managed to say quite easily, 'Grace.' That was all.

In spite of the noise, a woman heard him.

'What did he say?

'Grace.'

'Did he mean the name?'

But he was dead. It was too late to reply, 'You may well ask.'

Chapter 20

Two days later, James Ross-Gilbert was at home and busy when the phone rang, but he picked it up in the house already half dismantled since Marjorie's departure only to find himself immediately involved in a very difficult row with Grace. He did not want trouble. Neither had he absolutely, definitively, made up his mind that he did not want *her*. He protested again, 'No, I'm not packing. No, I'm not leaving England. Will you please stop shouting, my darling, and let me come and take you out for dinner.'

On the other end of the phone, Grace sat sharply down on the edge of the sofa, her eyes wide open, her heart thumping. 'Then why?'

'Why what?'

'You know Spencer killed himself?'

James also sat down now, although he had to choose a place carefully because the floor was covered with open suit-cases. 'What has that got to do with it?'

'He killed himself because of us.'

James was bored. She paused.

'Are you still there?'

'Yes.'

'Well, don't you see? He told me you were cheating. My God, I do so desperately hope you're not cheating.'

'I am.'

She laughed. She had obviously been drinking. In a classic gesture she lifted one shoe with her toe balanced loose just inside the tip. 'And if you are, I'll strangle you!'

'With kisses?'

'Oh yes.' She nearly fell off the sofa. 'Tomorrow.'

'Tomorrow what?'

'Dinner tomorrow. Not tonight.'

'All right,' he said. 'Goodbye, my darling.' He returned the phone to its cradle and stood up. It was extraordinary how life simplified itself, letting you no longer want what you couldn't have. Goodbye Grace. He would wait until Philippa arrived, and until then he continued packing.

'Mary,' said Roger Collingham, 'may I introduce Mr Mal Harris of Shipping Investigation Securities. This is Dr Mary Seymour.'

'Oh!' She didn't quite know what she meant by that. She jerked her nice bronze head backwards with her chin tucked in and her eyes showing frank surprise. She said, 'How do you do.'

Mr Harris's manner, on the other hand, was quiet and formal. He showed no sign of noticing her reaction, except that those who knew him well would have spotted the increase in his own expression of innocent gravity. And known that he was laughing. Outwardly, he shook hands with the solemn care his father would have used to greet the Minister's wife on a miners' holiday outing, his mild expression fixed tidily on her face. He didn't look as if he would be much use in a confrontation with a senior government minister. However, presumably he had the necessary information on ROSE, and it would do no harm to have him in tow. She gave Roger Collingham a slightly quizzical look as he stood there, having introduced this eccentric protégé.

'Thank you,' she said to him. 'I'll call you this evening and let you know what happens.' Picking up her briefcase, she went down, together with Mr Harris, to her car and drove over to Whitehall.

Half an hour later she looked at her watch and thought it was going to be extremely inconvenient if Kenneth kept them waiting much longer. She remembered a suit she had to collect for George, and Liz had been gone for almost ten minutes. If the problem was that Kenneth objected to her bringing Mr Harris, in spite of the fact that she had asked and received permission, she would just have to let him go. He had hardly spoken a word anyway from Holborn to White-hall, except to warn her just in time of a Mini on her inside lane going straight on when she herself was turning left. It was useful, but no substitute. But for the vital importance of her not quarreling with Kenneth, both from the point of view of her career and her relationship with George, she would just as soon not have come.

By the time Liz Hatch returned with the inevitable, 'I'm so sorry you've been kept waiting, will you come through now', she had lost half her patience. She advanced nevertheless into the room with her usual pleasantness. Sir Kenneth got up from his desk and came round to meet her, radiating charm. He accepted his introduction to Mal Harris without betraying a fraction of hesitation. He had had it explained to him that Shipping Investigation Securities was responsible for the research that had brought the ROSE shares to light, and he was as keen to negotiate with them as with Mary. Because, what it boiled down to, as he explained very eloquently, was an issue of confidence. If a public figure made this kind of a mistake – and it was very much a question whether he had or not – various considerations had to be taken into account. One could not damage the image of high office without doing a great deal of general harm. Now, assume just for the moment that the shares did change hands and that they had been issued in payment for investment out of embezzled funds. No one had known that at the time, except James Ross-Gilbert himself. As it turned out, the shares rapidly became valueless. Why make a damaging issue out of it when the government was doing a good job in so many areas, and this kind of a diversion could jeopardise their chances in the next election? The PM would consider it a personal favour if the matter could be allowed to drop. When he had finished talking, there was a silence.

Mary said, 'You mean, hush it up.'

Well, he could handle her being deliberately provocative. He assumed the intimate half-smile that let people know he regarded them as a special friend, and yet wasn't afraid to speak his mind. 'You know very well, Mary,' he said, 'that information is not necessarily always given to everyone who asks. One mustn't get personal about this. Discretion is a perfectly familiar burden we have to bear in high office.

She looked at him with a spark in her eye. 'Why do you think I'm being personal, Kenneth?'

'I'm sorry.' He was conciliatory at once. 'I'm sorry.' In fact it was his conversation with George that had given him that idea.

'Well, thank you,' she said. 'I do take your general point. But the accuracy of my facts are not in doubt, you know. Mr Harris has evidence of the paperwork.'

'Oh, really?' The Minister controlled an impulse to fidget by moving back behind his desk and sitting down. 'Really?'

'One thousand shares transferred at their par value, Minister, of one pound ten pence paid up, on 14th January 1984.' Mr Harris spoke quietly with a marked Welsh accent, but an unexpected and unmistakable steadiness. In circumstances like these, people were often over-eager or nervous, their self-control in inverse ratio to the breadth of architrave around the doors.

Mary's hair bobbed as she turned her head as if on springs of attention. It had never occurred to her that as a car-driver she frightened her passengers into silence.

'But there is no record in the Department of Trade. They are in a nominee name therefore?' The Minister put the question like that because it was a way of asking without, as it were, touching the actual query.

'The company was registered in Bermuda, Minister.'

'Oh yes. So it was. So it was.'

'And the shares were indeed made to a nominee name; it is Peetree Nominees.'

The Minister was shocked and angry; genuinely. It should not have been possible for Shipping I.S. or anyone else to find out the names of nominees. 'How did you find this out? Surely the Inland Revenue can't have made such a disclosure to a third party?' What on earth was the man talking about? Was no one safe?

But although Mr Harris looked quite conciliatory, there was no doubting the implied humour in his reply when he said, 'Not on purpose, Minister.'

'You mean you used unlawful methods to get this information?'

'I'm not at liberty to discuss my company's methods, Minister,' the astonishing little man said. 'I'm afraid we also sometimes have to be discreet.' He sat there, the timeless looks of the emaciated worker-poet reincarnated in a city suit which apparently clothed a personality as tough and effective as Genghis Khan. 'It's a matter of evidence, you see, sir.' He paused, and then said again politely, 'We have it.'

'I see.' Sir Kenneth put down the piece of paper he had been fidgeting with, and with it his manner of querulous asperity. He leaned back in his chair, and said again, 'I see.'

'And in the circumstances, therefore,' Harris went on, 'we would like to know the attitude your department takes towards James Ross-Gilbert.'

'How do you mean?'

'It's him we are interested in, sir. We want him prosecuted.'

'Why should we do it?'

Mr Harris let a long pause answer the Minister's own question. Then he said, 'Also,' as if continuing, 'he has committed fraud, and he intends to leave the country.'

'Oh, does he?' Both Sir Kenneth and Mary were brought to attention by that one. Her reaction was alert, his thoughtful. Once domiciled abroad, only the DPP could bring Ross-Gilbert back to face charges.

While Kenneth thought this one out, Mal Harris watched him. The deep-seated spark in his eye was observed by Mary, who held a glint in her own, the sensual ridge around her thick mouth sharpened as she pressed her lips together. He was reading Kenneth like a book.

'It would be unwise to depend on that, Minister,' he said, after a few moments' pause. 'A refusal by the DTI to prosecute might force my company to go back on any agreement to be discreet about ROSE.'

The Minister looked startled, and then annoyed. 'Not at all what I was thinking!' he declared revealingly. The fact that Mary Seymour actually smiled goaded him to add, 'I can assure you.' There was a moment of silence while he brought his mind back to the question of prosecution, and considered that. 'This man has committed other fraudulent acts and appropriated other funds entrusted to him, I take it?'

It was rather a nerve, Mary thought, for him to refer to his erstwhile yachting host as 'this man', as if he couldn't even remember his name from one minute to the next. She knew why he did it, of course; why he needed to distance himself.

Mal replied, 'Yes, sir.'

'Nevertheless, in an enquiry, an independent prosecutor would be bound to go through all the transactions, and this matter of the ROSE shares would inevitably be included. We couldn't then stop unpleasant publicity from that angle.'

'I think we could, Minister.'

'Oh?' He paused wisely this time, and then said, 'Really? May one know how?' Mr Harris had a way of widening his eyes like a maiden aunt about to wipe jam off a child's fingers when his intention was not to give an inch. He did it now, and to his credit the Minister forestalled him with a raised hand, as if in absolution, saying, 'No need to answer that. We'll take it as read. You could guarantee that this particular aspect of the activities would not appear or would not be available in the investigation?' He spoke thoughtfully.

'I must say,' Mary Seymour broke out, 'I think it is disgraceful that this sort of bargaining should be necessary. No, Kenneth, I'm sorry. You know my position on this sort of thing.'

It was difficult enough without this. The Minister, who genuinely liked his cousin's wife, was exasperated. Women! Notwithstanding all the so-called liberation, women just couldn't get to grips with the way the world was run. In his opinion there was no question of their altering any of the basics. It was simply that in the higher echelons of business and government men were just constantly having to make certain allowances for them, to cover up for them, and this was a case in point. He set himself now to convince her that it was better to lay by the heels a treacherous underwriter who had gulled his trusting friends for fourteen years and stolen millions than ruin the career of one misguided politician who had unwisely accepted a gift.

'To come back to what I was saying,' he reiterated when she had simmered down, 'you are requesting that we prosecute. Have you got evidence of the other irregularities?'

'I have, Minister.' Mr Harris took a file out of his case and held it. 'There is enough documented evidence here to warrant an arrest, and that is what we are asking the DTI to do.'

'Oh, I don't think we can take precipitate action!' Sir Kenneth pushed his chair sideways as he said it and recrossed his legs at an angle. 'The Department could ask for an arrest only when we had completed our own investigation.'

'But, in the meantime, Mr Ross-Gilbert will have left the country, sir,' He pointed at the papers he held. 'If the Department could be persuaded to examine this evidence in . . .' he paused, and seemed to choose a figure, 'the next twelve hours, they will find plenty to justify an immediate arrest on charges. If they don't do that, he will leave the country, and it will be necessary to get him extradited. A very slow procedure, Minister, which would not suit us. The DPP would involve a whole new basis of negotiation.'

Kenneth pulled his lip. It was only too clear what the man was getting at. The DTI had the means, if they acted immediately and a number of unfortunate public servants, including possibly himself, lost a night's sleep yet again, to have Ross-Gilbert arrested within hours and released on bail without his passport, and things could be carried on from there. Shipping Investigation Securities were in a position to insist that they do it. Blackmail was not exactly the word to use, but evidence of those shareholdings in ROSE amounted to something like it. He could be realistic. This was one thing that distinguished men from women, in his opinion, although, thank heaven, Mary Seymour seemed to have decided to fit in this time.

'Very well,' he said. He held out his hand. 'May I have the

file now, or do you have to fetch copies?'

'No. These are, in fact, the copies, Minister.' Mr Harris stood up and deposited the bulky stack of papers on the desk.

'I had better get onto this straight away, then.' Sir Kenneth rose to his feet but stayed behind his desk. 'An unpleasant business, Mary. I'm afraid it comes to all of us at one time or another.'

'That depends. Are you talking about death, Kenneth, or blackmail?'

He winced. He'd just have to make a joke of it for now, but my God, next time he saw George . . . He walked out into the middle of the room and patted her on the shoulder in an avuncular style as he shepherded her towards the door. 'We're all idealists, Mary, under the skin. You're not alone there, you know.' She smiled at him. 'Now, I have work to do.' As he handed them over to the waiting officer in the anteroom, he beckoned in his clerk.

Outside, it looked as if it was going to rain. Mary said, 'I don't consider that you played fair with me, Mr Harris.'

'I'm very sorry,' he said, looking up at her, and somehow, on account of the sincere sorryness of his expression, looking even less sorry than people often do when trotting out the phrase.

'You're not. You did it deliberately.' A glint of a smile appeared in his eye only. 'Still, I suppose we've got him cornered.' She meant Ross-Gilbert, not Kenneth. 'It looks as if it might rain. Can I give you a lift?'

'No,' he said hastily. 'Thank you very much, but I'll get a taxi. There are plenty about.'

'Don't bother to see me to my car.'

They shook hands and parted; and as they did so, twenty miles away at Heathrow, the plane with James Ross-Gilbert aboard, accompanied by Philippa and her two girls, rose into the air and began its long flight to America. It was a beautiful evening. Mary had got it wrong. In the west there was no hint of rain.

Chapter
21

'I PRESUME THAT string of Welsh swear-words means something has gone wrong, Mr Harris?'

In his shirt-sleeves behind a metal desk in an office near
Spitalfields, Mal Harris had not slammed the phone down or
spoken loudly, but it was true he had been swearing. The
Minister's PA at the Department of Trade had just given him
the news of Ross-Gilbert's disappearance. Five minutes later
he rang again to say that James's name, together with that of
Mrs Ross-Gilbert, Philippa Oakes née Dawson, was on the list
of passengers for a flight that had left Heathrow for America
at eighteen thirty hours the previous evening.

The loss assessor's clerk was holding out a paper for him to
initial. Mal said, 'Yes. We were just too late on something,
I'm afraid. What's this, John? The cargo damage contract?'

'Yes.'

'Right.' He initialled it. He waited for the door to close,
and then dialled the number of Collingham Ward Kaye.

For his part, Roger Collingham, when he had finished
hearing what Mal Harris had to say, picked up the Lloyd's
direct line and got through to the Chairman's office. One way
and another between a quite small circuit of contacts the
news got into circulation in time to make a small entry in the
business pages of the *Standard*'s evening edition. And among
those brokers and underwriters who didn't drink too much to

be able to work in the afternoon, it also spread. Not that the general reaction was immediately or universally suspicious. James had said he was going to live abroad. He'd retired. His admirers pointed out that he wanted to leave himself enough time to spend all the money. The disastrous, and as yet unexplained, suicide of Spencer Day had cast a shadow over the market that people in general were at pains to lighten, not add to.

Grace Derby, returning from a long session with the research department of a leading stockbroker, had been out of circulation, as far as other news was concerned, for the whole afternoon. When she got back to her own office, the first thing she did was to ring James. She had been wishing all day that she had let him take her out to dinner the previous evening. He knew how to be a good friend. He wouldn't have let her get into a state about Spencer or any of the paranoid suspicions that Spencer had tried to pass on. She looked at her watch. He wasn't in; but then he had a lot to see to, what with sorting out Marjorie after the divorce and getting things ready for the future. As for other worries, he had an answer for all the rumours, and frankly she didn't care. Her instinct was to transfer her professional attention for the time being to the Stock Exchange. She was in love.

While she listened to the phone ringing unanswered, she smiled to herself and examined the chipped varnish on one of her nails. She could take her time having a bath and getting ready. The prospect of the evening was delightful, like an exquisite garden laid out in the sun for their especial pleasure. The radiance of it spilled out to gild the last hours of the afternoon. She put down the phone with an indulgent smile, and left the office. She picked up a copy of the *Evening Standard* to read on the bus home, but spent most of the journey dreaming with placid happiness of James. When she got in, she put the kettle on to make a cup of tea, and opened the paper. Her attention was fragmentary and effervescent. She played for five minutes with her cat and felt the warmth of the kitchen table where the sun fell on it. And then, eventually, in a moment of casual attention, her eye fell on the column. She read it once meaninglessly, as if it were a railway timetable or an out-of-date gazette. The second time, notwithstanding the glacial numbness that crept through her body as if she had drunk hemlock, she was certain it was a misprint. Her heart pounding somewhere in the remote depths of her suddenly unwieldy flesh, she got up and went over to the phone. It rang. He still didn't answer. It rang. She read the column again, tearing it. Her breath was making a harsh sound which was the unconscious byproduct of pure pain, and her gestures were panicky and inaccurate, walking irrationally to a part of the room, hands shaking, getting up, sitting down again. She was trying to contemplate a version of events that couldn't be forced through the existing passages in her mind. She must ring someone who would know. Whom? In a panic – whom? There was that report in *The Times*. She went over to the stack of newspapers in her bedroom and found it and the name of the journalist on the article; someone she didn't know. Who was the editor of that section? She rang. She got a name, but not a friend. No phone number. She rang another friend. No answer. Another.

'Are you all right, Grace? Is something wrong?'

Yes, yes no. What is it? 087 2241. Dial again. No answer. She was sitting on the bed, looking at her shaking hands, aghast. Her experience was not all that dissimilar to Spencer's, because there came a moment when the confusion of the actual fall was over, followed by a dismembered stillness. After a long while she got up and walked into the sitting-room and poured herself a drink. She looked and walked like a different woman. That element of existence so indefinable and so variously described whether as the soul, or life, or fire, or wit, that being absent, the physical components of the body congeal into a corpse, had left her. She looked dead in her own way.

Finally she poured herself another drink and sat down by the phone. After some moments' thought, she chose more carefully whom to ring. She needed to speak to another financial writer whom she knew was interested in the investigations into Con-Re and other related dealings, and who would be likely to be up to date. She dialled Mary Seymour's number.

As she listened to what Mary had to say, her heart

recovered from its brief but devastating infatuation. Her self-esteem, on the other hand, as a journalist capable of intelligent dispassionate opinion or even instinct for news or even yet integrity, shrivelled. James had apparently registered the flight bookings under the names of Mr and Mrs Ross-Gilbert. Philippa Oakes. Who on earth was she? And it had become clear – clear enough to warrant an arrest that only this flight had pre-empted – that the rumours of financial scandal in Con-Re and others were well founded. It only remained to find out their full extent. By the time Grace put down the telephone, James Ross-Gilbert had another, and most indomitable, enemy.

Chapter 22

WHEN A MARKET crashes, what sound does it make? It must have one, like a plane or a car or a building falling to the ground, the physical impact of hard metals and stone and the poor soft human bodies trapped and crushed. Certainly not entirely dissimilar. One morning, two weeks after the departure of James Ross-Gilbert, Lloyd's bore a marked resemblance to the site of such a catastrophe. It was not just the main building in Lime Street that bore the brunt of it, but all the others – the Member's Agencies, the working Names, the brokers, the outside Names – and all lashed with constant and escalating reportage and comment in the Press. God knows what anybody in the market had ever done before to fill in their time, because now they had no time for anything else. Having set themselves to absorb the shock of James Ross-Gilbert's and Richard Trene's sudden disappearances coinciding with the discoveries being made about the running of their syndicates, it was briefly the fashion to say that at least the Names, if they had been cheated out of much profit, at least had not made losses. And then the enormity of the losses they had in fact made began to emerge, compounded by the disappearance of reinsurances designed to protect them, and the disappearance of 'investments', and all hell broke loose. Now at last a steering committee at Lloyd's began a meticulous enquiry into the entire background of all JRG underwriting.

In his capacity as a director of Merchaum, Ralph Scott, his temper soured to the point where he could almost make the bottom drop out of a bucket by looking at it, was requested to attend a meeting at Lloyd's. It wasn't a request he was at liberty to refuse, and he didn't make the mistake of thinking that it was. He went up to the eleventh floor, his handsome face, bony, crooked, aquiline nose, muscular mouth all dourly turned on silence; tall, thin, one hand in his pocket, not about to go and live in some God-forsaken foreign country if it could be avoided. He had his friends.

Philip Carrington wasn't there. The Deputy Chairman, Ray Banbury, and about eight members of the committee ranged around the table welcomed him, so to speak, and invited him to sit down. He felt like a schoolboy at an exam where he had expected to have a crib. Ross-Gilbert and Trene having absconded with such alacrity, he was left alone to try to brazen it out. It boiled down to two issues: what he had done himself, and what he knew, but didn't disclose that he knew, of the misdemeanours of others. As a principal director of Merchaum and shareholder in Con-Re, he had to admit to a certain knowledge. When questioned, he gave them an edited version of that meeting following Persian Arc's allegations. He said that he had discussed the re-insurance schemes with Mr Trene and Mr Ross-Gilbert and with reference to the Banque de Flors, and that he had expressed uneasiness about the propriety of the scheme. He had asked Mr Trene if his, Ralph Scott's, fund was sufficient to meet outstanding liabilities, and he had confirmed that it was. And he said he had then instructed Mr Trene to return the whole of his own part of the fund to the appropriate syndicates, although he had not ever checked to see if this had been done. He said he didn't know what subsequently happened.

The enquiry droned on about the fact that he knew that other members of the JRG syndicates knew nothing of these schemes and that there were other participants up to the same game. He knew the exercise was covert, and just assumed that others were doing likewise. In saying this, his thoughts walked briefly over the grave of Spencer Day just as his well-polished shoes, on the way to the entrance in Lime Street, had trodden the pavement now washed clean of his blood.

As for sitting in that chair and answering all those questions politely, it was arguable that for a man of Ralph's temperament the experience constituted, in itself, a real punishment. He disguised his secret loathing of those who questioned him, but he couldn't suppress his own tormented observation of their minutest quirks and habits: their hands, the way they breathed, the particular items of which certain of them took notes. When he had left, they would discuss him. They would argue for or against the probity of his word, the pressures he had had to bear. The snarl that he couldn't quite keep out of his eye he directed at the table in front of him. These men, who had trusted and admired James like fools for fourteen years, were suspicious of him now, after five minutes.

When asked, he gave a complete account of the reinsurance scheme under which reinsurance of syndicates would be handled. Mr Ross-Gilbert had mentioned that the scheme would alleviate premium income problems, and he had discussed it with Danvers and Bennett May – solicitors and accountants respectively of Merchaum. He had offered Mr Scott a 6 per cent share, and he had accepted, knowing that substantial profits would accrue to the participants with no real risk of loss, and that funds originating from premium paid by the reinsured syndicates would be transferred abroad and placed under the control of those who participated in the scheme.

It went on and on, there being no end to what they wanted to know, or the grave expressions they would pull at every word he spoke. The presents bought for his wife, even the name of the jeweller he paid in New York, what repairs had been made to the yacht, and whether contributions had been made to his brother's expenses. By the time he was allowed to leave for the day, he would need at least twenty hours to hone his temper back into edge. The last item was fourteen payments into his account, each one of which they itemised with a remorseless persistence, reaching a tally of sixty-eight thousand pounds from June to May.

However, they wouldn't bloody well find the rest of it! He defied anyone to trace funds that Richard Trene had had the hiding of. One day he himself would get a letter in the post with a few trustee names and addresses, and he'd go off on holiday to nice places like the Cayman Islands and Bermuda in his own good time, and collect what was his.

He got to his feet when eventually he received the word of dismissal and walked to the door, particularly conscious of the eye of Roland Pierce, with whom he and Sarah had gone on holiday on two occasions in the South of France. He had liked Roland's wife. And Roland. Still, one couldn't have everything, and Roland Pierce didn't have five million. He might have the right to sit in judgment on his old friends, but he probably couldn't damn well buy a decent yacht. Andrew Milstead the same. Would he please come back the following day at ten? Very well, he'd come back tomorrow. And he walked away, stoically scalding his own feelings in his own bile as he always had done.

Chapter
23

Mal Harris, telephone engineer, went into the offices of Merchaum on the Tuesday, accompanied by his mate, Jim Gardiner, to correct faults on the line that had been arranged by themselves the day before. It was no longer a happy place. The building had never, in itself, been attractive, and James Ross-Gilbert's style of not particularly informed but wealthy display caught the eye now for what it was. His former employees worked alongside the personnel appointed by Lloyd's to deal with the emergency with the bewildered resentment either of those who had taken him at his own face value or of those who expected at any moment to be confronted with evidence of their own complicity.

Jim Gardiner was, in appearance, the Cockney boozer type: rolls of stomach, a T-shirt and a British Telecom holdall.

'It's these three only, I think,' the filing clerk was telling them. 'This room and the two along.'

They plodded through, noncommittal, uninterested, as she was. You could have sworn that Jim Gardiner habitually spent days on end crouched inside a red striped tent with the flap hitched back, leering at bits of skirt, from the disappointed way he said 'OK, love' to Mrs Sweeney.

'Let reception know when you've finished, will you?' she said, and left them to it.

It took a while to locate which of the rooms they were after: a certain amount of opening doors and laconic apologetic interference with any work they found going on. But the files that Dick Trene had been so busy with and had regarded as his own were in a series of locked cabinets in the empty room he had so lately left. From top to bottom, running over the locks, they were each and every one of them bound with steel rods and sealed with the DTI seal.

'Well, take a look at that, boyo!' Mal breathed, in something like admiration. 'So nice and tidy. Let's have a screwdriver out of your handbag, Jim. Unravel some wires near the door, so that you'll be in the way of anyone coming in.'

He spread a canvas tool-pocket out near the bank of cabinets and laid some wiring and a spare phone out ready, and then unscrewed the backs of the cabinets one by one. He worked extremely fast with economy of movement, as if he had been trained for this particular task according to a time and motion study. It looked too easy, like a trapeze-artist strolling along a bit of string, whistling. Two interruptions were fielded with hardly a ripple of anxiety, presenting to the dispassionate attention first of a clerk in search of a different room and secondly a secretary needing something out of a desk drawer, the sight of two typical British Telecom engineers with fists full of coloured wires. When he had located and taken the ROSE papers and photographed and returned several other documents, Mal Harris rescrewed the filing cabinets, and they packed up and left.

By the time the pigeons were thinking of turning in for the night, lining up in rows along the facade of the building occupied by Shipping I.S. in Spitalfields, the papers were locked up in Mr Harris's office inside. He himself was sitting at his desk, and he could not rid himself of the idea that Sir Kenneth Dunphy had changed his mind about the need to cooperate.

Chapter
24

'SO THAT'S THE explanation, George.'

'Poor woman.'

'Mmm.'

George Seymour looked up at his wife, curious. He could recognise a certain lack of sympathy when he heard it. 'I thought you liked Grace Derby.'

'I did – until she turned me down when I offered her the ROSE investigation.'

'That's not a crime, is it?'

'I just find the motivation unappealing.' Mary was sitting at her dressing-table while George, still in bed, read the Sunday papers, 'After all if, as a financial journalist, you come across an organisation that increasingly looks corrupt, it's a bit pathetic to get a crush on the ringleader when you meet him and drop the whole investigation.' She took off her glasses and polished them on a clean handkerchief. She did not feel sorry for Grace. Nobody who knew her would waste sympathy on Grace when it came to affairs of the heart. What femmes fatales ever have shoulders to cry on when their own, rare, feelings take a knock? 'All the same,' Mary continued, 'she'll come in useful.'

'How so?'

'I'd like to feel that somebody with reason to stand up to the inevitable persuasions of interested parties –' they both knew she was talking about Kenneth and friend – 'is still on the Ross-Gilbert trail.'

'Do they need it!' George said emphatically, more as an explanation than a question, holding the full spread of his Sunday paper sideways to demonstrate his point.

'I've seen that.'

'"*Names public meeting to be held in London*" and breakdowns of expected losses and individual little family sob-stories.'

'The stuff of real drama,' she said with a wan smile. She was doing her hair, and had stopped to look at her reflection, directing the remark, to some extent, at herself. But she didn't know how right she was. Imagination was not her strong point. She could have told you that, on Ossie's calculation, Henry Allanport was presently down for £2,400,000. And she could also have given you some rough idea – something hardly anyone outside the direct working community of the market would have had the knowledge to calculate – of by how much and how quickly that figure would go up. But what she had no idea of was how it felt. To imagine the emotions of Henry Allanport after the funeral of his wife and when he had mastered the paperwork calculations of the value of his estates, the farm and other property, was beyond her.

On this particular Sunday morning Henry also was sitting up in bed, much like George, reading the same paper. His breakfast tray had been put down on that side of the bed where Delia had been used to lie. He read the paper intermittently, as he did everything since that awful day, as if negotiating some inhospitable element from which he had to rise at intervals and breathe. It was not noticeable. But the characteristic understatement of his manner belied the anguish that he felt. Behind the guard of his quiet lack of self-pity, only the hope of revenge stopped him from bleeding to death.

It might have struck some people as ironic if they had known about it, that by one person at least James Ross-Gilbert was being expected to pay out more than, strictly speaking, he owed, since the death of Delia had not been down to him. But from the point of view of Henry, who had left her to spend her last hours alone so that he could attend the Agency meeting, there was a debt to pay. And every mental image he retained of Delia anxious about the threat of this financial disaster, overtired while she kept him company with his calculations, unable to sleep, the secret poison in her system nourished by worry, or disguised, each memory condemned him.

In roughly equal proportions – although it is difficult to compare such disparate values – the prospect of the loss of his estates tormented him. He also knew that his current exposure of over two million pounds was only now and for this year, and that the losses could go up. He would not be able to survive the accumulated deficits, and only when his unlimited liability as an individual was exhausted, and he had nothing of value left, would the Lloyd's central fund step in and pay. There might be talk of levying assistance among the other Names in Lloyd's, but that would be against the basic rule of the institution . . .

'Each for his own part, and not one for another.' It would not get off the ground. And this meeting, announced so stridently in the newspapers and to which he would certainly go with the dual purpose of looking into the possibilities of legal redress and redress from the Lloyd's central fund – it didn't stand much of a chance. The Lloyd's Committee would argue that the central fund existed to secure the risks of the insureds, not the private fortunes of the Names themselves, and there would be argument based on reciprocal responsibilities. And so it would go on.

When he had read the relevant pages in that newspaper, including the individual family sob-stories, as George called them, he paused characteristically in the new way he had, and seemed to breathe a different air. Once again the contemplation of his decision revived him. The certainty of it quietened all his deliberations. By all means he would attend this meeting and participate in a collective effort to minimise their losses. But for him personally the solution had moved into quite a different sphere. What he intended to do was to seek out and kill James Ross-Gilbert.

He got up and dressed. Just as in the rarefied atmosphere of his particular personality, so uncompromisingly loving but light-hearted, there had been nothing to obscure the intensity of his affections, so there was nothing to hamper his revenge: no lack of nerve, or bombast, or self-pity, or shallow heats of fire made of paper. His luggage was packed, his local financial affairs all seen to. For the benefit of his household and employees and friends, he was taking a long holiday abroad. No one had the slightest suspicion of his intention to track down Ross-Gilbert, and he dropped no hints or half-clues. He seemed outwardly, in all this tragic mess, to have admirably retained his composure and his clarity; but the light that illumined him had, in this one direction, subtly changed in quality, and acquired a laser edge that kills. And, when thought of the unbearable miseries that had descended threatened to smother him, this private intention of his, this purpose, like a shield, held them back and gave him room to breathe.

In London he was met at the station and driven to Black's, where he had agreed to meet Rupert. Of the two of them, as they sat discussing the prospect of the meeting and eating their lunch, the bereaved brother appeared the more down-hearted. Rupert was still young enough to resemble a handsome puppy sometimes, and he looked like that now, but one who has been pining. He grumbled about the fish, ordered another bottle of wine and complained that the club was going downhill.

Henry, looking sympathetically at him, eventually said, 'What's wrong?'

Rupert gave him a surprised look, since everything was.

'I mean what extra? Something especially bugging you?' He hesitated. 'Work?'

'Damn broking.'

'You do it all the time.'

'Ha ha! My God, I don't know how you can crack jokes, Henry.' He said it with admiration. He wasn't criticising.

'But what is it?'

'If I tell you, you'll think I'm like the rest.'

'Something you broked to Merchaum?'

Rupert flung himself back in his chair, a slight flush tinge-ing the lower curve of his jaw. He said, 'The trouble is that in a situation like this everything looks different.'

'In what way?'

'Well . . .' He swept aside the straight thick mass of his brown hair and let his wrist fall heavily back on the edge of the table. 'Ross-Gilbert did people favours, you know. Brokers; fellow underwriters; everybody thought so well of him. If he had told me that an irregular procedure was a jam tart, I'd have believed him!'

'So what did he get you to do?'

Rupert said, 'Oh, nothing', and kicked the side of his chair, shifting his weight round at an angle to the table.

'I know you wouldn't do anything dishonest.'

'No, I bloody well would not!' he burst out. 'But . . . on one occasion, Ross-Gilbert accepted some lousy business from me on condition that I placed some reinsurance, which seemed perfectly genuine. Well, at the bottom of those slips there's a section marked "Information", and I just accepted what he told me; didn't check it.'

Henry said, 'Should you have?'

'No, the reinsurance market does operate on trust, after all.'

There was a silence. Henry turned the stem of his wine-glass in his fingers, which were thin and long, not like Rupert's strong farmer's hand, and then looked up at his brother-in-law. 'So what have you got to worry about?'

'The information he gave me left out some essentials I won't bore you with. But it invalidates the policy. If Ross-Gilbert was still here himself, he'd probably have talked his way out of it with charm or bribery. That man could make birds come out of the trees and sit down on the ground and purr!'

Henry gave a short laugh. 'As it is, I've got to go and explain to the Committee how a whole new section of uncovered over-exposed risk needs to be added to the night-mare total they're compiling.'

'But he didn't pay you for doing it?'

Rupert's hangdog expression changed to momentary belligerence. 'No brown envelopes, no. But he did something, didn't he? He did me a favour by completing the cover on the dud slip I'd been toting round for weeks.'

'I see.'

Rupert shook his head, and said, 'I don't think you do.'

'What else? Will they hold you responsible?'

'No. No, it's not that. As far as they're concerned, I can't be blamed at all. Privately, I know that I let an element of bargaining arise where my job was to get the best deal for both clients, whose fortunes were in no way meant to be interdependent.'

'You sound as if you're quoting.'

'Forget that. The point I'm making, apart from the lousiness of how I feel, is the subtlety of Ross-Gilbert's methods. He's probably got other members of Lloyd's entangled in some way or other. You and your fellow Names are going to be trying to get a prosecution going and build up some case for shared responsibility with the ruling body of Lloyd's, aren't you?' Henry nodded. 'They say they're out to help you. But at the same time there will be an undeclared percentage of them who are afraid of the moment when their dirty linen gets washed in public, and every item picked over and the name-tapes all read. What if *their* names are on some of them? They thought JRG was perfectly straight, and now that they look at it a bit more carefully and from a different angle, they see he did favours for them which involved subtle irregularities: subtle enough to confuse the stupid or tranquillise the more intelligent.'

'That's that, then,' said Henry. 'We'll just have to try.' He smiled at Rupert. His heart warmed to him. In so many ways he closely resembled Delia; but it was not for that alone he loved him, as if he was merely some device through which could be played the cracked and distant echo of a piece of music gone for ever. They had always been friends. 'Don't worry,' he said again. 'No one is going to confuse your motives.'

But nevertheless, as they climbed into the taxi a while later and drove down to the Royal Festival Hall where the public meeting was taking place, he reviewed the conversation in his own private thoughts from another point of view and realised that without himself to reckon with, James Ross-Gilbert's chances of escape from retribution might have been quite good. He had muddied the water round his own activities so well and timed his disappearance so exactly that, but for the existence of one implacable enemy, who was to say that he might not have escaped. And, in a manner of speaking, Lord Allanport smiled to himself.

Chapter
25

AT THE ROYAL FESTIVAL HALL an atmosphere prevailed such as that you might imagine if, having had a large ship pointed out to them which was known to be about to sink, a thousand or so perfectly healthy individuals, of their own free will, clambered aboard. Viewed as such, the members of Lloyd's and all Names involved on the Ross-Gilbert syndicates who gathered for this meeting bore up as well as they could, although the threat of financial extermination somehow lacked the raw material of heroism. Add to that the fact that many of them had been at the Agency reception so short a time ago; had, within two months, wrung James Ross-Gilbert by the hand and called him a dear friend. It didn't help.

John Fairchild, the elderly underwriter and member of the Committee appointed by Lloyd's to head the new takeover Managing Agency, sat with several others on the stage facing the audience of over a thousand Names and opened the meeting with funereal calm. He did not mince his words. He had been appointed to carry out the syndicate's current business and run off* old years, but the problem they were dealing

---

*Run off. Syndicates in Lloyd's work three years in arrears in the sense that a year's business is normally 'closed' at the end of each year but not accounted for for another twenty-four months. When, therefore, trading in certain syndicate numbers abruptly stops, as in those managed by James Ross-Gilbert, business of the preceding two years and the remains of the current year must be 'run off', i.e. managed through to their conclusion.

with today was fraud and larceny. He said this in spite of the fact that a number of the JRG underwriters and brokers who had participated in the business under discussion were present.

He paused, having made that statement, and looked at various men in the audience. 'They are here not necessarily by any means as former perpetrators of these crimes. Many people ...' He paused, and his audience could not but acknowledge the justice of what he said when he continued, 'Many people were taken in by James Ross-Gilbert and his partner Richard Trene.'

Ralph Scott, seated not far from where Henry Allanport and his brother-in-law had happened to find seats, set his teeth, not knowing where Lloyd's currently placed him between the fox and the hounds.

'You will have an opportunity to put your questions to them later,' continued John Fairchild. 'But now I hand you over to my younger colleague, who will explain the situation to you as we perceive it at present.' He gave the name and credentials of a competent-looking handsome man, who rose to his feet and started to address the meeting.

Henry Allanport listened, unlike many other members of the audience, with a combination of acute attention and indifference. He listened in fact with the detachment of an executioner. Strained comprehension, fearful anger and frustration rose from the minds of the audience around him like bodily heat and charged the atmosphere in a way that his sympathetic nature monitored and understood. There was something in his expression that caused the light to reflect in much the same way as it might off the blade of a drawn sword.

The speaker matched his account of the minutiae of underwriting losses with information (in so far as it was yet available) of stolen money. He dexterously kept the two sources of disaster in simultaneous play, constantly relating the loss-making non-marine underwriting to the reinsurance which should have protected them, but had been stolen or dishonestly or unsuccessfully invested. But as soon as he had completed his account and opened the meeting to questions, the tensions of the audience rose. It was the scramble for the lifeboats – Lloyd's central fund, legal redress, the responsibility or otherwise for Names to pay up when fraud rather than bad or unlucky underwriting was the cause of loss.

Henry, who had decided beyond argument where the blame lay and to whom he owed the debt of revenge, and who had settled on a private course that was independent of anyone else's cooperation, listened with detachment. Not far from him the progress of the debate had a different reception altogether from Ralph Scott. His position was so dire that one might wonder how on earth he had been persuaded to attend the meeting. The answer lay in his desperate hope to avoid the necessity of having to go and live abroad, by appearing to cooperate. He was prepared to be taken for just a fool. Now, however, the questions being asked all around him came nearer and nearer to his quaking skin, more and more the name of Cleave & Engels starred with Merchaum & May as the brokers who had broked the most disastrous of the high premium long tail liability risk business. It would be only a matter of time before one of them pointed out that if the perfidious underwriters had absconded, at least the brokers responsible could offer some sort of an explanation. What exactly had they gained from it? Why had they involved the syndicates in so much potentially dangerous business on such a high risk basis?

It was a youngish man in the audience who linked his question to one of the brokers he spotted in the audience. 'The broker provided the business,' he pointed out, 'and the underwriters took it. It's a team effort. I'm a direct Name, and I think I have a right to know from Mr Victor, who I see is in the audience here, why he, as a broker for Cleave & Engels, conducted so much disastrous business through the syndicates.'

The end of his sentence was already muffled in the upsurge of sound from the audience, who all moved in their seats to look in the direction indicated and murmured or called their agreement. It was a vile moment, and not only for Nick Victor. Henry could sense Rupert's dismay, and for his own part his nature shrank from the impulse to set on another man as a pack, however guilty he might be.

As for Ralph Scott, he had thought it would be him. His face blenched with the determination to hate more than he was hated, and he had nearly risen from his seat before the young man had got to the point of naming Nick Victor.

Nick Victor, apprehensive and cautious about his own safety as he had always been, always on the brink of refusing Ross-Gilbert's schemes and always, in the end, allowing himself to be persuaded, stood up now because he had to. His knees nearly bent under him. He gave a few weak explanations, but the audience sensed the uneasy cause of his timidity. He looked about him in a blurr that mercilessly cleared and showed him, in the upturned faces all around and the angry voices, the position that his actions had given him among his fellow men. Formerly when, as an apparently unusually successful broker, he had enjoyed the admiration of his peers for his house, his car or his wealth, the sensation had been pleasant; but in proportion, by no means sweet enough to set beside the gall of this. Magnified by the almost certain prospect of future disgrace when more was found out about the various arrangements, his suffering was terrible.

Henry Allanport, seeing this, stirred uneasily. He was loath to take part in any way. He had come only to observe; and then only because London was a staging-post to his departure abroad on the track of James Ross-Gilbert. But he stood up. Immediately the Chairman noticed him, and gestured to the attendant with the microphone, who came to the end of the row and put it in his hand.

'I don't think . . .'

There were some calls of 'Name?' to remind him to introduce himself, but the Chairman bent to his own microphone and said, 'I think it's Lord Allanport, isn't it?'

'Yes.' There was again a silence. 'I wanted to put in a plea for Mr Victor. I don't think we should subject individuals here this evening who have, after all, had the courage to attend in response to the request of the Committee, to the sort of hostile questioning that few can respond to rationally.' The audience seemed to concur.

The Chairman, scanning their faces from side to side like a

tennis umpire, said, 'Very well. Then I think the question was yours, Mr Henderson.'

The Name who had stood before repeated his query to Nick Victor in more reasonable terms, and the wretched man launched on a reply both stumbling and evasive, knowing he was doomed.

When at last the meeting came to an end, among the first in the audience Ralph Scott got up to leave. It was his intention to cut the reception being held in the foyer. Others could have his glass of poisoned champagne. He was getting out. But no sooner had he emerged from the auditorium than he saw, on the fringe of the space prepared for the reception, the television cameras pointing his way. The last thing he wanted was to be caught in front of the cameras in the van of this event. He turned, as if he had forgotten something in his seat. No one had recognised him yet. It needed only a second or two for him to be able to re-emerge into a room crowded enough to hide him. He was coming out for the second time and starting a circumspect detour of the reception when Marjorie Dunne saw him – the very woman who had accosted Henry at the Agency party with such dazzling ineptitude.

Now, as if she saw a chance of a cosy chat with someone who would actually want to talk to her, she seized his arm as he was slinking past, and said, 'Mr Scott! I'm so pleased to see you. Isn't this terrible! I don't understand half of it, and Paul's so worried he won't explain. Can you tell me?'

The wretched man, from a force of habit more powerful than any other, did not dare to bring himself to be rude to such a woman. He stood like a man in torment, but one not able to get away.

The television cameras moved inexorably in the crowd. Those Names who agreed to do so answered questions put to them, presenting for the first time to the outside world the collective face of a group commonly thought to make money without risk or effort.

'It will put the record straight over that, at least,' Rupert said to Henry.

Henry shook his head. No records ever get put straight. At that moment he saw Giles Anderson. It took him a moment to remember who he was, and with the memory came a sharp stab of referred pain from the moment when he had first heard of the death of Delia. He watched him now stride and push his way across the room, a head taller than those around him, a dangerous intentness in his direction. Ralph Scott was standing to one side, his head half-turned away, but his companion saw Giles Anderson before he did.

She said apprehensively, 'I think this man's coming to talk to you.' And Ralph looked up in time to see the tall and massive figure bearing down on him, too late for him to get away.

'Ralph Scott!'

People standing near by took a squeamish step away, and Marjorie Dunne frankly panicked, turned her back, and took two or three paces towards the door. Ralph Scott stood his ground because there was nothing else to stand on, but he did not look upright in any other sense of the word.

'I've something to say to you!'

Ralph said nothing. Even the venom of his expression was diluted with fear. One of the TV cameras had picked up on the scene brewing and had him nicely in frame.

'When I saw you last,' Giles Anderson thundered, 'Lord Allanport, as I remember, asked you a question about long tail American liability risk, and you made out you knew nothing about it.'

'Oh, did I?' Ralph sneered. 'I think you may have mistaken the background detail of our conversation.'

'No, I did not.' He stood over him, his big-boned Northern body immaculately dressed, his massive neck showing red where the greying crop of his hair stopped short. 'I'll have you know that I remember that conversation word for word, and I have given it some thought since. It seems you not only knew about this part of the underwriting portfolio, but you broked about half of it yourself. You lied. And, by God, this is what I call a bit of well-deserved hostile questioning!'

He drew back one massive clenched fist as he said it, and hit Ralph Scott full in the face. At the same time with the other hand he reached forward and seized his coat to stop him falling down. Ralph Scott, fairly dangling from the fistful of cloth by which he was held, received a second crashing blow into the already blood-spattered mess of his face before being dropped unconscious to the floor.

Giles Anderson, not even breathless, stood, and taking a clean handkerchief out of his left-hand trouser pocket, carefully wiped the blood off his right fist. In a room that had become almost silent, he said, 'If anyone wants to sue me for assault, Lloyd's has my address.'

No one spoke. And then, without another word, he left.

Chapter 26

SIR KENNETH DUNPHY at the Department of Trade and Industry took a call on Tuesday that threatened effectively to spoil his week. For obvious reasons he had told his staff that he would deal personally with the queries being raised by Mr Harris of Shipping Investigation Securities, but it was with a pleasant conviction of having the upper hand that he pressed the cut-out button on his private phone before saying Hello. In fact what he said almost immediately was, 'Ah, Mr Harris, I'm afraid my department is out of this one now.'

'I'm sorry,' Mal Harris replied. 'I'm not quite clear as to your meaning, Minister.'

'Naturally we will continue our enquiries,' Sir Kenneth continued, 'but I'm afraid the circumstances are changed.'

'In what way, sir?'

'The question of the evidence of your allegations: it's taken on a different perspective now in the light of the disappearance of the individual concerned. The Department has had the records sealed, and in due course they will be investigated.'

'I see,' Mr Harris said. There was a silence, and then he added, 'What shall I do then, sir, with the papers from the James Ross-Gilbert syndicates investment file?'

'What?'

'The papers from the JRG investments file,' Mr Harris said

again. 'The correspondence between Mr Ross-Gilbert and his friend acknowledging receipt of the ROSE shares and the index numbers of the investment, showing from which set of Agency reinsurance premiums the money came to buy them.

Sir Kenneth simply said 'I see', but in a tone of voice that well conveyed his anger. 'In that case, Mr Harris, if you are in some doubt, perhaps you had better come and see me. I presume this was what you had in mind.'

Sir Kenneth duly received Mr Harris at five o'clock, sitting at his desk unsmiling. If John Ruskin had given his 'Sesame' lecture in our day instead of 1864 he would have had to have men like Sir Kenneth Dunphy in his audience still to be able to declare 'a false accent or a mistaken syllable is enough, in the parliament of any civilised nation, to assign to a man a certain inferior standing for ever.' From such a base the Minister's deep-seated sense of superiority in general and over Mal Harris in particular largely derived, and was the main element in his character that gave him the courage of his convictions. From that point of view, knowing that Mr Harris had somehow managed to get his hands on the real evidence of this scandalous transaction in spite of his own prompt move in having the filing cabinets locked and sealed, he nevertheless suffered from no sense of being at a disadvantage.

'I am not accustomed to dealing with matters in this kind of way, Mr Harris,' he announced with a certain loftiness, 'but I suppose I must congratulate you.'

Mr Harris made a gesture of polite acknowledgement, but said nothing.

'As things stand, I don't see what you expect me to do. The man's gone abroad. To live. It wasn't deliberate, but there you are. We missed him. Now it must be in the hands of the DPP if he's to be brought back.'

'True, sir, but the DPP will act on evidence presented to them by your Department?'

'And we'll give it fairly. No point rushing us now.'

'It depends, Minister, on what you call a rush.'

Sir Kenneth gave him a curt look. But he persisted. 'The problem is that James Ross-Gilbert, Richard Trene and others have created a situation which is too urgent to allow of delay. Their combination of bad underwriting and mis-appropriation of syndicate funds will cause such a scandal that it could seriously damage Lloyd's as an institution. Britain can't afford to have its international influence and earning power decimated.'

The Minister nodded an acknowledgement.

'Also, there are Names whose losses will ruin them. They must have some help and some redress, Minister. They are not just shopkeepers going into liquidation. They are peers of the realm, landowners, powerful men.'

If Mal Harris wanted to know what Sir Kenneth thought, it was that he should have put it like that before. Nevertheless, there was still this appalling problem of the ROSE involvement.

Mr Harris looked up with an expression of modest respect. 'I think we have made that safe now, sir,' he replied.

The Minister gave him a cool stare. 'And then?'

'Locate the funds where they have been secreted abroad, sir, and recover them.'

'Is that easy?'

'Not at all. Secret names, trustees unaware of the source of the funds they hold, no records. But my firm is equipped for this work.'

'I see,' Sir Kenneth said. There seemed to be no obvious problem, provided that the discretion of the holders of the evidence of the share transactions mentioned above was to be absolutely relied upon. For the first time, putting aside the obstruction of his own career interest in the protection of his Master, he acknowledged his actual inclination towards justice in this whole affair. The man James Ross-Gilbert had always been an outsider, even when he, Kenneth, had chosen to ignore it. In some extraordinary way this fellow Harris, in spite of his Welsh accent, wasn't – quite. The thought cir-culated well below the radar of the Minister's conscious mind, but nevertheless it was there. The bell on his desk buzzed, and he pressed the switch to hear his PA ask if he would like drinks brought in.

'Can I offer you a drink, Mr Harris? Whisky? Gin? White

wine? Two glasses of white wine, thank you, Oliver.' He settled back, and said, 'Where were we? Recovery of stolen funds abroad. Right. Has anyone put a figure on it?'

'Provisionally, forty-eight million.'

'As against?'

'A hundred and thirty.'

He gravely shook his head. 'It won't go far. No time for investment.'

Mr Harris said, 'Maybe the Japanese could be persuaded to accept some reinsurances. It's happened before.'

Sir Kenneth actually smiled. It was balm to a Trade and Industry Minister to be reminded of a day when someone in the City had got the better of the Japanese. At that moment the white wine was brought in. 'So,' he said, taking his glass and savouring the cool delicious impact of a good Sauvignon at the end of a day's work, 'all you require from us is the readiness to process the evidence you produce, document the other contents of those filing cabinets and rubber stamp the go-ahead to the DPP.'

Mr Harris also enjoyed the wine, and perhaps it was responsible for the sharpened gleam in his eye as he looked across at Sir Kenneth holding the stem of his glass resting on the back of his left hand, and said, 'Not quite. Not only that, sir. I have a favour to ask of you.'

Every parliamentarian, let alone minister, knows the meaning of the word 'favour'. It means work, inconvenience, attention to something that one would far rather ignore, and sometimes it refers to an ill-conceived debt of some kind.

The unfortunate Minister experienced a sudden evaporation of that sense of wellbeing that the last half-hour's conversation had produced in him, and he said in a tone that was very nearly querulous, 'Of course the Department will do whatever they can to help. What had you in mind?'

'The Swiss bank,' Mr Harris said. 'The Banque de Flors, owned by James Ross-Gilbert and four others. Naturally it is protected by Swiss law, but it is, like others of its sort, a repository for accounts that are held in secret, and we are sure that a large proportion of the money belonging to Lloyd's Names is deposited there.'

Sir Kenneth followed him so far. He couldn't for the life of him see where this was leading.

'I would like the secrecy ruling to be waived and the accounts opened for inspection.'

The Minister frowned slightly as people who are slow-witted often frown when they are spoken to, slightly hostile to the effort of understanding. In this case, it was incredulity that inhibited him from taking in what was being proposed. Eventually he said, 'Forgive me if I misunderstand you, but surely you cannot possibly be suggesting that a Swiss bank should disclose secret accounts? They'll never do it!'

Harris said nothing. Sir Kenneth pushed back his chair. He smiled, but not particularly pleasantly. He said, 'You do expect the earth, don't you, Mr Harris.'

Mr Harris smiled back at him. 'Perhaps,' he said.

'Well, I'm afraid I can't help you. In what way do you imagine I or my Department can influence Swiss law?'

'In an unusual way,' Harris said. 'I thought that the Prime Minister could persuade the Chairman of the Swiss regulatory body.'

'Why should he? Or, more particularly, how could he?'

'Well,' Harris said, 'it is a fact, I believe, that last year one of the largest Swiss chemical firms was in competition with the Italians over a very important patent. Now, strictly speaking, they should have lost, but someone over here managed to arrange things so that the Italians were pipped at the post.' Sir Kenneth said nothing, but kept his eyes fixed on his guest. 'You may not have heard about it, Minister, but it was worth a lot of money. And prestige.'

'I did hear about it.'

'Right. Well . . . I think that, in return, the Prime Minister, or yourself, could persuade the Chairman of the Swiss regulatory body to let this search of the accounts of the Banque de Flors go ahead.'

'I doubt if he'll think it an important enough issue to use such top-level pressure, Mr Harris, and risk causing offence to a foreign friend.'

'Well,' Mr Harris said quietly, 'if he doesn't think Lloyd's is a good enough cause, perhaps you will have the goodness to remind him that his own reputation is at stake.'

'What exactly do you mean by that?' Sir Kenneth demanded.

'I think you know what I mean, Minister,' he said. 'I have no wish to be troublesome. But I have two aims before me at the moment; one is to bring Mr Ross-Gilbert to answer to British law for his crimes, regardless of who are or have been his friends; and another is to locate the stolen monies and restore them to their rightful owners. It would in my opinion be insulting to presume that you or any other government department involved would not have precisely the same objectives.' He was already standing. He put his glass down without a tremor.

'Very well,' Sir Kenneth said. 'I will raise this question with the appropriate people. But I make no promises.'

He pressed the bell on his desk, and Oliver came to the door. 'Show Mr Harris out, will you, please?' he said, and then as soon as he was gone, he threw himself back in his chair to contemplate, with no satisfaction whatsoever, the prospect of what he had to do.

Chapter
27

IT WAS Celia Merrin's idea that Henry Allanport should meet Mal Harris. Ossie's information about the involvement of Shipping I.S. in the Ross-Gilbert enquiries seemed, according to her, to offer her cousin the means of getting some re-assurance before he left on his holiday. On that account she had persuaded Ossie to bring Mr Harris to lunch in a restaurant off Marylebone High Street.

There, arriving on his own, Ossie struggled across the crowded floor towards her, exlaiming, 'Dear Heart, how I must love you! This is very inconvenient for me.'

The spark of humour, that would have lit Henry's eye at the sight of someone like Ossie threatening to sweep everyone else's lunch off their tables with his draperies as he burst in from the street, was dead. But he had a reason to acquiesce, to let his time be filled.

'But where is Mr Harris?' Celia was saying. 'No Mr Harris, no lunch, Ossie.'

'He'll be here soon, I assure you. Lord Allanport, I presume, Gordon Hollander. If our tyrannical friend is not going to introduce us, we must help ourselves.' And having shaken hands, he sat down and applied the same principle to the wine.

'I suppose you know all about yesterday's meeting in the Festival Hall, Ossie,' Celia said.

'Oh, were you there?' Henry asked politely.

'No.' He shook his head lugubriously. 'But one hears about these things.'

'I wish I'd been there,' Celia said. 'I'd have liked to see that awful Ralph Scott get a bloody nose!'

'Cruel Child,' Ossie said, pronouncing the word 'cruel' in two distinct syllables.

'Cruel, indeed! Don't forget I spent a whole weekend with him on a yacht.'

'Nevertheless, to know someone deserves punishment and to enjoy watching him get it are two different things. Otherwise Lord Allanport would not have rescued Mr Victor.

'Did you rescue him, Henry? What from? He was the broker responsible for nearly half the most damaging liability business broked to the Ross-Gilbert syndicates!'

'But I thought,' said Henry, 'that nobody even knew that the syndicates were taking on American liability business at the time.'

Ossie shook his head. He said, 'Someone always knows.'

Celia ate the last of the nuts in front of her and said, 'Don't look now, but there's an adorable little man coming in at the door who looks as if his job is something like trapping moles in Wessex or writing poetry down a coalmine. Good heavens! I think he's coming over here.'

Ossie put aside his napkin and shifted his body in a polite gesture that implies getting up without actually doing it, and introduced Mal Harris to Celia and her cousin. Celia's candid eyes were open wide, where he could read, behind their apparent astonishment, a challenging ironic gleam that he was more capable of detecting than she thought.

'Ossie has been giving you a rave notice, Mr Harris,' she said as soon as he had sat down.

He replied, 'That's very kind of him, Lady Celia.'

'He says you beat a combined force of Greek shipping criminals, a Russian chemical warfare experiment and the PLO almost single-handed last year.' He just raised his eyebrows and ducked his head to one side. 'And shred steel bars with your teeth and fight sharks for fun.'

He smiled at her, and said, 'Do I look as if I could?'

She laughed. Henry looked at him appreciatively and sipped the wine that the waiter had just poured.

'I gather you're investigating the Merchaum Agency scandal, Mr Harris.'

'Yes.'

'I'm a direct Name, you know.'

'Mr Hollander mentioned it,' he said. 'Very unfortunate.' His tone was politely funereal.

Ossie, who had been drinking wine and reading the menu from end to end with all the oblivious concentration of a happy man, sat back now with a sigh. Perhaps being such an eccentric himself he was quite unaware of the unusual impression made by Mal Harris, who did not look remotely like a man with the expertise or background needed to make headway in an international business enquiry. Why choose him?

But then, as Henry reminded himself, what did it matter? If Mr Harris could simply be persuaded to give him details of Ross-Gilbert's exact whereabouts, it was all that he, Henry, required of this meeting. That, and something to eat. Celia's determination to arrange the encounter was the sole reason that they were all here.

'Unfortunate, indeed,' intoned Ossie, 'but not necessarily beyond repair.'

'Do you think not?' said Henry.

They were interrupted by the waiter coming to take their order – an elaborate process at any table that included Ossie.

'What course of action can be taken, then?' said Henry, as soon as they were free to resume the conversation. 'I mean beyond persuading Lloyd's to take a general levy of Names, or submit to a legal action for damages against themselves for failure to enforce their own by-laws, what else can be done?'

'Recover the stolen money, for one thing.'

'Oh, I see.' He was showing nothing more than a polite interest. Mal Harris, quietly sitting there like a rather dull and inappropriate guest, watched a man with two and a half million at stake pretending to care about the recovery of it.

'How can they do that?' Henry continued. 'I was told it was all put in trust funds abroad with no record of the names of the trustees or of the funds. Plus Swiss bank accounts.'

'Precisely.' Ossie seemed to feel he had made a mysterious point. 'Not an easy task, but possible. And Mr Harris is an expert.'

'Ah!'

Henry took this in with the courteous gravity of someone making a deliberate response to an audience they wished to indulge. But like a magician's trick that unaccountably falls flat, Ossies's declaration had obviously failed to arouse the flagging conversation. Henry sensed this himself, and said to Mr Harris, 'What chances of success do you think you have?'

'Well . . .' He seemed to calculate. He put down his knife and fork tidily. 'A lot depends on finding Mr Ross-Gilbert himself.'

Henry's attention shifted into an altogether different level. 'Indeed.'

Mal Harris perceived it, but he tended to keep his eyes away like a nervous man.

'So will you look first for him or for the money?'

Mr Harris seemed to choose quite carefully as if the option were before him at that very minute, but more like a bet on a horse than an order with any intrinsic merit in it. Lord Allanport waited, and as he did so, he tensely spun the stem of his glass between his thumb and forefinger.

'I'm not sure, to tell you the truth,' Mr Harris said, and looked up with sudden and unexpected directness and saw, quite clearly before he had time to adjust his gaze, the intensity of the look that Henry had settled on him. 'Which do you think is the more important, Lord Allanport?'

Henry saw at once that it had been intentional. A rare flick of anger momentarily hardened the semicircular crease around the corner of his mouth. 'You're right, Mr Harris,' he said. 'I am very interested in the whereabouts of Mr Ross-Gilbert.'

Mal Harris acknowledged what he said without a trace of timidity. 'I'm not surprised,' he said quietly. 'You have every right to be interested, Lord Allanport. That man is going to have to answer for what he has done.'

Henry was silent. A waiter hovered near by, but getting no

encouragement, he drifted off again towards the bar.

'Who to?' Henry eventually said.

'The law.' A distant look came into his eyes. It was the nearest he would come to a contradiction.

'Perhaps you were thinking, Lord Allanport, that these men would be allowed to get away because of the influential people who were their friends?'

'Perhaps.'

'That won't happen.'

'No?'

'I intend to see that it doesn't.'

'You mean you are going to get him first?' Henry accidentally put an emphasis on the second 'you'.

'Who else, Lord Allanport?'

He gave no answer. Celia looked at him in surprise.

'What are you going to do, Henry? Kill him?'

'Yes, I should think so.'

'Watch out, Mr Harris,' she mocked. 'He probably means what he says. If you need James Ross-Gilbert's signature to any of those trust documents, you'd better hurry.'

Chapter
28

'I'M SORRY, HENRY. Maybe that wasn't such a good idea.'

Celia was driving Henry to Heathrow directly after leaving the restaurant, stopping off on the way at his house in Holland Park to pick up his luggage.

'What do you mean?'

'The lunch; dragging you along to meet Ossie and his friend.'

'Ah well!'

'You don't like him?'

Henry paused on the brink of saying what he thought, looking at the trees in Manchester Square, feeling the newly familiar friction of unhappiness snarl the smooth progress of one event to another in the day. 'Like him? Yes, I did, in fact. Very much. Weird fellow.'

'Mal Harris, you mean?'

'Yes. Ossie I'm not so keen on, but his friend; his inconvenient friend . . .'

'Why inconvenient?'

'Perspicacious.'

Celia took the turning into the Bayswater Road with her lips pressed tightly together in an unconscious reflection of how she was calculating her next remark. She said, 'Henry, I know you need a holiday.'

He just turned his face to her and smiled that cool ironic

smile, the length of his eyes intensified, the golden-brown surface of the iris spaced fractionally away from the bottom lid, his lips in a straight line until the upturned corners; so familiar, so previously light-hearted that now the almost facsimile of his former ways caught the heart of the recipient of each smile like a thorn. 'Go on.'

She said, 'Are you going to Florida to find that awful man?'

'James Ross-Gilbert?'

'Yes. Is that what you're going for?'

He didn't answer at once, and then he said, 'Celia, do I look like the sort of person who would go and sit on a blasted beach in California three weeks after my wife had died and enjoy it?'

'We weren't talking about enjoying it. And, besides, I thought you were going to stay with Phoebe Lennox.'

'What gave you that idea?'

'I don't know,' she said. 'But one thing I do know is that James Ross-Gilbert is no pushover. Do you remember I told you once that I wouldn't like to meet him on a dark night if he had anything against me?'

'Ah yes. That was a long time ago.'

'Maybe. But it's not one of the things that's changed, Henry.'

They had arrived. He held open the front door for her. Inside, it was cool and shady. It was full of the absence of Delia, redolent of the atmosphere that had belonged to her, but going to waste like dying flowers. Standing in the hall, a feeling almost of shame haunted both of them, knowing Delia was not in the house, not on her way home.

'I'd better just speak to Mrs Cullen,' Henry said. 'Go into the drawing-room, love, and pour yourself a drink. Or would you like some coffee?'

'Neither, thanks. It's all right. I'll just wait for you.' She went in and stood in the shadows. The room, west facing, was subjected to the heavy probing golden fingers of the late afternoon sun. Suddenly aware of Henry's real frame of mind, the realisation made her thoughtful.

Later, as they drove to the airport, she said, 'If you're not really going to stay with Phoebe Lennox, Henry, where will you be?'

He took a piece of paper out of his breast-pocket and handed it to her. 'Wrote it down ready, but I'll be moving around.'

She glanced at it and handed it back, saying; 'Can you put it in my bag?'

There was a silence between them. Celia would not cross-question him. They were already half-way to Heathrow.

Henry said, 'I can't sit about and do nothing, Celia. Everyone else will do nothing.'

'Not Mal Harris.'

'You heard him. He's after the money, not the man.'

'That's not true, Henry. The man as well. He said so.'

'I don't trust him.'

She didn't answer. Driving due west, she screwed up her eyes until her lashes almost met in a double fringe. The light caught on them, too, as if raked up.

'Or, if I trust him, I don't trust him enough.'

'All right.' She sounded angry although it was really no more than a pretence. 'All right.'

He reached over and took her left hand off the wheel and held it briefly against his face. 'Where's Simon?'

'Oh, Simon! Paris, I think.'

'When I come back, love, I'll bring you a clever rich handsome Argentinian polo-playing poet for a present.'

She laughed. 'Remember,' she said, 'before you promise to bring me back presents, that there's nothing so empty-handed as a dead man.'

Chapter 29

THE FOLLOWING DAY, in the busy traffic in the Lloyd's building, Mal Harris stood unobtrusively in the back of one of the main lifts going up to the fifth floor. He was escorted by a pass-holding member of the Collingham Ward Kaye office. This was not one of the outside lifts from which Spencer Day had taken his last view of the world; Mal Harris emphatically did not share his indifference to heights.

When the lift stopped and he eventually got out, he nearly passed by a broker waiting at the fifth floor. At the last minute the young man, who had been talking to a colleague, caught sight of him out of the corner of his eye, and called, 'Mal! Mal Harris!'

Mal Harris stopped, and a delighted smile slowly spread over his face. 'Hello, Leo,' he said. 'Good to see you, boyo. How are you?'

'Good to see you. What are you doing here?'

'Didn't your brother tell you?'

'I've been away. Has Roger got Shipping I.S. on to something?'

'Yes,' he said. 'The Merchaum Agency scandal. James Ross-Gilbert. I'm on my way to the Collingham Ward Kaye office now.'

'James Ross-Gilbert! Well, if Roger's set you on to him, Mal, I can find it in my heart to feel sorry for the bastard.'

'Say what you like, Leo,' he said with a wry look. 'Mind you, it's worth a bob or two on my personal total if we can get some of the money back.' He was referring to the sum of all that he, personally, in the exercise of his profession to date, had managed to snatch back out of the grasp of the various would-be perpetrators of insurance frauds.

'Are you going after Ross-Gilbert himself?'

'Not as such,' he said, recalling to mind the face of Henry Allanport at lunch the previous day. 'I've an awful feeling someone else is doing that. I'm after the money. Are you coming in?'

They went in to Roger Collingham's office together, but Collingham himself, looking up from his desk and seeing both of them, said, 'Leo!' and then very drily, 'To what, I wonder, do I owe this pleasure?'

'I just happened to bump into Mal in the lift.'

'What a coincidence. All right, pull up a chair.' He got up himself and walked over and closed the door that his young half-brother had left open.

Mal Harris, slightly shaken by the unexpected encounter with the sheet-glass wall that gave, to one entire side of the room, an unimpeded view of the drop down from the atrium onto the main underwriting floor, sat with his back to it, and said, 'The Department of Trade had sealed the filing cabinets in Merchaum's.'

'So you didn't get the files?'

'Oh yes. We unscrewed the backs.'

Roger Collingham looked relieved, but at the same time not entirely pleased. 'I can't get used to your methods, Mr Harris,' he said, but he smiled.

'And the Minister?'

'He agreed. The British ambassador should have seen the Chairman of the Swiss regulatory body yesterday.'

'I suppose you know, Leo,' Roger said, 'that Ross-Gilbert and Trene put syndicate money into a Swiss bank. Re-insurance premiums went in as well; probably other funds. The Banque de Flors.'

'Have the Swiss ever allowed disclosure?'

'No.'

'Collingham Ward Kaye shouldn't have to be commissioning this enquiry,' Leo said critically. 'How about Lloyd's? And the DPP?'

'Oh, well . . .' His brother didn't want to go into all that. 'You're all right, Leo, you're a broker. My Agency has twenty-five Names on the Ross-Gilbert syndicates. At least ten of them can't pay, and one of those is a widow with two children in school.'

Leo said, 'I was telling Mal, I shouldn't be surprised if one of the Names didn't go and shoot the bastard.'

Mal looked curiously at him. 'Neither would I,' he said, 'especially if his name was Henry Allanport.'

'Henry Allanport? Good Lord, is he involved?'

'A direct Name.'

Roger was writing out a cheque, and now handed it to Mal, saying, 'Geneva on Friday? Or did you say next week?'

'Tomorrow, if I can. I'll be ringing the embassy in about an hour.'

'I won't ask you how you expect to be able to persuade him!' Roger was himself, by choice, a dealer only in the most straightforward processes sanctioned by tradition. 'But there you are. The Swiss accounts will almost certainly give evidence for prosecution as well as restoring funds. We can't do without them.' He stood up, looking at his watch. 'I'm sorry, I've got to get back to the Box. Shall we all go down?'

They left together, Mal and Leo continuing to the basement for a cup of coffee. Not many people were there. The vast oval concrete pillars, reminiscent of ships' funnels, were beginning to show signs of their great age. After more than two whole years *in situ,* the surface was rotting slightly. And yet the overall style of the place did some honour to a noble institution hitting back at the twentieth century.

'You've got your eye on something,' Leo said.

'I have, mun.' He put the coffee-cup down carefully. 'Can you tell me anything about your friend Lord Allanport?'

'Not a lot, really. He was at school with me, as it happens, but five years younger. Very well liked always. You say he is a direct Name with Merchaum?'

'Yes. And the direct Names stand to lose more than anyone else has ever yet been asked to pay in the history of Lloyd's.'

'He's not all that wealthy, as I remember. Family estates, but not real cash in modern business terms. How did you meet him?'

'Ossie Hollander; or rather, his ex-broker cousin Celia Merrin, who knows Ossie Hollander.'

'I see.' Leo waited for Mal to say more. 'So what were they after from you?'

Mal shook his head. 'Information; some indication of the prospects of recovering money from stolen funds, that's what I thought. But . . .' He held his head sideways in a speculative gesture as if weighing something uneven with his eys. 'I think the poor man has lost more than his wife and his peace of mind.'

'What do you mean, his wife?'

'She died. Very suddenly. Complication of pregnancy, and worry. He seems to bear it well, but I could feel something there. That man is in a murderous frame of mind.' Leo said nothing. 'Now I hear he's gone away on holiday.'

'You think he's gone after James Ross-Gilbert?'

'Yes.'

'I wouldn't be in that wretched underwriter's shoes with you and Henry Allanport after him!'

'I hope I get to him first,' said Mal, with bloodthirsty solemnity. 'I'll need his signature before his heart stops beating.'

Chapter 30

AT GENEVA AIRPORT Mal Harris was met by Miles Cotton, the Commercial Secretary for the British Embassy, and driven straight to the Swiss Federal Banking Commission in Berne. The diplomat was not encouraging. 'You won't get much out of Victor Hahnbrugger,' he said.

'Won't I?'

'Mean as a twist of lemon. We can't understand here why your office in London has gone to the expense of sending you over.'

'Perhaps they know something you don't.'

He took no offence. The official car was into the streets of Geneva in no time and checking off the landmarks of their progress with spiritless precision. The sky had become leaden and grey, all trace of summer fled. 'If you get their permission, you'll be back with some accountants, presumably?'

'That, too. But I want some information now.'

At the Bureau, Miles introduced Mr Harris, and beyond that his usefulness and his inclination were both arguments in favour of his being free to leave and return to his own office. He left Mal Harris in the company of Victor Hahnbrugger and his deputy, Joseph Baal. Victor Hahnbrugger re-seated himself behind a large desk, with his deputy standing to one side and Mal Harris in the chair in front of him. Marooned in the vast high-ceilinged monochrome interior of the office,

Victor Hahnbrugger looked like the official photograph of a man taken in perfect focus. His grey-brown light-weight check suit fitted his body with uncompromising exactness, not the smallest gap between the bottom of his buttoned waistcoat and his trousers. This absolute lack of space seemed to be characteristic: his eyeballs gave the impression of being crammed against the lids of his eyes, his teeth – although small – against the inside of his lips, and his body every fraction of space within the skin. Although he was essentially quite a good-looking man, his physical appearance had something in common – one could not quite tell what or why – with the density of a corpse. Joseph Baal, lingering to one side of him, his taller, thinner, frame printed in tones of sepia, bore out the prevailing style to its last detail.

Herr Baal slid a pile of papers in front of Herr Hahnbrugger, who glanced at the top sheet and took off his spectacles, at the same time as pronouncing his guest's name, in a cinematic series of routine gestures. He said, 'Please excuse me one moment', and picked up the phone. He dialled an extension number and spoke a series of brief sharp questions and answers in German. 'There is a note on this file to refer me to you in connection with the British request for access to the Flors account. Yes.' He listened. 'I see.' Again, 'But this is not my concern.' Pause. 'I see.' He put the phone down.

'Mr Harris.' Again the spectacles in their thin rim of gold were handled in gestures sacred to the colourless worship of authority. 'Your request has been given attention, and I have taken into account the fact that your government feels that some assistance was recently given to a major Swiss firm in need of special help, and that we should reciprocate. But the law of confidentiality of an account in a bank registered in Switzerland is a law that, once broken, would seriously and permanently damage our client confidence.'

Mr Harris, at the end of this speech, said nothing for fully five seconds, and the two men at the desk began to prepare for the next phase. The idea of such a serious request being dismissed with one dry reference to the rule-book seemed not to strike them as incongruous, although for an official of greater standing than Mr Harris they would have talked for longer.

'Herr Hahnbrugger.'

At the sound of Mr Harris's voice, he looked up, co-operative, courteous, limited in his intentions.

'Yes?'

'This is a very serious matter. The Prime Minister himself has requested that you should cooperate. The Banque de Flors has accounts held by men who have stolen millions.'

Herr Hahnbrugger said, 'Are these account-holders being prosecuted in Britain?'

'Not at present.'

'Then, Mr Harris, when they are, perhaps the request could be repeated.'

It sounded reasonable. Mal Harris said nothing at first in reply, but this time the two Swiss officials did not seem to expect him to leave so abruptly. They seemed to have understood that he intended to fight it out. He said, 'Unfortunately, we can't wait until the prosecution is under way, Herr Hahnbrugger. Neither should the considerable favour extended to the Swiss company in the matter of the patent be looked on as something over and done with.'

'That's not our concern, Mr Harris. This is a separate department.'

'It's not so separate that you, personally, didn't have a large shareholding that tripled in value when the patent came through.'

Hahnbrugger and Baal did not look at each other. But across the space that separated him from them, Mal Harris could feel the sudden tension between the two men exposed to each other's observation by this private insight.

Herr Hahnbrugger said with repressive formality, 'I deplore the implication that there was anything improper in the incident you refer to, Mr Harris. It was a pure coincidence.'

'Really?' Herr Baal looked uneasy. 'Your trade department,' Mal Harris said, 'does not know of this transaction? Or rather, is it that the Minister doesn't, but that the young man who is his private secretary does?'

Herr Hahnbrugger's expressionless face simply developed a pair of white lips without any other change taking place. Mal Harris stood up.

'Interdepartmental rivalry in your government is no concern of mine,' he said. 'But the matter I came here to deal with, Herr Hahnbrugger, is not just a bloodless formality. There is a great deal at stake. You must not be surprised if we take the trouble to seek out arguments that will carry some weight with you if you find the prosperity of Lloyd's of London and the pursuit of justice so easy to sweep aside.' He took out of the breast-pocket of his a coat a folded sheet of paper, opened it, and laid it on the desk.

Herr Baal leaned forward to look at it, made an exclamation in German, and glanced angrily at their guest. 'What is this?'

'A letter on your own department's letterhead.'

'I can see that!' he exclaimed.

'It's a permit,' Mal continued in the same level uncompromising tone. 'You will see it is in the correct wording: the same as when in response to the Spanish scandal of 1968 your predecessor waived the secrecy ruling. If you would be so kind as to sign and countersign it, I should be most grateful.'

There was a silence.

The three waited as if each of them expected the other to make a move. The cream-coloured walls, highly polished and grooved dark wood of windows, bookcases, desk, chairs, combined with hard shiny leather, neutral carpet, uncurtained windows with just a slip of white mesh against the long rectangular exposures of dull sky: the very large room, lit with photographic half-light – all preserved a drama slightly staled with time. The colossal ennui of the tidy streets outside seemed to penetrate, and threatened to douse, the fragile flame that Mal Harris had succeeded in lighting.

Herr Hahnbrugger slid the paper towards him with one finger. It seemed suddenly pathetic; an inadequate try at coercion based on too small a point. But, in thinking that, Mal Harris definitely erred. The rivalry between departments in a bureaucracy can be intense, and would in fact have still amazed him. He hoped it was sufficient to oil a wheel. It was enough to loosen the whole mechanism within a fraction of flying out of control. To stop the head of the rival trade department from knowing that he had had unofficial access to a confidential trade matter and had made a personal profit from it, Herr Hahnbrugger would have signed a death-warrant for his own grandmother. He took his pen out of his breast-pocket, unscrewed it, with his eyes bent on the work in hand signed the text, and initialled the rubber stamp.

Herr Baal watched him. He it was who picked up the paper and handed it across the desk. Mal Harris took it, pre-occupied, now that his main objective was achieved, with the formalities of the inspection and the timing of what he had to arrange. It made him less observant. His instinct for danger — that unaccountable subcutaneous awareness of shifts in the electricity of hate or fear that prick the skin — was dulled. He folded the paper and put it back in his breast-pocket and left the room, unaware that of the two men he left behind, one was careful not to watch him in case the hatred in his eyes should give away his intentions.

Chapter
31

THERE IS A frequency to the muted background vibrations of the air-conditioning system of Geneva airport that equates to some activity unsympathetic to human life. Mal Harris noticed and disliked it. He was looking forward to getting out.

He set off for the Departure gate. There were only two other men, one in the uniform of a Swiss Customs officer, apparently going in the same direction down the long sterile corridors. Now that the tourist season was over and the new terms had begun, presumably traffic between London and Geneva dwindled. As he walked, the passenger behind started to gain on him. Mal glanced over his shoulder and then at his watch, checking the time. It was not instinct that warned him, but the exactness, though so often suppressed, of human observation that could tell the difference between the sound of a man's steps when the trajectory of his path aimed or did not aim to take him past. In this case, Mal spun round, suddenly aware that the man was aiming for him. Ahead, the Customs officer had also turned and started back. Not a word was spoken. As the first man lunged forward, Mal caught his arm above the wrist and spun round, pulling him forward in the direction he was already going. At the same time, he blocked his feet. The man crashed to the ground, sliding on the polished surface, ridiculous in his suit and lace-up shoes, but hardly hurt. The second, who had been carrying a folded sheaf of papers, now held a gun fitted with a long silencer, and fired. The dull phut of the muted impact snapped a corner off the wall, leaving an ugly gash for the decorators to deal with. He took aim for a second time. There was nowhere that Mal could run for cover nearer than the bend in the corridor thirty yards away. But, against that, he knew that to hit a moving target with a small hand-gun is not as easy as they suggest it is in films. Mal turned and ran.

Up ahead of him, at last, another passenger – a woman – rounded the corner with a piece of hand-luggage on wheels like a toy. She looked curiously at the scene in front of her, and then screamed. Her voice drowned the placid explosion of the bullet, but Mal felt it like a wasp's sting suddenly slice against the side of his neck. Both men were still in pursuit, the woman lying on the floor. He had time to hope she'd fainted before hurtling down an unmarked passage to his right. Fruitless to retrace his steps to the Departure lounge with an armed 'Swiss Customs officer' just behind him, or to the Departure gate, for that matter. He took a series of unmarked turns, marvelling at the maze of corridors and empty walkways. Suddenly there was a shout of '*Gehen Sie nach rechts!*' over to his right, and running feet to the left could be faintly heard. They were cornering him. He turned. A door with no marking and a heavy iron latch caught his eye. The time taken to try it would be the death of him, if it was locked. One set of running feet approached the corner in front and to his right. He grabbed the door. It opened. A bullet richocheted off the just-opened angle above his head with a squeal like a knife catching on a plate. He slammed the door behind him, and looked for a bolt. There was none. He gripped the handle to stop it from turning, and saw at the last moment a levered metal slide that could be kicked up from the floor to lock it. At last he turned.

He was in some sort of utility room, the far wall of which was a partition that stopped three feet short of the ceiling. He heard the sound of a cistern flushing and running water on the other side. He took off his belt, slotted it through the handle of his briefcase, and retied it round his waist. Then he jumped. He got a purchase on the top of the wall with his hands and started to pull himself up. It would have been easier if there had been an overhang. His polished shoes got some grip on the roughened concrete. To one side, a bolt set into the wall for some long-obsolete purpose provided the one point of leverage he had to have. If his luck held, it would also turn out to be the Gents and not the Ladies. It was.

From his postion on the top of the wall when he reached it he could see into the row of cubicles. Only one small boy directly below him was just pulling down his trousers but snatched them up again with a speed uncomplimentary to the climate of morality at his school. Mal suppressed a laugh, but manoeuvred himself to one side and dropped down on to the seat of the lavatory in the next-door cubicle. His pursuers had not yet found their way round. Cautiously he went out into the room. Unusually, there were two doors at opposite ends, and as he pondered the reason, a man came in at one side and murmured, '*Excusez-moi*', as he made his way past. Mal went over to the other end and opened the exit door. Outside and to the left stretched a long counter-top with car-hire facilities and telephones on the near side, and across the walkway showed another direction-tab pointing towards the very gate he had been heading for in the first place.

Standing in the area between, with his back to him, checking out the surroundings with his head moving in short observant jerks like some sort of unpleasant automaton, was the gun-toting 'Customs officer'. Mal stepped back discreetly. Once inside the washroom, he walked quickly across the interior, seeing briefly, in passing, the reflection of himself in the glass. The blood from his neck had soaked his shirt-collar and stained the darker fabric of his coat. There was no sign of the small boy. Perhaps he didn't dare to come out. Just as he reached the door, the Swiss 'Customs officer' came in at the other side. Seeing Mal, he immediately reached into his coat-pocket, but paused. He didn't dare to shoot. A yard away from Mal's foot, the second exit gave on to French soil. The cloakroom was built on the frontier, and, like the airport itself, had a Swiss half and a French half. The Frenchman came out of one of the cubicles and washed his hands. Mal smiled once, mockingly, at the guard, who continued to stand in the Swiss exit and then, taking his time, he stepped out into the open. He turned up the collar of his coat to hide the bloodstain, and wondered what reaction he'd get if he said he'd cut himself shaving. And he wondered what Sir Kenneth Dunphy would say if he were told that rather than have the accounts of the Banque de Flors inspected, someone in Switzerland, probably either Hahnbrugger or his deputy, had been prepared to murder the man accredited as his envoy.

Chapter
32

RALPH SCOTT WAS at home when he was arrested. Oddly enough, Sarah seemed to have become much more fond of him of late, as if his public unpopularity had stirred a forgotten vein of compassion. She sobbed as he was taken from the house, and the passport she had been requested to find and hand over was slippery with tears. A certain military precision governing the exercise, Nick Victor was already waiting to be charged at the station so that they could be 'done' at the same time. That same day, the papers that neither of them had yet had time to read carried the news of the Swiss concession granted a week earlier relating to the Banque de Flors, and went a long way toward explaining the timing of their arrest.

As for James Ross-Gilbert himself, he had not, so far, really enjoyed his retirement. Before receiving the news of the latest developments in London via *The Times*, delivered a day late to his new residence in Bermuda, he had shaved slowly, listening to the sound of Philippa organising her girls for the day. A general impression of grande luxe surrounded him in a house full of polished marble, expensive furniture and extravagant accessories, where even the sunlight coming through the windows seemed done over with a proprietorial gloss.

All this he enjoyed. And he enjoyed Philippa. The one thing

he did not enjoy was his loss of status in no longer being the hero of a market, the Chairman of a company, an important wealthy businessman whose influence was still courted and recognised. What he did not enjoy was being a private individual with no empire to command beyond the temporary trivial range of a table in a very expensive restaurant. This had dealt his sense of wellbeing an unexpected blow. To put it right, he had started to make overtures to the business insurance community in Miami. He had been flatteringly received; but their secretaries kept him waiting. He remembered hearing, some time earlier, from a friend who had retired as Chairman of a large advertising company and tried to set up a new small enterprise of his own in another field. When he had to make his own phone calls, he couldn't believe the way he was treated: told that the buyer was too busy to speak to him for five minutes, asked to call back, laboriously-made appointments cancelled because they were no longer convenient. He was a nobody, and they were busy people. This galling story had not made much impression on James at the time. Then, it had the limited interest of something that was happening to someone else, but now he went in to breakfast with his inward eye focused, as it were, on a spot on the horizon that might grow into a real storm-cloud.

Nevertheless, a person's right to occupy an elevated position in the world is, in the end, borne out or demolished by their intimate private character. To some extent this vindicated James Ross-Gilbert's past prestige, because his self-discipline was absolute. He scorned to protest, and never did. The only version of an objection known to him was the capital solution, and until he pronounced sentence, he tolerated disappointments, even inadequacy, with the rigour of a perfect master. He didn't discuss his problems.

Philippa, beautiful, young and deliciously slightly common, wearing fine gold chains and a light fluffy jersey, had no idea that James was having second thoughts. She had not quite yet started to miss England herself, except that she regretted having to abandon opportunities that might have resulted from her breakthrough in TV advertising, where she had won a contract as the model for a brand of floor-polish. A product that could give a wonderful shine in the hands of someone who looked as if she hardly knew how to get the lid off was a winner. But then again, if Philippa got restless, the Americans would probably be quick to recognise her talent over here. The version of a comedown for her – having to catch the underground from Kensington to Piccadilly – was not on the cards.

On the other hand, although educated in the British tradition that deems it unsuitable for the state system to pass on to members of the working class useless information about Keats, Plato, Beethoven, Rembrandt, Homer and so on, Philippa was not at all unintelligent. She saw now that James had come across an item in the paper that had upset him, but she asked no questions. They never discussed James's business, and she let him suppose that she believed in the explanation that their rather sudden departure from England was down to horrid Marjorie. She had already organised the household here so that it ran with comfort, and now, with a faultless instinct for how to respond in a crisis, she went out into the garden to pick flowers. By the time she came back, James had retired to his office and was on the phone to London.

The first time James rang the Scott household there was no answer, Sarah having driven to the police station to fetch Ralph, whose bail had just been arranged. James reread the item in the paper. If the Banque de Flors accounts were laid open, the British could see, but could they touch? To make either of these concessions went very much against the grain. Disclosure would leave him without one shred of credibility as far as his reputation in London was concerned. A realistic observer of James Ross-Gilbert's career to date might have assumed that there was nothing left to salvage. And yet he had cherished hopes that would have made an honest man laugh. In this, at least, the knife he honed for other people cut himself.

Half an hour later, he rang again and got an answer. It wasn't good timing. Ralph, cornered and shaken, was not in what the Americans might call a thinking mode. Explaining the morning's experiences, including the confiscation of his passport and the certain promise of a future engagement at the Old Bailey, his normal tone of acrimony was heightened to a pitch that threatened to unhinge him and certainly rendered him comparatively useless to his friend. He had no idea how the Swiss bank accounts had been breached. He had not heard of Shipping Investigation Securities, and Hahnbrugger, who might have been expected to get in touch after the fiasco in Geneva, had gone on holiday to Morocco with his wife.

For Dick Trene, who was next in line for a phone-call from James, Ralph Scott's predicament was a compensation for everything. But when it came down to protecting all their various funds and accounts, his attitude was different. The plane that would bring a team of investigative television reporters down to film Dick snarling at his villa gates had not yet left London. But, whenever it did, he had his V-sign ready to give the folks at home. In reply to questions like, 'Mr Trene, are you aware that your former co-directors Ralph Scott and Nicholas Victor have been charged with conspiracy to misappropriate funds at Lloyd's?' and, 'Mr Trene, what have you to say to rumours that you and James Ross-Gilbert stole millions of pounds from Names on your syndicates?' he said, understandably enough. 'No comment.' And, when pressed, gave that V-sign that looked so impressive on the small screen.

Now, in conversation with James on the phone, he could explain without any problem exactly how the Swiss accounts had been tapped, and he used on Mal Harris and Shipping I.S. some of the vocabulary researched in his days of combat with Ralph. How he kept so closely in touch was his business, but he warned James to expect his share of the bills. Everything – the Swiss accounts, the old offshore investments, the trust funds in their various havens – needed looking after. But the prospect of being pilloried in London worried him not at all. No one could physically get at him where he was, and the bubble reputation was, in his view, a combination of squeezy washing-up liquid and hot air.

James thought long and hard when he put down the phone. He could not pretend to quite the same indifference as Dick

Trene. Immediately before him on the desk was a letter containing a flattering response to his enquiries from one of the leading American insurance companies. But such reactions would not survive brutally unsympathetic exposure in London. He sat in his chair exuding, even in private, that combination of elegance and consequential firmness that never let him down. After ten minutes he decided whom to ring, and his choice was ingenious. The hapless Minister for Trade and Industry, asked if he would take a call from James Ross-Gilbert, picked up the extension in three different minds as to the attitude he should take.

But James had no such problem. He called him 'Kenneth', thereby firmly laying claim to a past history of friendship the Minister would have preferred to forget, but at the same time his tone was hard and domineering as if he and not Sir Kenneth was in a position to state terms. He explained simply but effectively what Lloyd's and the City could expect from him if any attempt were made to prosecute. He drew a fine picture of himself in the role of Samson bringing the financial temples of London down in ruins with him. But where he really made his mark was in respect of the ROSE shares. There he made it clear that, if prosecuted, he would supply any deficiencies in missing paperwork from memory, and members of the government needn't look to locked filing-cabinets or unconventional security operatives to protect them.

Since Mal Harris, in his role of defender of Lloyd's, and James Ross-Gilbert in his role as predator, both threatened the same results if their demands were not met, Sir Kenneth could be excused if he concluded, on putting down the phone, that he could do nothing right.

Chapter
33

'PICTURE TO YOURSELF an emaciated, rather poetic, hill farmer with a Welsh accent,' Sir Kenneth Dunphy said indignantly, 'and you tell me if you would cope well with having him suddenly turn round and analyse your share portfolio!'

Kenneth was having the conversation he had promised himself with George. He accepted a glass of whisky and soda, and took a grateful sip. 'Where was I? Oh, yes . . . And before I had a chance to orientate myself to this blasted Alice in Wonderland character, he'd managed to slip a dose of mixture into the conversation and there wasn't a damn thing I could do about it. I had to come to terms.'

George said, 'Let's sit down, Kenneth. There's no one around here for the moment.' They were in the Garrick club.

'Well, where on earth did Mary dig him up? And why did she have to set him on to me?'

If George had a weakness, it was that he enjoyed the role of confidant to men like Kenneth. He said, 'She seems very set on this James Ross-Gilbert affair.'

Kenneth eyed him with a certain canny silence. He was wondering how much Mary confided in her husband. He himself could get a lot out of talking to George without actually making the mistake of being indiscreet. He hoped George knew nothing of the real details of the ROSE affair or of Mal Harris's intervention.

A group began to gather at the other end of the room: presumably another member of the club giving a small cocktail party. George, noticing them, said, 'Shall we go into one of the private rooms? We can come back in here just before Mary arrives.'

Kenneth was about to agree when a woman came in who caught his attention. This they very rarely did; but his bachelor status was the result of lack of interest, not competition from young boys. Being rather handsome, from time to time he had a little fling, but his heart was never in it. Now, with his eye on this extraordinarily fine woman, he said, 'I'd as soon wait here. Don't let's bother to move.' He looked at his watch to make it seem as if it wasn't worth disturbing themselves.

'So what has he achieved, this Harris fellow?'

Kenneth decided he could tell George about the Swiss bank. He was himself still ignorant of the degree of desperation that had nearly resulted in Mr Harris being murdered on his way home. He gave an account of events, with one eye on the woman who had been greeted and handed a drink and now stood, exceptionally graceful and alluring in a tailored cherry red skirt and high-heeled shoes.

'And what happens now?'

'There are various possibilities,' he said, rather distractedly. 'One is that Mr Harris collects the information he needs for us to prosecute the account-holders and return their assets to the rightful owners.'

The party at the other end of the room now consisted of about eight people grouped around a member of the club whom Kenneth knew by sight. George had never seen his cousin so distracted, but really couldn't credit the idea that the girl he kept looking at had anything to do with it. When Mary finally arrived, there was only time for a very brief drink before setting off for the theatre. But, as chance would have it, the other party broke up first, and as the girl walked past, she saw Mary and stopped. Kenneth couldn't believe his luck. He stood up. What would have been perhaps no more than a passing acknowledgment was turned into an all-round introduction by the strategic way Kenneth was blocking the exit. He only heard that her name was Grace Derby, and had the fleeting chance to shake her hand before she was forced to rejoin her friends who were hovering, waiting for her just past the door. But in response to his quite legitimate subsequent enquiries, he now had from Mary a fairly complete account of her.

The absent-mindedness that George had noticed before stayed with Kenneth through the play and throughout dinner and still derived from the same cause. Something in the girl's looks, her way of moving, her clothes, those wonderful ankles, the ingenuous glances with which she met one's eye, pre-occupied him totally.

'He can't have been smitten, surely!' Mary exclaimed as she sat at her dressing-table that night brushing her hair. She sounded none too pleased.

George gave her a shrewd look. 'Don't you worry about Kenneth,' he said.

'I'm not worrying. Just wondering.'

Kenneth, for that matter, was doing the same thing. He lived in a large palatial flat in Artillery Mansions, which he shared with his sister Ann, who just at the moment was away in France. He had been impatient for dinner to be over, and he sat now alone in the drawing-room drinking brandy and soda and wondering how best to approach the business of getting in touch with Grace the next day. Since she was on the Ross-Gilbert story for her paper, he decided he could easily make contact on that basis; even invite her to lunch. The graceful vista of the room with its pillars, fine paintings and quiet lights perfectly complemented his state of mind. He had always said to himself, if with a certain bloodless lack of urgency, that if the right girl came along, he would know it. Now, it seemed, his confidence in himself would be vindicated.

The next morning, as soon as he had dealt with urgent questions in his office and it being then already ten fifteen, he asked his secretary to call *The Times*, and if Grace was not there, the Covent Garden offices of the *The Independent Financial Digest*. Just because he had not devoted a great deal of his attention to chasing women was not to say he was not good at it. Now, he cleared the hurdle of getting Grace out to lunch with great panache and he decided from the first to do it all in style. He sent the ministerial car to pick her up at ten to one, and he himself took a taxi to the Fleur de Lys, where he would be treated with very distinguished attention which was, at the same time, discreet to the point of secrecy.

Grace had accepted the invitation with the innocence that characterised all her responses to the results of her own extraordinary attractions. It seemed perfectly reasonable that the Minister, wishing to promote his views of the latest implications for Lloyd's of the JRG affair, should seize on the fortuitous opportunity of their chance meeting to brief her. In one sense she had recovered from the way Ross-Gilbert had treated her, but not from the shock. She wanted revenge, and she went into any situation likely to yield information about him with a certain professional avidity that was not sensitive to other messages.

She arrived at the restaurant, and Kenneth, already installed at his table out of sight of the door, could have judged of her approach if he had been more used to her by the ripple of silence that flowed along her path. He got up from his chair, his expression, unknown to himself, one of boyish enthusiasm. The head waiter escorting Grace noticed it, but Grace herself did not. From her point of view she was on a professional assignment. Perhaps, if the assignment had had to do with any other aspect of finance besides that of the James Ross-Gilbert syndicate irregularities, she would have laid more store by the ministerial car and Sir Kenneth's own distinguished appearance. As it was, she shook hands in a business-like way and sat down with her mind on her job.

Sir Kenneth, intimidated but not at all put off, suggested disposing of the problem of what to eat first. The menu, limited and unpriced, made Grace cast one sideways look at Kenneth, and finding his eyes fixed on her face, smiled intimately and said something pleasant about having always heard that senior members of government knew all the best restaurants. Poor Kenneth, who often had sandwiches at his desk, accepted the assumption that he came daily and, if necessary, alone to the Fleur de Lys with besotted courtesy. He skilfully persuaded her to choose a dish which he knew would be superb and lowered his own menu momentarily to look over the top of it with an expression of limited patience in the general direction of the room, which ploy immediately brought the waiter to the table.

Grace, watching and also subsequently receiving the waiter's apparently devoted attention, privately thought to herself how agreeable it was to receive such treatment. She looked more attentively at Sir Kenneth, seeing him for the first time less as an essential milestone in her pursuit of James Ross-Gilbert's downfall and more as a man in his own right. She liked powerful men. She found them fascinating. The attentiveness of the waiter increased her awareness of his importance, the glamour of his position, and she admitted to herself that he was handsome. By this time the food and wine had been chosen and they were alone again.

'Well,' she said. The paradox of her divine looks and her prosaic manner struck Kenneth as the most perfect combination he'd ever come across in a woman.

He smiled at her encouragingly. 'Yes, now. Back to Lloyd's. Shall I first outline my Department's present position, and then you could ask me any questions you wish to add?'

She reached down to her bag on the floor and took out a small pad. 'Do you mind if I take a few notes?'

He did not. 'My Department's attitude,' he began, 'is that the appalling situation in the Merchaum Agency is symptomatic of basic problems in Lloyd's and less a matter of personalities. As you know, we have already instituted certain reforms aimed at this very type of exploitation. These events quite usefully confirm the absolute necessity of divestment. But they also point the way to further measures in the essential regularising of accounting and disclosure procedures.' He carried on for a further ten minutes, eloquent, flatteringly confiding in his manner, pointing out just how the private institution must conform to that pattern whereby great value, however generated must submit to the rules of treasure-trove to a degree. It was all very well to say that Lloyd's was more a private club than a business, and that any irregularities, those of the JRG syndicates included, were limited in their repercussions purely to in-house damage, as it were; members ripping off (he used a different word) other members, with no question whatsoever of the public suffering. But the government could not longer accept that. In the national interest, Lloyd's must be protected; if need be, from itself.

This line of reasoning completely diverted Grace from her awakening interest in Kenneth, in that it was unwelcome. As Mary Seymour had predicted, Grace's personal feelings altered her commitment as a journalist from disinterested reporting to bias. She would have liked it better if the Minister had seen the problem more from the angle of personalities and less as an institutional issue. The poor man was about to be subjected to yet another attempt to influence his course of action, and this time with a leverage even more difficult to resist.

The waiter had brought their second course, lobster à la fin d'étude. Kenneth struggled to eat his, but, good though it was, he simply felt he didn't need it. Grace, the soft curve of her cheek tinted only very slightly with the combined stimulus of champagne and intellectual effort, was thinking of Ross-Gilbert.

'Nevertheless,' she eventually said. She had put down her fork and, as it were, reflectively, broke off a piece of bread, her delicious rose fingernails immaculate and delicate. 'Nevertheless, personalities do come into it.'

'Oh, of course.'

'It was, after all, a unique achievement to date for James Ross-Gilbert to have exploited the system so long and so effectively for his own ends.'

'And Richard Trene and his fellow Ralph Scott and Victor. Rather a combined effort,'

'He was the ringleader,' she said firmly. Kenneth nodded, apprehensive. 'Our readers are anxious to know what official steps are being taken to prosecute them.' This was not a lie. The readers *were* interested.

'Oh – two men arrested only last week!' Kenneth said. 'You know that, of course.'

'But how about James Ross-Gilbert and Richard Trene?'

'Well, of course, that's up to the DPP now. We have no extradition arrangement with Spain at the present.'

'And Florida?'

'Florida? I don't quite understand.'

'Florida is surely where James Ross-Gilbert is rumoured to be at present.' Rumour had it wrong, in fact.

'Ah, Florida!' He said that as if it were some new brand of ice-cream just brought to his attention. Grace wondered what on earth was wrong with him. She saw him as always operating like this in the Ministry, sitting behind his desk in a haze of wellbeing on the brink of becoming hilarious. He responded hastily to the reproof he could see in the recesses of her expression. 'There again, it's down to the DPP and the Americans' disposition to cooperate.'

She pretended to make a note of it in the hope of frightening him. The small pad she kept by her plate was indecipherably littered with little shorthand signs which Kenneth found fascinating. He had never thought it of the slightest interest when his secretaries wrote shorthand. But now his essentially hierarchical nature responded to the device in the more elevated hands of a clever financial journalist, irrespective of her additional attractions.

'How productive is that likely to be?'

For a moment he was aware of having completely lost the thread, but surfaced just in time. 'Naturally, the Department of Trade will put pressure on them,' he promised extavagantly.

'On the DPP and the Americans?'

'Oh, yes.'

She looked at him with approval. 'Because there was a rumour that some unorthodox share deal or other could cause the government embarrassment, and they might stay their hand?'

Sir Kenneth took this heroically. Schooling himself to observe her dispassionately for a moment, he concluded that she didn't know about ROSE in detail. She was just fishing. And, in truth, when she had reapplied to Mary Seymour for more information along the lines which she had so cavalierly rejected only about a month ago, Mary had not cooperated. The realisation of what a part ROSE now played in the bargaining between Lloyd's, Shipping I.S. and Sir Kenneth deterred her from giving Grace any further clues.

'Any department of Her Majesty's government,' he said with slight return of pomposity, 'has a vested interest in justice and maintaining the rule of law.'

She smiled at him, which so far she had not done much. She liked the gravitas of that declaration, and was reminded of the status of the man who made it. He was very good-looking, and his personal interest was beginning to penetrate the intimate insensitivity with which her effect on others was balanced. It crossed her mind that such a lover would be very interesting. For the rest of lunch she took no more notes.

Chapter 34

NOTWITHSTANDING THE assurance with which everyone referred to Florida as James Ross-Gilbert's new home, that was not where he was living. The house in which he and Philippa had settled was in Bermuda, and he had quite deliberately not notified his former friends of this ultimate address. The wisdom of this policy was quickly borne out by the fact that Henry Allanport, arriving in Florida, could not find him, and there seemed to be no forwarding address.

Miami was not a place that Henry would ever have come to for pleasure, but now, when the very principle of pleasure was absent from his plans, it was far less irksome a place to him than it would have been to any of his friends. He was tempted just to do nothing. It wasn't that he had lost heart. The splintered remains were still stuck there, jarring against every movement that turned him towards home. But in his settled programme of retribution, he did not grudge Ross-Gilbert another day or two.

His first thought was to make enquiries back in London, but of whom? Mal Harris or Celia would respond with suspicion and immediately guess his purpose, had they not already done so. He opted instead to ring *The Times* and contact the journalist, Grace Derby, who was covering the affair. But this was unsatisfactory. Because although, as it happened, he was lucky in reaching her, she promptly informed him that Ross-Gilbert was in Palm Beach, Florida, at the Sherry Netherlands Hotel.

He would simply have said 'Thank you' without contradicting her, and put the phone down, if she hadn't then said, 'I'm sorry, I didn't catch your name.'

'Henry Allanport.'

'You're calling from the Association of Lloyd's Members?'

'No.'

'Oh, I was expected a call from the ALM. I thought when you rang . . .' Her voice tailed off. Something about the name Henry Allanport rang a bell, but if he didn't respond to her obvious invitation, she couldn't very well ask.

At this point the hotel operator chose to get her lines crossed, and there was a tangled interruption of small electronic explosions. 'I'm sorry, sir. Yes, madam, Florida. New York? Florida speaking.'

Grace Derby finally got a chance to say, 'Are you still there? If you're calling from Florida yourself, Mr Allanport, I don't understand.'

'I am,' Henry responded, 'but Mr Ross-Gilbert isn't at Palm Beach. Your information's not right, there.'

'Oh.' She was longing to ask him what he wanted with Ross-Gilbert, but was too taken aback to assemble her thoughts quickly. She simply said, 'Are you trying to locate him?'

'Yes.'

'Could I ask you to let me know if you do find him, or at least say that I should be interested in any information?'

'Certainly.'

'Thank you, Mr Allanport.'

He put the phone down. His room was high up overlooking the sea. Through the still and somewhat heavy air was diffused a torpid glitter of playground luxury. He decided to look up the name of an enquiry agency in the local Press and hire them to do the necessary research. This slow activity, minimal and uncomplaining, lay lightly on the shattered structure of his life. Time itself seemed to carry him ever closer to his prey.

Unaware of any such respite, James Ross-Gilbert told

Philippa that he was going to have to be away for a week. The time had come to visit Richard Trene in Spain, and he wanted to get it over. Faced with the business-like researches of Shipping Investigation Securities and Lloyd's, he needed to round up his finances, and to do it, he had to have this meeting.

Richard's car but not Richard himself met him at Granada airport. Their relationship had never been exactly convivial, but now, when the business element might have been considered secondary to their association, it was all too obviously the last thread that held them together. Even Anne, Richard's wife, had not bothered to meet him. He looked out with disapproval from the back of Dick's air-conditioned Rolls-Royce at the harrowed coastal landscape of Spain between the airport and Marbella. But Marbella itself came up to scratch. This kind of environment suited Dick and himself as did Palm Beach and Bermuda. As he had always said when he was at the height of his career in Lloyd's, this was the sort of place for a successful man to retire to: unashamed luxury and a good climate.

And, in fact, he was given a better reception when the car drew up at the end of the short drive, and Anne, looking well and thriving, came down the broad flight of steps from the house. They were to have lunch by the pool, and Dick, his fingers already curled round a large drink, walked across the emerald grass looking jovial and pleased with the prospect of entertaining his guest.

As James allowed himself to be led down to the water, it didn't occur to him to notice how like a hotel swimming-pool it all looked. A small group of strangers, incurious, cheerful, relaxed, submitted to the introduction. His name, that would have made a stir in some places, made no difference to them. He was just Dick's former partner. In the reflected glory of that association he was accepted. James, who had had a long journey, didn't really care. For the moment he was too tired to bother who Dick's associates now were or on what he spent his time. The fact was that Dick, who in Lloyd's had been an indifferent if devious underwriter and a fractious member of the board, had exactly what was needed for this phase of the game. He had discovered in himself a natural talent for the criminal's way of life. Making money, he had lagged in the second class. Guarding the proceeds, shifting them from one place of safety to another, tax havens, funds, trustees, secrecy and, if necessary, corruption and coercion, all came naturally to him. He had, as it were, come into his own, even if, in another sense, most of it was other people's.

The evening that finally found Dick and James on their own with the privacy to talk and do business was towards the close of what had been a busy day. An afternoon on the yacht had further bronzed and burnished their little group of friends, and in the early evening, while Anne struggled to extract a decent dinner from the Spanish cook, they retired to Dick's office. By no means a small room, Dick had lined it with electronic equipment, some of it set in consoles: computers, safes, telecommunciations of every kind, fax, telex, safe lines, cut-out systems, video-assisted monitors, financial market softwear – he had it all. The room measured twenty-five feet by thirty. A glass desk mounted on a pair of huge Chinese terracotta horses, soft leather sofas and a bar more or less completed the furnishings. James took it all in with a discriminating eye. It didn't look like the room of a man who was planning a quiet retirement.

'All right, isn't it?' Dick said with grim satisfaction, noticing that James was impressed.

'Excellent.'

Dick was pouring whisky, and the ice clanged with larger-then-life impact against the rich glass.

'Do you plan to use all this?'

He turned and handed James his drink.

'Of course.'

James nodded. He wasn't going to ask any more questions. But he felt a slight twinge of apprehension.

'Now, to business.'

Dick had prepared a stack of papers, and James sat opposite him at the desk where, one by one, the forms, certificates, letters, etc., could be examined. After several of the items were dealt with, Dick would lumber over to a spanking new photocopying machine and run off the necessary duplicates.

'And how about the Swiss accounts?'

James brought this up as Dick was standing with his back to him replacing some and extracting other paperwork from the wall-mounted safe. Dick turned. He was actually silent, but the expression on his face implied a sound stifled only by its own ugliness, and James remembered clearly, for the first time, the distaste with which their past association had been tinged.

'Steady on,' he said. 'They may look, but, as you pointed out, can they touch? I think not.'

'Do you know who manoeuvred that bit of underhand business?'

'No.'

'Roger Collingham.'

James was surprised. 'He hired this little creep from Shipping Investigation Securities, and somehow they got to lean on the Chairman of the Swiss Federal Banking Commission, but you know that. The point is, he got away with a signed paper in the pocket of his bloody little jacket, and that fool Joseph Baal and the hit-man I bought for him let him through Geneva airport as if they were there to give him safe passage.'

'What do you mean, "the hit-man"?'

'Oh, the hit-man missed, that's all.' Dick had no wish to cross the Ts and dot the Is if James was going to be slow-witted.

'I don't understand,' he persisted. 'You mean you hired somebody to mug him and get the paper back?'

'Mug, my foot! My instructions were to shoot the bastard. Don't look so shocked, James. An eye for an eye. He only went there to foul our pitch.'

'That's ridiculous,' James said. 'You can't be serious!'

'I certainly am,' his friend sneered. 'If we could have got the first paper back, Hahnbrugger wouldn't have made the same mistake a second time. Neither would I. I was caught on the hop myself.'

'So what happened?'

'The Shipping I.S. fellow ran and got away. Simple as that. And it will cost us, I can tell you.'

James was looking at him, concealing his own feelings,

knowing that it was useless to try and sway him. But the man was in fact an out-and-out criminal in a way that James himself had certainly not sanctioned. It was not in these terms that he saw himself, and such present expedients cast a most unpleasant light on the activities that preceded them and called them into being. It was a shock to him; an unpleasant alteration in his own status to which he couldn't see his way to adjusting.

Dick, following the progress of James's thoughts in the fastidious downturn of the corners of his mouth, seemed to derive a coarse satisfaction from it. It was as if this was his opportunity to expose the sham implicit in James's recent reputation in Lloyd's, and in which Dick himself had never had a fair share. He said, 'Do you want me to leave you completely out of it?'

'Out of what?'

'Well – presuming this fellow hired by Lloyd's gets near some of the trust funds, for example, you'd better realise I'm not just going leave him to it.'

James looked astounded. 'How could he? Even the trustees themselves can't make any connection between our nominee holdings and the Lloyd's claims – assuming they read about them in the papers. How on earth should that lawyer in the Caymans, for example, guess that Geranium is one of ours, or that our pass signatures have anything to do with Ross-Gilbert or Trene?'

Dick looked at him as if he was wondering whether to let something pass. He didn't like to hear names even mentioned. Why do it? He said 'You wouldn't have thought they'd nobble the Swiss, and yet look what's happened. Learn from that. Shipping I.S. has already spoken to the Samad brothers. I got word yesterday from Gibraltar. It's the same fellow called Harris, the one that went to Geneva. He's after the whole bloody lot – and us, too – but you first, I shouldn't wonder. Now ... I wasn't letting it worry me.' He made a gesture towards all the equipment, like a general pointing to his troops. 'It's not my way just to sit around like some ruddy virgin waiting to lose my all. But if you want to go it alone, you can. It'll take a week or so, but we can split everything up and we can redeploy.'

James considered. He drank from his glass, letting Dick wait. Finally he said, 'I'll let you know in the morning, may I?'

Typical! That reminded him of what it had always been like: somehow James, the smooth bastard, always managing to treat Dick like a second-in-command. He nodded. All right. One last time. 'Very well,' he said, with slightly exaggerated patience. 'You let me know in the morning.'

Chapter
35

THERE IS AN AREA in Speightstown, Barbados, where the buildings, such as they are, have to climb a hill, and they do it like a group of cripples, a bit haphazard, losing balance. Small businesses hang out there, shops with roll-down grids to protect a random collection of electronic parts, or a door with some brass lettering on a wooden plate. The tarmac of the road has an occasional worn or dug-out patch through which the sand shows, and there is an atmosphere of decay and laisser-faire. It's not so much a question of having lost a grip on something as never having wholeheartedly subscribed to the notion of its value in the first place. With a certain haphazard condescension, the locals, part of the time, pay lip-service to European methods.

But not all. Samuel Hanley, although not a successful lawyer, took a great pride in the dignity and traditions of his profession. It was not just lip-service with him, but devotion. One of his great-grandparents had been British, and in a manner which could not but touch the heart of anyone with a sense of humour, he earnestly behaved with all the integrity and some of the arrogance of the nation he admired. The web spun in the days of Empire held him, a bit threadbare but touchingly honest, in its dusty thrall.

He made hardly any money. The local people were too poor to need lawyers, or if they did, they paid him almost nothing. He did a little property, odds and ends for the smarter firms in the prosperous business quarter, but his life was lonely, and economically only just viable. He would come out of his office building invariably alone, his close-cropped dark hair sleeked down, his narrow hips in their brown trousers, an incongruous yellow shirt, tall, thin, close-boned, ungraceful and solemn. Nobody disliked him. He locked his office door on to the street and went down the hill to eat at a café with an English paper, where from time to time some friendly incumbent of a richer firm would see him and pass him a few scraps of business.

On a morning when the sky was the colour of a dirty white bath-towel for the seventh day running, causing some consternation among the new tourists who didn't know what to expect, while sipping his coffee and reading *The Times* he made an unlucky discovery. He had read of recent events at Lloyd's. This section in the business news referred to some of the movements of money connected with the Merchaum Agency syndicates, and he realised, his mind making an intuitive leap which he subsequently had to go back on, to label, as it were, the stages properly, that he was a trustee for one of the funds. As soon as he imposed logic on himself, he was less sure.

The history was as follows: Felix Tubbman, M.A., telephoning some months before in the afternoon to Samuel's office – not unheard-of but unusual – had a client wanting a discreet home for a trust. This regular customer had specifically asked him to recommend a separate firm – again unusual, but not unheard-of. Sometimes someone wanted an egg in another basket. Would Samuel do it? The client had called later that day: a small dapper Barbadian who described himself as an agent, and the business was done. There was no hint of anything underhand, or Samuel would not have taken it on. He had filed the pass name for the surrender of the documents under 'D' for 'Daisy'.

What now stirred his suspicion? The dates, the correspondences between certain figures, the names; precisely that combination of coincidences and intuition that Dick Trene feared and James Ross-Gilbert thought couldn't happen.

With a slight sense of consequence, as if his hour had come –
and who's to say it hadn't – he rang Felix Tubbman as soon
as he got back to his office. Mr Tubbman advised him not to
mention it to anyone else until he had had time to look into it.

Whereas Samuel in his office, with the brown lino floor-
covering and two filing cabinets, had peace and quiet to think
in, Mr Tubbman was harassed with many clients, some of
them rich and not one of whom he wanted to lose. Samuel
would have been surprised to see him ten minutes later going
out of his office with his hat on, his light beige suit over a
white shirt spotless, throwing his cigarette on the road before
getting into his car. His driver took him out of town to where
a large house built in a modern copy of the old colonial style
overlooked the sea. He was there for half an hour, and when
he left, he felt more or less confident that he had limited the
damage.

Damage was in fact an appropriate word to use. It had to
go somewhere, and deflected from Felix Tubbman, it all
happened to Samuel Hanley. When it was dark and he was on
his way home after an hour in the bar, at the weed-snagged
back door of the old house he had shared until her death with
his mother, two young men were waiting. When they spotted
him, their limbs slackened even more with a lethal careless-
ness. There was a moon. Its light picked out dark bright
lettering against the black shirt of one, like advertising. A
bulging shoulder-muscle, a quick glance, a surreptitious
snuffing of a cigarette under the toe of a white running-shoe.
Samuel was within three paces before they stepped into his
path with the sudden purposefulness of evil intent. He said,
'What do you want, man?' but neither of them had the
decency to answer. They went silently to it, scooping
Samuel's life out of him like hard workers, one with his knife
and one with his arm like ropes to hold him down. Halfway
through, the spindly street-lamp on the corner, that had been
out for months, suddenly came on. It frightened the knifer,
who jumped back, pulling his fist out of Samuel's stomach
with the gesture of a scaled cat. Samuel fell out of the arms
that slackened and dropped him to the road. Still silently, the
boys ran down the hill, the knifer with his hand out,

fastidious, not to spoil his clothes. And in the more than silence that they left behind them, Samuel Hanley very soon died.

Chapter
36

PHILIPPA, DRIVING TO meet James at Bermuda airport, on his
return from Spain, was not quite the happy girl she had been.
She was essentially too much of a good sort to say so, but she
wasn't absolutely sure about Bermuda. Rotten Marjorie had
had a hell of a good time in London, being on the committees of
charity balls and being photographed for magazines. Rotten
Marjorie had met the Queen at the opening of the new Lloyd's
building and had a box at Ascot. After a week on her own in the
house in Bermuda, Philippa felt an aching desire to go shopping
in Harrods with her mother and take the Rolls-Royce on a spin
around Richmond Park. She would ask James, as soon as
there was a chance, if they could go home on a visit at Christmas. In her white jeans and high-heeled shoes with a fine gold
chain around the ankle, she waited restlessly until he came
through the Arrivals door, and then realised that something
was wrong. He was a man who had always, from the beginning of their acquaintance, been utterly complete. There was
no other way of expressing it. He always seemed able to
encompass every situation, to master those who came within
his range, even if the only point at issue was the purchase of a
cup of coffee.

But, now, something was wrong. She went up to him,
pretending to be as usual, and the little jangle of artificiality
seemed to escape his notice. The driver took his cases and

James put an arm round her shoulders, but he seemed to lean on her slightly. She didn't like that. She made a fuss of him in the car and prattled about small things. Instinct warned her not to mention the Englishman who had called asking for him earlier in the week and gone away, promising to come again. She would have expected him, once they reached the house, to take her into the bedroom. She had to some extent planned for it, in that the girls' Nanny had met the children from school and taken them to play with the Costellos.

But James said, as soon as he was inside the door, 'I'm sorry, Pussy. I've got a little bit of business to attend to.'

He tipped her face up to kiss her in his special way by coiling his fingers in her marvellous hair and pulling it gently. For a moment he gave the kiss his full attention. She tottered forward on her high heels, letting herself be pulled towards him, her good-natured enthusiasm reawakened. But, 'I won't be long,' he said. 'Just one or two phone-calls.'

He went into his room and closed the door, walked over to the table, and laid out the newspaper he was carrying. It was turned to a certain page, and he put it out flat. Then, reflectively, as if carrying a number of heavy thoughts, he moved over to the sideboard and poured himself a drink, and sat down. He was trying to come to terms with the news about Samuel Hanley.

Richard Trene gets a phone-call in Marbella, while James is still there, saying that an obscure Barbadian lawyer – stupid fool – has made an unlucky guess about one of the trusts, and even been naïve and officious enough to expect to do something about it. What were Mr Trene's instructions? His instructions were to get rid of him, and then between himself and James there had been a row, just as in the old days there had been rows with Ralph Scott. In the past, James had always managed to rise above those situations, but he seemed to have lost something of his touch. Out of England, out of London, Richard Trene seemed to have shed the restraints that had induced him to follow another's lead. Now he was running things his own way, and he reminded James he could either stay on board or not, exactly as he pleased.

But if Samuel Hanley had been his responsibility, what

would he, James, have done? And if he was not a signatory himself to Dick's various funds and trusts, might he not be in danger himself from such a man as Trene, who obviously had no compunction about eliminating risks to his own security? An informed ex-partner would constitute such a risk. Having thought it over in this way, he had decided to tell Dick that things could be left as they were. The remaining days had passed pleasantly. And then in the plane he had opened a copy of the *Caribbean Times* and read of the brutal murder of a small-time Barbadian lawyer.

Now in his own quiet office at least half an hour elapsed before James picked up the phone. Dick's butler answered it in Marbella, and very soon Dick himself came on the line. 'Good. Good,' he said meaninglessly, in response to a few tentative thanks. 'But I'm glad you called. No, I've got some news for you. Or perhaps Philippa has mentioned it?'

'No,' James said. 'Nothing.'

'Well, she may not have realised who it was, of course. Lord Allanport. He's out there, looking for you.

James couldn't immediately take this in. He said, 'What do you mean?'

'Draw your own conclusions. Henry Allanport is looking for you, and he called at your house while you were down here.'

'How do you know this?'

'Let's not go through all that again!' He sounded uncompromisingly, unpleasantly, curt. 'I know. Leave it at that. If you want me to help, I can sort him out.'

'Sort him out?' James had regarded Henry Allanport as a friend, once. He had been, as it were, proud of him. But he also remembered the last time they had met, and in the light of that memory he felt fear and dismay. His heart seemed to swell. Absurdly, his feelings were deeply hurt.

Dick's tetchy voice said, 'Hello. Hello, there! James? Have we been cut off?'

'No, I'm here,' he said.

'What say, then? Shall I put someone on to him, or is he fairly harmless? I can't believe he's flown all that way to thank you for the losses that I gather he's about to make on his underwriting.'

'He's harmless enough,' James lied. 'Leave him alone. And that other matter, Richard. I've changed my mind about the whole arrangement. I want out.'

'You want *what*? Well, that's fucking inconvenient! You'll just have to come down here again.'

'I will,' he said.

'Thank you very much! I'll tell Anne. I'm sure she'll be delighted.' But by the time he'd finished slamming down the phone, Dick had already seen the bright side.

James got up and went out into the main part of the house. The palatial hall, leading past a pillared open entrance into a yet more palatial drawing-room, was occupied only by a servant who was on some errand. James decided not to ask for Philippa, but to go and look for her. He ran her to earth by the swimming-pool, where she was teaching the cook's little boy to dive.

She leaned forward and clapped her hands, and said, 'Neow!' and then, 'Good boy! That was very good, Mano.'

James smiled warmly and went up and put his arm round her – but well, this time; the style of the happy master back home. He did this consciously, hiding the disquiet in his heart. 'Time for treats,' he said. 'I've ordered champagne cocktails, and Willy and Caroline are coming over for dinner.'

She was as pleased as could be. 'And I've been thinking, James,' she said. 'Can we go home for Christmas? Just a visit?'

He had stretched out on one of the reclining chairs, and she was perched beside him. Had she really not realised that he would probably be arrested if he turned up in England? And had he? 'We'll think about it, darling,' he said.

'Oh, please, James?'

With a supreme effort he tickled the end of her nose, and said prophetically, 'I dare say you'll get what you want, Pussy.' And then, when he was sure that she was happy and without arousing her suspicion, he drew from her the story of the visit of Henry Allanport.

Chapter
37

KENNETH DUNPHY HAD fallen in love with Grace. Nevertheless, he had the good sense to continue for some time to use Lloyd's as a pretext when he wanted to get in touch with her. But now he felt the time had come to change that. He was good at letting his grandeur show, to flatter and charm Grace, seeing without resentment how the magnetism of status drew her to him. She liked powerful men. But he considered power as part of himself, and therefore no insult to be valued for it. Stuffy, boring, slow-witted and vain as he had always been, his feelings for Grace had transformed him. Seeing him with her, even Mary Seymour had to admit he was a different man. Excitement made him amusing, love made him modest.

If he was still stuffy, then so also, in her way, was Grace Derby. George was given the job of persuading Mary to invite them both for dinner. Kenneth had planned this to put their relationship on a new footing. George had persuaded Mary not to introduce one single note of sabotage. The guest-list was not to be less distinguished than usual, or too small. His cousin was suitably grateful. In the drawing-room after dinner, when he walked in with the other men, he noticed, not for the first time, how Mary did in a way resemble Grace. If she had been fifteen years younger and the features they both possessed – thick, gold, wavy, short hair cut in much the same style, the intelligent sensible mind, the healthy body – had received the same magic touch of gracefulness and proportion, Mary might have been a twin. Unconsciously he had hit on the very reason, besides her defection over Ross-Gilbert, for Mary's attitude to Grace. To her, the resemblance between the two of them was even more obvious than it was to Kenneth. Grace was a living, walking, object-lesson in how the self-same elements that combined in one way produced beauty, could, combined differently, result in ugliness. They wore the same size in shoes. They probably wore the same size in gloves; and it wasn't as if Mary was a gardener or had to do the washing-up. And the face, the neck, the shoulders; blunt blond features, white teeth, large blue eyes combined with such a different result. And as if that were not enough, Mary, who was frankly heaven to make love to – witty, sensual and uninhibited – knew with the certainty of an expert that the waves of sensuality that lapped about Grace probably left her high and dry when it really counted. Too nice a woman and too intelligent to let herself drink the poisoned elixir of real jealousy, nevertheless the sheer injustice of it all made her spit, and she was hard on Grace.

'Do you know, I think he'll marry her!' George said, when everyone had gone. 'Whoever would have thought it!'

But Kenneth himself, saying goodnight to Grace, had his first real encounter with the splinter of ice in her heart. She wasn't encouraging. But then, he didn't need encouragement. He was sure she'd have him in the end. He went home quite happy.

Grace also knew that, in the end she'd have him. The evening had been a great success. She had felt herself to be at home, accepted by the distinguished company as an appropriate cadet; essentially one of them. But against all this she could not help occasionally recalling the ruthless sensuality of James's stare, and an altogether different reflex went through her. For her, that had been something else.

In the silence of the flat, she stood now taking her makeup off in front of the bathroom mirror. No single issue occupied her mind. The phone rang. She looked at her watch with a wondering frown. Her friends didn't normally call at midnight.

She hurried across into her sitting-room and picked it up.

There was a momentary pause for connection, and then James Ross-Gilbert's voice said, 'Hello. Is that Grace?'

Her skin reacted as if the receiver had given her a slight electric shock. She didn't want simply to answer. What could she do? Disconnect? But then curiosity got the better of her, and she said, 'Speaking.'

'Hello, Grace. I'm sorry to ring you at such an unsociable hour. Is it midnight in London?'

'Yes. That's all right,' she said frigidly. 'What exactly can I do for you this time?'

There was a pause.

He said, 'I don't blame you for being angry with me.'

'That's really very understanding of you, James.'

He let it go without comment, as if taking what she said at face value – a lousy trick that lent him, until she could think of a riposte, the false credit of an absolution. He said, 'I notice you are covering various items of Lloyd's news and the Merchaum Agency problems (he called them 'problems') for *The Times*. That's right, isn't it?'

'Yes.'

'Well, I want to give you some information.'

She listened in stony silence.

'It has, of course, been a great shock to me to learn of losses that have arisen on past underwriting, and the dispersal of funds needed to cover those losses. I have made an offer of restitution to the Committee of Lloyd's, but they have turned me down. Had you heard of it?'

'No.'

'Well, this is why I'm calling you. I want you to report the fact that I have made an offer.'

'How much?'

'It's a matter for negotiation,' he said.

'Very well,' she conceded. 'I'll do that. But if it's a genuine offer, I can't see why Lloyd's have turned you down. Or were there strings attached?'

'Strings? What do you mean, "strings"?'

'You know what strings are, James.'

'I don't want to be prosecuted, if that's what you mean, or

pestered by Roger Collingham's bloodhounds, or anyone else.'

'You mean Henry Allanport and Shipping I.S.?'

'How do you know about Lord Allanport?'

'He rang me at my office, wanting to know where to find you. I checked him out after he put the phone down and found out who he was. Where are you, by the way?'

'Leave him out of it,' James said. 'He's just an old friend. It's S.I.S. I won't tolerate.'

'You're not in a position to call the shots,' she said. 'And if Lord Allanport heard you call him an old friend, I think he might wish to contradict you rudely.'

'You've changed,' he said, after a pause. 'I've never liked bitchy women.'

'And you haven't changed. But I wasn't so practised at recognising a dishonest man.'

'How dare you!'

She laughed, but briefly; for effect only. She was shaking.

'Well, just pass the word around,' he snapped, 'and tell them, if they're in doubt, to mention the word ROSE to that tight-arsed nincompoop Dunphy at the Department of Trade.'

'What do you mean? James? Can you explain that?'

'Goodnight, Grace,' he said, ignoring her. 'Sweet dreams.' And the bastard put the phone down.

With rage, pure rage, she could just refrain from screaming out loud. She flung down the receiver. And Kenneth also had let her down, with his selective briefing, not mentioning something important, using her obligations as a journalist merely to get an unfair advantage. Her resentment flared in every direction that her mind turned. If she had remembered the man in Sainsbury's meat department at that instant, she would have included him. And then she stopped. The image that she had hurled from her mind with all her strength until it broke in tiny pieces reformed, like a nightmare, shard on shard, until the memory of James stood once more complete before her: his body, his dominance, his cool charm. Others had called him shifty, but she didn't know that. She sat down and wept.

Chapter
38

'I'M SORRY,' Celia said. 'I'm coming with you.'

'Of course, Lady Celia, you must do exactly as you want.'

She looked at Mal Harris, working him out. 'You said that on purpose.'

He made that characteristic half-turn of the head, his face solemn, his blue eyes not. He was packing. He said, 'For someone who has just walked into a locked bedroom and found a beautiful blond inside, I think I'm behaving very well.' He deftly folded a couple of shirts, then rolled his shoes in newspaper. 'I think that's the lot.' He glanced round the room, snapped the case shut, and said, 'Well – if you'll excuse me.'

'Of course,' she said. 'I'll see you on flight PA 937 to Miami.'

He turned sharply round from the entrance towards where she still sat, slapping his hand to the tickets in his coat-pocket.

But she was up and walking past him, and side-stepped through the door, saying, 'Sorry, I haven't got much time', and was off.

He went thoughtfully downstairs and checked out of the hotel. He thought he had just about identified the porter who had let Celia Merrin into his room and went over to tip him, holding a two-hundred-franc note. When the man was already putting out his hand, he put away the two hundred reflectively, extracted a fifty, looked him carefully in the eye, and handed him the smaller note. The porter blushed, knowing exactly what he had done wrong. Then Mr Harris picked up his suitcase and walked out of the door.

At Orly airport he cashed in his flight ticket, bought a replacement for London in the name of Collett, which tallied with one of his passports, and settled down to spend the intervening time in a local hotel. The change of plan was not essentially inconvenient. He had been in two minds about returning first to London, anyway.

As he ate lunch in a little local brasserie, the cream paint and tiles, the mahogany vanish, the men knocking back their *digestifs* at the bar, he was quite content with the way things were going. He had ten of the James Ross-Gilbert funds accounted for, including four in Gibraltar, the Swiss accounts under investigation, and business at the Bank suspended. Nevertheless Richard Trene, amateurish and heavy-handed as he was, was learning his new trade fast, and it wasn't realistic for Mal to expect to be able to collect the remaining names on the list without trouble. He knew now that he personally would be far more popular with Mr Trene when dead. Also, to locate and unravel a fund was one thing, to liquidate it another. He now needed some signatures and information he wouldn't get from Richard Trene, and which neither Scott nor Victor were knowledgeable enough to give. The time had come to get to Ross-Gilbert, and before harm came to him from another source. That other source could only, as he saw it at the time, be Henry Allanport. He overlooked, for the moment, the likely security of Ross-Gilbert if he had any difference of opinion with his former partner and he hadn't thought of the British bureaucratic interest in Ross-Gilbert's survival or otherwise. He wouldn't remember it until later.

At that moment a voice said, 'Hello, Mr Harris. You were followed.'

He looked up, and said, 'So it seems.'

Celia Merrin stood at the table, exasperatingly attracting the attention of half the people in the room. 'Not only by me,' she said. 'That creep put something in your coffee. I shouldn't drink it, if I were you.'

He kept his eyes on her face, and didn't glance at the cup. '*Diawl eriod,*' he said.

'What on earth does that mean?'

'It means that was very clever of you, Lady Celia, and I'm extremely grateful.'

'Extremely patronising, you mean!'

He grinned, silent, and then said, 'It means "the devil for ever", in Welsh.'

'Shall we go, then?'

'Yes. I think we'd better.'

He got up. The bill was already paid. Half an hour on, they checked in for the later flight to Miami.

'That's two cancellation fees you've cost Lloyd's, Lady Celia.'

'That's tough, Mr Harris.'

She smiled at him. If she wanted to go to the rescue of her cousin Henry, who had disappeared but was known to be trying to find Ross-Gilbert, and Mal Harris, with the advantage of intelligence backing and personal expertise, was doing the same thing, there was logic in her determination to attach herself to him. For the moment he was going along with it because he couldn't do much else, and he owed her something for the coffee.

'You know you suggested I should keep an eye open for the poisoner?' she said.

'Yes.'

'He's just going into the Departure lounge.'

Mal stopped to open his briefcase and took out his paper. 'Blue tie?'

'Why mention his tie, when he looks like a frog with his ears chopped off?'

'Stupid of me!' he said. 'I've got him now.'

'Do we do anything?'

'No, I don't think so.' They started forward again. 'It's a full flight. We'll go to the gate in a crowd, and there's not much harm can come to us. It's the other end we need to plan for. I think I can manage that with a phone-call.'

They went through the barrier. She looked as if she was enjoying it, and privately he gave her a caustic thought, knowing very well, better than she imagined, the few easy triumphs in the theatre of nonconformity that gave her such panache. Which was not to say she'd be no good. But only time would tell.

From the call-box in the Departure lounge, he called his office in London and gave an outline of the situation. Shipping I.S. had part-time links all over the world in a deliberate imitation of the system of Lloyd's watchers. The London office now agreed to alert their contact in Miami to be at the airport. He said Thanks, gave the flight number, put the phone down; he turned, looking across the room, putting a spare coin back in his pocket and there, large as life, was Celia standing thirty feet away, talking to the poisoner and accepting a cigarette from his packet of Gauloises.

'Mr Harris,' she said as soon as he approached, 'this is Monsieur Paul Grandi – Mr Mal Harris. Monsieur Grandi says that the stuff he put in your coffee would only have made you go to sleep. Then they would have thought you were drunk, and his friend in the uniform was going to take you off in his van.'

'Oh!' Mal said, nodding politely. 'That's it, then. Right.'

Since Grandi was holding out his hand, he shook it, thinking he recognised in the chap's bemused state something with which he sympathised. He no doubt was unaware of the name of the man whose ends he had been hired to serve, but Mal Harris guessed that it was Richard Trene.

'Another of his friends is waiting in Miami,' Celia explained.

The man was smiling like a lunatic. There was a brief silence of drawing-room calibre, until he said in the stilted manner of a rather desperate host, '*Voulez-vous prendre un boisson?*'

'*Très bien. D'accord,*' Celia said at once. 'Will that suit you, Mr Harris?'

'*Mais oui. D'accord,*' he said, turning on her an expression of indefatigable endurance, and trailed gamely along behind the two of them. In this way they kept each other company until the plane left, shaking hands at the barrier with all the attentive politeness of old friends.

'You heard what Monsieur Grandi thought of the fellow in Miami?' Celia said as they walked down the corridor. 'He sounded rather worried about him.'

'On his behalf, or on ours?'

'Ours, of course. He might try to harm us. What are we going to do about it?'

'My office is sending a man to meet us.'

'Oh, good,' she said. 'You should have mentioned it. It would have stopped poor Monsieur Grandi worrying. But never mind. That's all right, then.'

Mal tried to read her out of the corner of his eye. When eventually they were sitting in their seats, he said, 'Lady Celia, I take my hat off to you.'

She didn't ask him what he meant. She knew perfectly well it wasn't the coffee or making friends with Monsieur Grandi.

Chapter
39

CELIA WALKED FROM Customs into Miami airport alone, pushed her trolley to a side wall, and waited. Somebody with instructions to do so could easily have picked out an English girl in a slightly crumpled linen suit with no gold and no dog, in spite of the mêlée, but whoever it was, he was looking for Mal Harris. With that thought in mind, Mal had asked Celia to go ahead and wait for him. It was getting dark. The short twilight of tropic places was homing in. With it, or possibly there already, came a tinge of loneliness. In all the crowd, one middle-aged woman in a white piqué short-sleeved blouse and brilliantly set yellow hair went backwards and forwards looking at one board, looking at another, stopping porters.

'Oh my!' she gasped, fetching up at last alongside Celia. 'I hate this place. And if he doesn't arrive, I'll kill myself. What was that I said, dear? Don't take any notice of me. I'm just silly . . . I never could stand waiting. But then, if I was late, who's to say I wouldn't have missed him? You see? Either which way it's trouble. I tell myself, you be happy, Ellen. You've got it all. And then what happens? I find I wasn't listening. What time is it, dear?'

Celia looked at her watch. What on earth was keeping Mal Harris? She said, 'Two thirty.'

'Two thirty!' She paused. 'Oh, you're English. Oh, you're so cute. No, no. It's . . . Now let me see . . .' She looked in her handbag. She couldn't read her watch without her spectacles, which was why she'd asked in the first place. It was very small, surrounded with diamonds. 'Here they are.' She put the glasses on. 'It's half six, dear. You see . . .' She held it towards Celia. 'Half six.'

'Yes, so it is.'

'Are you waiting for someone, too, dear?'

'Yes.'

'From New York?'

Celia was getting desperate. She said, 'I think I'd better go and check at the barrier. Goodbye,' and rushed across the floor.

At that moment Mal emerged from Customs. She saw him carry his case through and stand a moment. A man some distance from the barrier, who subsequently turned out to be the S.I.S. watcher, put his paper under his arm and started towards him, but so also did someone else. He drove a fork-lift trolley loaded with twenty cases of bonded liquor that never should have left the Customs shed, but no one had noticed, with his uniform and all, what he was up to. Before Celia could do anything to warn him, and before the Shipping I.S. watcher had finished folding his newspaper under his arm and taken more than three steps, Mal Harris was hit from behind by the truck and thrown forward hard on to the floor. Because the driver had just had to alter his line of approach to dodge another member of the public, he didn't hit Mal fair and square, but a glancing blow that did much less damage. Hit and miss, to pun a phrase, is a factor of grievous bodily harm because it is difficult, in the heat of the moment, to be accurate. No sooner had Mal landed on the floor than the truck-driver jumped down and ran, unhindered by the astonished people near by, ignored by those further off as he reached and passed them.

Mal was lying on his face, dead still. Celia reached him just ahead of the first uniformed official, the S.I.S. watcher, and several dozen others.

'Do you know this gentleman, ma'am?' the official asked. 'Don't move him, please. We must be very careful in cases like this. Further injury could be caused. I have sent for the doctor on duty.'

Celia stood looking down on him. He stirred. 'Mr Harris,'

she said, bending over him. His face was slammed to one side, where the impact with the floor had thrown him at an angle. He wasn't going to be a pretty sight in the morning, assuming he regained consciousness. She hadn't seen whether he had saved himself at all with his hands as he fell. She had only seen the astonishing impact, a human body treated like an insect, swept aside with a deliberate blow from something far larger than itself. After all their careful planning, it had been absurdly simple.

A white-coated man, announcing that he was the doctor on duty, had arrived in response to the airport official's call. He crouched now on the ground beside Mal, opening his medical bag and saying nothing.

'Is he going to be all right?' Celia asked, 'He's not dead, is he?'

The doctor had hold of Mal's wrist, but seemed to be in a tearing hurry. 'Concussed,' he said.

'So what are you going to do?'

'This man's in a state of shock. He's got to have something to restore his blood-pressure before it collapses.' He had taken out a hypodermic, and now bent to where the inside of Mal's wrist, turned upwards where he lay on the thrown-out arm, showed the blue veins against a skin white as fish.

The Shipping I.S. watcher who had been on the look-out at the barrier, but not carefully enough, had mended his ways. Now he took a sudden step forward. For an instant his movement didn't break the concentration of the little crowd around the body on the floor. And then the toe of his shoe came forward very neat and sharp and kicked the hypodermic out of the doctor's hand as it was about to puncture the skin. A collective gasp went up from the crowd. The doctor froze, and then lashed round, indignant anger but also something else confusing the message of the outraged professional. Some hurrying passengers going past the outskirts of the disturbance halted in their stride, uncertain if they could spare the time to find out what was going on.

The official said to the watcher, 'What do you think you're doing there?' and spoke a few urgent words into his hand-phone before coming forward again.

'I'm sorry, Doctor,' the watcher said quite politely, but his tone of voice was not apologetic. 'I'd like to see your credentials before you give treatment.'

'Who are you?' the official asked. 'What right have you?'

'I'm a friend of Mr Harris here.'

'I thought this lady . . .'

The man looked across at Celia.

'He may have more than one friend. People sometimes do.'

But the doctor had stood up. He closed his bag. He seemed outwardly very calm, angry, but the finger closing the latch quivered, and it didn't shut the first time. He spoke English with a heavy mixture of Spanish and American.

'I'm sorry, Doctor,' the official cut in. 'He must be shocked. He doesn't understand.'

'Is this doctor personally known to you, sir?' the watcher asked the official.

'No. But the on-duty doctor. . . .'

'Ask to see his identification,' the stranger demanded.

The official asked, but at that moment Mal Harris sat up. It looked as if the process was as painful as coming out of a twenty-four-hour lotus position, but he did it. There were two men with a stretcher approaching. As they saw him sit up, they stopped with expressions of confusion and, without explanation, turned and hurried away.

Seeing them, Celia said, 'What on earth's happening?' She bent down. 'How are you, Mr Harris?'

'I'm going to be sick, mun.'

'Oh.' She stood up and said to the official. 'He's going to be sick. Where's your doctor?'

'Ma'am, this is really beyond me,' the man said. 'That guy just walked off.'

'I don't mean him,' she said. 'Your real doctor.'

'Excuse me, please. Excuse me, please.' A small college boy in a white coat was pushing his way through. He held an airport personnel ID card out with his photograph on it and waved it briefly in front of anyone who might be interested, including the airport official. 'Dr Sillitoe. Stand back, please. Is this the patient? What's your name please, sir? Do you have an insurance number?'

The marines had arrived.

Chapter
40

'GOD SAVE ME from amateurs,' Mal Harris said miserably. 'I much prefer a broken limb to concussion. I had a terrible night.'

He was sitting up in bed in a large bedroom in the Two Americas Hotel in Miami, and Celia Merrin said from her chair by the window, 'I'm really sorry, but I do think that's a bit unfair.'

'Oh, I don't mean you. Or Ben. It's Richard Trene. He doesn't think like a proper criminal. He's too inventive. When someone's been at it for a while, they get into a sort of rut and you know what to expect.'

In fact Ben Farrell, middle-aged businessman dealing in the supply of groceries to the smaller hotels, and the registered local watcher for Shipping I.S. who had been waiting the previous evening at the airport, still looked solemn and unhappy with himself when he arrived at the hotel half an hour later. The first thing he did was to apologise.

'How are you feeling, sir?' he asked. 'I sure am very sorry.'

'Not your fault, Ben. Sit down. Have a whisky.'

He was about to sit, when Celia came back into the room and he stood up again, his forehead divided horizontally into two deep earnest lines of polite appreciation. A genius could not have guessed that he was a man who, faced as he had been with the situation at the airport, could act fast and unconventionally. 'Well, thanks,' he said, referring to the whisky. 'That would be very nice.'

Celia poured it.

'Have you been able to make some enquiries about Ross-Gilbert's whereabouts yet?' Mal asked.

'Yes, Mal. I have.'

He drank a great gulp of the whisky, put the glass down and said absolutely nothing.

'Well, come on, boyo,' Mal said eventually. 'Is he in Florida or Spain? Or Alaska, maybe?'

'Alaska?'

'I knew that would be a mistake,' Celia said in a wicked *sotto voce* as she handed Mal his glass.

'Oh,' Ben said suddenly. 'Bermuda. Here's the full address.' He took out a piece of paper and put it on the table beside his own glass.

Mal looked astonished. 'How on earth did you manage that so fast?'

'Happy to oblige. Business contacts. Every man's got to eat, Mal, even if he is in hiding. This Mr Ross-Gilbert's very keen on caviare, and they have to import that into Bermuda. Sturgeon don't swim around there, no, sir.'

'I see.' Mal smiled. He had a very charming smile, as Celia observed to herself; even a spectacular black eye and a graze right down the side of his face couldn't spoil it. 'Well, I'm very grateful to you, Ben,' he said. 'We're in a hurry, you see. Not a minute to lose. We can go tomorrow, now.'

'Good,' Celia said. 'I've always wanted to visit Bermuda.'

Both Mal and Ben looked at her. The American said, 'Is that wise, ma'am?'

'Yes,' she said. 'It is.'

Ben cleared his throat and looked at his glass. There was a silence. Mal said, 'Are you free to accompany us, Ben?'

'Can pass you on,' he said. 'We have a watcher in Bermuda name of Geoff Mulligan. Shall I notify him for you?'

'What's he do?'

'Chandler's store in the marina.'

Mal looked at his watch. 'I don't suppose we could make it tonight?'

'Better in the morning. There's a flight at half nine. If I see you on to that, and Geoff is at the other end . . .'

'All right. You get the tickets, will you? And get Geoff to hire a car.'

'There aren't any cars in Bermuda, except for taxis and one car per resident household.'

'A taxi, then.'

'OK.' He drank down the rest of the whisky. 'I'd best be going.' He stood up, just as there was a knock at the door. 'Shall I see to that for you?' He strode over as if ready to knock it down, but in fact opened it, and only the waiter came in, wheeling lunch on a trolley.

Celia looked ravenously at it. Oysters, cold white wine, brown bread and butter, lemons, a huge pile of fruit and something under a silver dish. She stood over the waiter while he pulled out flaps and turned the whole arrangement into a table. She was wearing a blue knitted cotton sleeveless T-shirt with a small white seagull embroidered on one side of the neck. Mal watched the waiter watching her at the same time as trying to do his job. She looked up to say goodbye to Ben, and the waiter nearly broke his thumb on one of the latches. 'Are you all right?'

'Yes, ma'am. Thank you, ma'am.'

'Let me see that.'

'I'm all right.'

'You're bleeding.'

'No, I'm not, ma'am.'

'What's that red stuff coming out, then?' The boy looked desperate. She took a clean handkerchief out of her pocket, and said, 'Come here.'

You could see that when, many centuries ago, the Spanish invaders had conquered South America, someone somewhere had had a baby which was the starting-point for the arrival of Juan Duez to work as a waiter at the Two Americas Hotel. But his hidalgo features had worked their way down incongruously into this narrow, very pale-skinned, face surmounting the body of a typical American adolescent. And he looked scared.

'What's the matter?' Celia said, dabbing at his hand. He

237

had another go at saying nothing. 'Has someone asked you to do them a favour?'

'Not really, miss, not a favour. He's gonna pay me.'

'What for?'

'Letting him collect this trolley when you and your friend have finished lunch, miss.'

'Thank you very much,' she said. 'You can go now.'

He looked thunderstruck. He said irrelevantly, 'Don't you want your handkerchief?'

'You can keep it.'

'But . . . Are you going to tell the hotel manager? I'll lose my job if you do. Please, sir!'

He turned for the first time to Mal Harris, who was watching in silent amusement, not saying a word. He still said nothing. He left it up to Celia to arrange everything, and by the time she'd finished, they had acquired a bodyguard for a really very reasonable fee who would probably die for them, and would certainly see them through safely until they left the hotel.

When Juan Duez had gone, Mal at last said in tones of awe, 'How on earth did you know?'

'I didn't.' She looked bored. 'It's a trick I learned in my prep school. You stare at someone and they begin to get uneasy, and if they've got a guilty conscience they begin to think you know about it. Eight-year-old little girls can be pure poison, I can tell you! Let's eat lunch.'

'But did something make you suspicious?'

'We ought to be suspicious of everything and everybody at the moment, shouldn't we?'

'Yes, but . . .'

'Mal,' she said, 'you're not a woman, and you never will be. Now eat.'

Chapter
41

JAMES ROSS-GILBERT had come to the reluctant conclusion that if he wanted to avoid a meeting with Henry Allanport, he would have to leave Bermuda for a while. Now might be the time to return to Richard Trene in Marbella and complete the paperwork for separating their assets. He felt a real urgency about winding up that relationship. But from Marbella he could not risk returning 'home'. He found himself faced with the question of where to go, and one of his new business contacts supplied the answer. His reputation had given the major American insurance firm of Karnak Securities, based in Florida and New York and internationally known as K.S., the idea of appointing him to negotiate a deal in Iraq. They had written. He had phoned back. He now returned from a meeting, sitting in the back of his Rolls, feeling better than he had done, his ego massaged by a brief return to the stage and a very convenient timetable sketched out for the immediate future that answered his personal problems. K.S., in common with insurance companies generally, liked to maintain a good geographical spread. A share of the Iraq National Insurance treaty was one of several targets on their agenda, but an important one. They aimed at no more than one or two lines and a swap deal, but it involved sending a knowledgeable senior negotiator to Baghdad, someone persuasive, prestigious and experienced.

Certainly James Ross-Gilbert met two of these requirements. K.S. thought he met them all, and they were as pleased with themselves for having foisted the job on to him as he was pleased to get it. He would have all the usual arrangements: the first-class travel, the suites of rooms in five-star hotels, and he was pleased. It would be all right, Richard Trene, Henry Allanport and Baghdad could all fit together and he would come out on top, where he belonged. The question now was, would Philippa come with him?

He stepped out of the car, noticing how much colder it had become. He could hear the girls calling from somewhere in the garden, and as he walked up the broad stone steps, the door opened from within as the butler spotted his arrival. He said that he would like drinks to be served on the back terrace, and went through the house just loosening his tie, looking out for Philippa.

The partly-glassed terrace had been very beautifully designed and, ironically, like a sad tune cropping up in inappropriate places, was not altogether unlike Delia Allanport's conservatory. It faced west, and a beautiful sunset now promised to blossom over the sea where the water lay distant but visible in a fold of land.

He stood waiting for Philippa and waiting for someone to bring the drinks, reviewing yet again his present position. His mind was filled with calculations, but he was satisfied. Everything was doing very well. He withheld his attention, with his accustomed inflexible skill, from vantage-points that spoiled the view.

When Philippa appeared, she approached James coming from the herb borders, where she had been collecting lavender. She carried a little basket which, in fact, had been suggested to her by an English country magazine, and the sun behind her caught in her hair in a truly beautiful haze of burning bronze. James smiled with all the charm of the handsome mature lover – pure Mills and Boon – while the butler, just arriving, set out the drinks on a silver tray. James would have ordered champagne if he'd thought of it.

'Would you prefer champagne, Pussy?' he said, as she reached him, putting his arm lovingly over her shoulder. She always did prefer champagne. It seemed right, somehow. The butler went to fetch it. 'I decided to accept the job,' he said.

She hadn't much idea what reaction was expected from her. As far as she was concerned, as long as James didn't actually need to work, it was all right for him to do it. 'We don't need the money, do we, darling?'

'No, no,' he reassured her. 'It's just that – it's rather flattering to be asked, you know.'

'Will it mean your going in to work every day?'

'No, Pussy. Those days are over. This is more like being sent as a sort of insurance ambassador to negotiate something.'

'You mean, abroad?'

'Yes.'

'England?' She was absolutely delighted. Her eyes danced, and she straightened her back as she sat within his embrace in a way that very nearly made him spill his drink.

'No.'

It took her just a second or two to get over her disappointment. 'Oh,' she said. It was all too obvious.

'I don't think you'll guess it. Shall I tell you?'

'Yes,' she said, trying to sound bright again; and young and enthusiastic.

'Baghdad.'

'Baghdad!' Her mouth fell open. She said it again. 'Baghdad!'

'You don't seem to have a very good impression of Baghdad,' he said drily.

'Oh no. I suppose it's – very interesting.' She paused. 'But it's dangerous, isn't it? And the Arabs pester you and bang on about women being so inferior the whole time. Angela told me. Angela Makepeace, you know. She lived in Wimbledon until her husband Bob got sent to Bahrain, and she had to go too.'

'I don't think it's quite the same thing,' he said. 'Apart from anything else, Bahrain must be thousands of miles from Baghdad. And I'm not suggesting going to live there. It's just two or three weeks.'

She nodded. 'And when do you have to go?'

This was the tricky bit. Because of the urgency of disappearing before Henry Allanport should have the chance to come back, James had manoeuvred the directors of K.S. into thinking that immediate action would be particularly advantageous to themselves. Because, he said, of the time of year and also various Lloyd's tenders which he, James, had claimed to know were in the pipeline, negotiations couldn't be started too soon. They had ended up nearly doubling his fee to persuade him to do what he had induced them to believe would be a good idea – namely, to get to Baghdad within the week. It was already Wednesday. He had decided to stop off in Spain, so he could leave on Thursday evening.

When he unfolded this to Philippa, she saw her way out. She burst into tears. She was truly very reluctant to be left behind so soon on her own again when James had only just come back from Marbella. but wild horses couldn't get her to go to Baghdad. Not now. Just like that. And she couldn't leave the girls. Everything was too new. It wasn't home yet, and she couldn't possibly leave the girls. Take the girls to Baghdad? How could James possibly be so inconsiderate as to suggest that? It was term-time. And Baghdad wasn't safe. What did he expect them to do all day while he was working? Her eyes flashed. Perhaps it was going to be a real row.

The sun had gone down without their even noticing it. The champagne in its blasted bucket dripped water everywhere. Sometime earlier, the butler had noiselessly returned and switched on the groups of small candle-lights that burned like fireflies under the glassed area, and that just about saved the situation. When Philippa whirled round, about to snap down her glass and storm into the house, the sight of it all looking so pretty softened her heart. She had a soft heart anyway; soft and practical. She had married James for what he offered in the field of money, sex and elegance, in that order, and here it was, after all. As she might have said, Let's be fair. She started to cry again.

James could resist women's tears perfectly well, in certain circumstances and certain women. But for the moment Philippa was a delicate investment for him, and one he needed to look after. He took her in his arms and tucked her face against his neck. He felt solid as a rock. He smelled nice. He had shaved before driving in to his meeting. He said, 'There, there. There's no need for you to come, Pussy. If you won't be too lonely here without me, I'll only be gone a week or two.'

'Don't go!'

He sighed. She still hadn't got the point. He *had* to go. It was unpleasant even to be forced to put it like that to himself, and he was simply not going to say it out loud. He had to leave Bermuda for a while, and he could not visit England.

She pulled away enough to look up into his face, and said, 'Please James? I don't want to be left alone again.'

She saw the look in his eye that meant 'no go', and her temper flared again. But she weighed things up. Her mother had taught her to count to ten, and although she now dispensed with the arithmetic, the principle was in her blood. James felt her body stand off for time to think, the little alien frequencies making a barrier between them. He liked to have in his arms the docile, slightly rapacious, mistress of his London days. With the thought, a little fragment of the virus of longing got past his guard. But she had come to her conclusion. She dropped her head back on his shoulder. He wove his rather thick fingers with thoughtful habit into the wavy undergrowth of her hair.

'All right, darling,' she said. 'No more fuss from Pippa. It's all right.'

But it wasn't.

Chapter 42

THREE DAYS LATER at around midday the butler announced that two people had called to see Mrs Ross-Gilbert, and was she 'at home'? Philippa at the time was in the swimming-pool, but she was thrilled to have visitors. She already called the butler 'George', when James had said to use his surname. In time she would have got round to eating ginger-nuts with him in his pantry and possibly even taking him to bed.

Now, she said, 'Please get them to wait, George. I won't be long.'

She didn't have time to dry her hair properly or to put on anything smart. It seemed rude to keep someone called Lady Celia Merrin waiting too long; and Mr Harris. Consequently, when she walked hurriedly into the great marble stone and silk drawing-room, where the servants had lit a small fragrant wood fire to show that the seasons had changed, she looked natural and rather elegant. She had only had time to put on her little high mules, and the clacking of their tiny heels reminded Celia for a long time afterwards of a moment, an instant between one event and another, that she was never again able to pin down.

'Oh, hello. I hope George . . . I mean, George has given you a drink. How do you do, Lady Celia, Mr Harris?'

She locked her fingers together after shaking hands, standing and smiling.

Celia was taken quite aback. She said, 'I do apologise for just barging in on you, but . . .'

'Never mind, never mind,' Philippa interrupted. 'Sit down. It's so nice to see someone from home.' Just saying it made her realise how thoroughly homesick she was, and she marked a little trace of anger go past the background of her own mind like a spark across paper.

Celia smiled. 'Do you like it here? It must be lovely.'

'Oh, of course, it's wonderful.' She paused. 'My husband's retired, you know. But I'd like to go home for a visit soon. Are you staying in Bermuda on holiday? Or –' she had a new idea – 'do you live here?' The hope in her voice was so revealing that Celia felt as if she was administering a punishment when she said No. And Philippa's lips did straighten in a little gesture that would have become habitual if she had had to learn, permanently, how to restrain disappointments. 'Oh, well,' she said, she said, smiling brightly. 'Did you come to see my husband? I'm afraid James is away.'

'Oh, what a pity.'

'You're the second person who's called to see him. It's extraordinary, really.' She laughed. 'I thought it was going to be lonely at one stage, but maybe I hadn't given it a chance. At this rate it may perk up.'

Mal Harris, although in the circumstances, being neither female nor aristocratic, was perhaps invisible, but he was not blind and deaf. So that when a moment later Philippa said, looking at her watch, 'My goodness, it's almost lunch-time. Why don't you both stay and have some lunch?' he spoke, before Celia could refuse:

'That would be lovely. Really kind of you, Mrs Ross-Gilbert.'

Philippa looked startled, as if she hadn't expected him ever to speak at all. And then he had a Welsh accent. But Lady Celia was smiling, so it must be all right. 'That's wonderful!' she said. 'Wonderful. Will you tell cook, please, George. We'll have it on the terrace.'

She took them to see her rose-garden and explained the plan, and then they returned to where the table had been laid out, and she seemed to consider that there was no need at all for an explanation of why these total strangers had turned up on her doorstep.

Eventually Celia said, 'Did you say someone else had called this week, asking for your husband? He must be very much in demand, down here.'

'Oh, this wasn't an American businessman. Nothing to do with those local insurance companies.'

Cook had provided lobster and some very good mayonnaise and salad, and it took up a person's attention.

'But I'm afraid I wasn't very friendly. James had just gone, you see, and . . . Well, to tell you the truth, I was a bit annoyed with him for going.' She laughed and pulled a face, 'Naughty of me really. Are you married, Lady Celia?'

'No, I'm not.'

'Well, I don't suppose you need to be,' she said, smiling brilliantly. 'James and I have been married now for three months, almost exactly. That's all. That's why I was annoyed, I'm afraid. At being left. So I was quite rude and didn't offer him a drink or anything – the man who called yesterday, I mean. He was very polite. It's the second time he's called, too. Alan something.'

No one dared to interrupt her in case she stopped. Celia concentrated rudely on her lobster.

'He wanted to know where James had gone, so I told him . . .'

'And where has he gone?' Celia asked. 'I mean, Mr Ross-Gilbert. Mr Harris and I were hoping to interest him in an insurance network to do with holiday sporting activities.' She was very proud of this invention afterwards, considering it had been made on the spur of the moment, and it was entirely acceptable to Philippa, who might have believed a Lady Celia if she had said that Christmas Day fell in mid-June.

'I don't know if I should tell you,' Philippa said. 'Please don't get me wrong. I don't mean to be rude. But . . .' She sighed and made a face. 'I forgot, you see, that James told me not to say. I went and forgot when that Mr Whatever-his-name-was, the Englishman, called. After all, he'd been here before, hadn't he? And it's not as if it makes any difference. I mean, he's hardly going to go to Baghdad to talk to him, is he? Oh!' She clapped her hand over her mouth. 'There you are! I've said it. I'd be no good as a spy, would I?' And she laughed her head off. 'Don't say I told you, will you?' she added. 'If you see him when he comes back?'

'No, of course not,' Celia said. She let George refill her glass. 'That lobster was fantastic. It was wonderful of you to produce it so suddenly.'

'Isn't it good!' She was immensely pleased. 'Would you like another? It only takes ten minutes to do. The fishermen bring them in, and we keep them in a tank. Can you imagine! Have another?'

'I couldn't. I've eaten such a lot.'

'Tell me,' Philippa said. 'Where do you live in England? I'd love to hear about your house and your family. I've always wondered what it would be like – you know.'

They stayed most of the afternoon, talking about riding, and charity balls and Ascot, until at last Philippa reluctantly let them go when the light was fading and the girls were ready for their supper.

Chapter
43

FOLLOWING ON THE dreadful night when James Ross-Gilbert had rung her up, Grace Derby felt two urgent and conflicting priorities about what to do next. Having slept only very briefly from six until seven a.m., she sat at her kitchen table, worn out, over her toast and coffee. Her face looked bruised with tears and lack of sleep. And there was no one she could turn to. For reasons explained before, there was no one who would put their arms round Grace Derby and console her.

Except for Kenneth. Even if she explained why she had been so upset – which would be tactless and not really necessary – he would still do it. And for this reason she longed to be able to go to him, and it had caused her to make her mind up. She would marry him, and that as soon as he liked.

But, in direct conflict with that train of thought, she wanted her revenge: or at least, she remembered James's vile remark, 'mention the word ROSE to that tight-arsed nincompoop at the Ministry of Trade, Dunphy', and was at least determined to demand an explanation for exactly why Kenneth had withheld essential information about the Merchaum enquiry at the same time as professing to want to reveal all. Since she knew perfectly well what his reason was – that the whole subject had always been merely an excuse to get to know herself – her determination to ask the question might seem disingenuous. But she was not going to allow her identity as a career journalist to be compromised by that sort of treatment. And she wanted to know. She wanted, as James had so viciously recommended, to mention the word ROSE to Kenneth.

After she had looked at herself in the glass, she rang the newspaper and the Covent Garden office and said she wouldn't be in today. Then she went back to bed and slept for three hours. When she woke, she ran a deep bath and telephoned Kenneth's office. He was available. She asked him if he could possibly manage to see her in the afternoon – four or four thirty. She had some data to check on the Lloyd's theme, and, by the way, thank you for last night. It was such a good evening. She was about to ring Mary.

Kenneth was delighted.

By the time Grace had bathed, eaten a sandwich for lunch and made up very carefully, she looked as beautiful as ever, but tinged with a faint vulnerable shadow that would prove Kenneth's final and complete undoing. He waited for her in his office, rushing to get through his work but distracted, and inaccessible to new ideas on items he hoped to process before she arrived. When his private secretary eventually rang to say Miss Derby had come, he put aside what he hadn't finished and stood up as she came through the door, instantly aware of a change in her. When they were alone, he stood very close to her with his hand on her arm, wanting to kiss her.

She said, 'I've called on business, Kenneth,' but with a slight smile and an adorable glance that softened the blow of her taking a step away and looking for a chair.

He drew one up for her and sat down himself at his desk. 'Has Roger Collingham been in touch with you about Barbados?'

'No,' she said. 'The phone was ringing as I left. Is it something I should know?'

'A lawyer has been killed in Barbados, and apparently there is some evidence that it was on the orders of Ross-Gilbert and Richard Trene.'

She was speechless.

'Surprising, isn't it? But apparently, according to that weird little fellow Harris in Shipping Investigation Securities, the lawyer had discovered the real source of a trust fund he held, and was going to contact the authorities.'

She finally managed to say, 'I can't believe it.'

A person's reaction to news of a murder varies tremendously, according to its context. Where some group has established murder as a local norm, such as perhaps in Ireland, the first frisson of shock at the announcement of a killing can be substantially and quickly damped down when that turns out to be the place in which it happened. Conversely, this news of Kenneth's hit Grace a terrible blow. She felt something like despair. Thinking that all feeling for James had been burnt out of her the previous night, this frightful new dimension found some hidden remnant and crucified it. Kenneth momentarily was not looking at her.

'Well, I'm afraid there's progress in crime, as well as in everything else,' he said. 'I must say, I found it hard myself to imagine James Ross-Gilbert lurking in the dark with a knife in his hand.' Not an image that, months ago, Celia had found any difficulty in raising, as she had said at the time to Henry. 'Nevertheless,' Kenneth continued, 'I don't mean to be flippant. He'll have ordered someone else to do it, of course. But it comes to the same thing.'

Poor Grace struggled, unobserved, to recover. Both her feelings for James and the fact that she had ever had them equally tormented her, and she longed for the certainties of Kenneth's world with all the confidence with which it has always been said that lightning never strikes twice in the same place. She eventually pulled herself together, and said, 'Actually, Kenneth, I came about another matter. I received a phone-call – it isn't important who from – advising me to ask you a question, and I am going to do so. Can you tell me about ROSE?'

He was dumbfounded. In the first place he had half-thought she knew a little about it – Mary Seymour, and so on – and had tacitly avoided finding out more. And secondly, a phone-call implied a leak, and such a leak the direst consequences imaginable. Almost for the first time he thought of his own career from a working rather than from a purely decorative point of view when in her company. He picked up his reading-glasses and put them carefully on the left instead of the right side of his blotter, and then refolded them.

'I don't know,' he said, 'if I can disclose details of that involvement to you, Grace.'

'Does it have any bearing on the Merchaum enquiries and the prosecution or otherwise of Ross-Gilbert?'

The miserable man couldn't lie to her. He said, 'Yes. I suppose I must admit it does.'

'Then what is the point of my writing articles on the subject and setting myself up as the expert, at least in journalistic terms, if all the time you're holding out on me over a piece of information as important as that?'

He shifted desperately. 'I don't think it's that bad. A private matter.' He said that in an emphatic good-hearted sort of way, looking up at her at the same time to see if she responded.

'I can't accept that, Kenneth,' she said. 'You've told me yourself often enough that Lloyd's has transcended its own original private club status. It's apparently become a national asset too valuable to be allowed absolute autonomy.'

'True.'

'And now here is some issue that none of us knows anything about, which closely affects Lloyd's even to the extent of being a deciding factor in the prosecution of an underwriter known to have acted criminally, and you say it's private!'

'Well, I don't quite say it's private.'

'In that case, tell me about ROSE.'

'Off the record?' he bargained desperately.

'No.'

'Grace – I can't!'

She looked at him stubbornly. He got up and walked to the window, fidgeting with his spectacles, calculating. But, however he looked at it, it simply could not be told. Grace herself felt her heart sit in her ribs like a stone. She hadn't expected a rebuff. She'd expected denials, apologies and then coming clean; and a story she might have kept out of the paper at her own discretion. She stood up, and said, 'Well, in that case, I suppose there's no more to be said.' It was a statement that covered, to their mutual dismay, other ground.

He couldn't bear it. He said, 'Please, Grace.' He strode over to her, 'Please believe me. Let me think about it. Let me think it over.'

'You mean you may be able to tell me and you may not.'

He stood there nonplussed, his common sense absolutely numbed at the thought of losing her. 'You must realise I love you, Grace.' It was the last way he had wanted this to happen, but he couldn't help himself. 'I want to marry you, more than I've ever wanted anything. But you surely wouldn't want me to destroy my career, just to prove it?'

His last sentence was an unfortunate lapse into male chauvinism at the wrong moment. She was objecting to his failure to be candid about ROSE as it affected herself as a journalist. There was no question of making the claim as a girlfriend.

She said stonily, 'This conversation isn't about our personal problems, Kenneth.'

'We haven't got any personal problems,' he said desperately.

'We have now.'

'You mean you'll hold this against me?'

'Yes.'

He looked directly at her, but he couldn't be angry with her. He saw, despite her rigid expression, the vulnerable shadow of the tears she'd washed away. Perhaps he even thought they had been for him. He said gravely, 'It's not myself I'm protecting, you know.'

'Oh, so it is a question of protection?'

'In a manner of speaking,' he said reluctantly, caught.

'Wasn't it Mary Seymour who invented the phrase "Gentlemen's Mafia" to describe this sort of thing?' She smiled, bitterly. 'Over three hundred private backers of the most famous insurance market in the world facing possible financial ruin, one person has committed suicide, another murdered. Who is this friend of yours, Kenneth, who is so important that to protect him the penetrators of these crimes are not to be prosecuted?'

'It's not an individual,' Kenneth said. 'It's the government.' But even to his ears, put in that way, it did sound a wrong bargain. There was a silence. He was thinking. He turned his back to her for a moment to clear his mind. All they needed was for James Ross-Gilbert to be dead. He had threatened that if he was prosecuted he would disclose from the dock details, ROSE among them, that would gravely harm the government and the financial institutions. It was that that had stayed the hand of his own Ministry and the DPP in the end. They had reached an understanding with Shipping I.S. and Lloyd's, but Ross-Gilbert himself had stated his terms, and in all fairness one could see he wouldn't change. Not this side of the grave. In which case, what about the other side?

Kenneth's mind was made up, but the conscious layers of his mind absorbed the facts laboriously and with a desperate effort. Resolution and distress in equal measure moved him. He mentally called on that many-faceted image of murder, such different sides of which had appeared to himself and Grace earlier on in their conversation, when discussing the fate of poor Samuel Hanley. He needed that facet now, which reflected the impersonal decisions of state; and to get the whole thing at exactly the right angle so that there would not be a disturbing flash of reflection from a yacht in the South of France, or a beautiful girl turning away from him, but only another official decision taken. Presumably it could be done, if he could persuade Hugh, and Hugh could persuade the Foreign Office to persuade . . . He turned slowly.

'Grace, I can't tell you – in your capacity as a journalist, that is – about ROSE. I can say this much: it has to do with an error of judgment made by a very senior politician, but a small error, which is being cleverly used as a threat against government. Now, it is perfectly right that we should try to stop that.' He thought of pausing, and saying, 'Don't you agree?', but decided against it. 'But I agree that to refrain from prosecution on that account is no longer a reasonable option.' He paused, 'If I tell you that we will prosecute – that I will myself personally put in train the procedures to begin this very day – will you withdraw your demand to know the exact details of why that prosecution was delayed?'

'You mean ROSE?'

'Yes.'

'And you will start immediate action through your own Department and the DPP?'

'Yes.'

She hesitated, for form's sake. She said, 'Very well.' She sounded extremely tired. It had been one shock after another. Without entirely understanding that, his heart was wrung by her distress. But he held back for renewing his offers on the personal level. His decision weighed too heavily on him. It was a course of action that would impose a moratorium on developments in his personal life until it was done. Or perhaps 'moratorium' was an unfortunate word to use. He sighed even as he stood in front of her and kissed her cheek. She turned, and left his office.

He nearly called her back. He nearly called 'Grace', and she would have turned, or half-turned, her face perhaps still grave, her hair swinging over so that she reached up and tucked it to the side. And he would have said, 'I made the wrong decision just now. Come back, I'll tell you about ROSE, and I won't do the other thing.' 'What other thing?' 'Instigate the prosecution of a man publicly, but secretly have him murdered before he can be brought to court – where he would do so much public damage to important people. You see, ROSE was an excellent idea for an international business security scheme . . .' But he was talking in his mind to shadows. Grace had gone. The door had closed behind her. He had to do the other thing.

He lifted his phone and told his secretary that he wished to speak to the following people: Hugh, Morgan Trench at the DPP, and James Blacker at the Foreign Office. He spent some time explaining what sort of a meeting he needed with Hugh and James Blacker. He wanted this to be arranged as quickly as possible. He wanted the die to be cast.

Chapter 44

PHILIPPA WAS ABSOLUTELY right not to want to go to Baghdad. On his first morning, James was escorted out of the luxurious standard European insulation of the Mediteran Hotel by the representative of K.S. East, who had come to fetch him. There, outside, he stopped short. The vast heavily concreted boulevards which dissect modern Baghdad teemed with military vehicles, but in another way were curiously uncrowded. It was as if the unlovely parodies of modern architecture which made up the city centre somehow concealed the population, or at least at first sight. The door of the limousine was being held open for him, and James stepped in. And with that gesture and the starting up of the engine and the smooth glide out into the mainstream, prosperous normality, the continuation of his role as a wealthy and successful man, once more took over his attention. But it wouldn't quite have done the same for Philippa.

The job that James had come to do was genuinely interesting. Insurance being a nationalised industry in Iraq, these negotiations involved contact with government, and there was no need for James to concern himself with the limitations of the city itself. His attention was adequately taken up from the word go by the task in hand. If he could impress the men concerned with a wish to please himself, he would do well. This was always James's way in negotiations. But as the K.S.

representative who travelled with him pointed out, that wouldn't be easy.

The Ministry of Finances was housed in a fourteen-storey block in the centre of Baghdad. As a negotiator for K.S., bidding for a share of business, James's reception was nothing like that of his Lloyd's days. He had already encountered the fact that the individual man participates in the prestige of the firm he works for, and that none of that gilt actually sticks to his own skin and travels with him. But in this case he traded it off in his own mind, as he stood unattended in the lofty unlovely reception area, against the embattled conditions of the country itself and the inevitable tone of slight belligerence that must tinge their every foreign encounter. All this modern rebuilding smacked more of cannibalism than regeneration, and he allowed to creep into the impassive expression of his face a hardness that served him in good stead.

When eventually a junior colleague of the Deputy Minister dealing with insurance came to collect him, he followed him into the lift with stern courtesy. Arriving at the upper floor, he began the negotiations unchanged. All the unyielding tactics of his Iraqi opposite numbers glanced off him like air-gun pellets off armour plating. By the end of the first week, when he smiled for the first time at the Deputy Minister, the man instinctively felt a surge of optimism as if he personally had had a great success.

The evenings, too, were taken care of. James was not left to his own devices, and the modern casings of Baghdad had not always altered the contents. The men still went to *cantinas* and got as near as possible in this life to the Koran's somewhat surprising version of the virtuous man's reward: 'vineyards and high-bosomed maidens for companions and . . . an overflowing cup.' But in ten days, for James himself, the potential of both were exhausted. Above all, the business was successfully done, and James was ready to go back to Philippa.

On this evening he rang her as always from his suite in the Mediteran Hotel. He felt well and restored, and his frequent contacts with 'home' had all been good. Philippa knew how to give the impression that she had settled down, and her warm-

hearted nature prompted her to be romantic on the telephone. Somehow behind the vibrations of ordinary sound
James could swear he picked up the relaxed hum of
Bermudan life, and he congratulated himself with renewed
confidence on the future prospect it gave him.

It was at this point that Philippa told him she had given his
address in Baghdad to Henry Allanport. 'Are you there,
darling?' Her small but carrying voice could have been heard
by someone standing five feet away, so still had James
suddenly become. 'Are you there?'

'Hello,' he said. 'I think perhaps we were cut off for a
moment.'

'Oh, good,' she responded meaninglessly.

'When was this?'

'When was what, darling? Oh! I do hope you're not cross
with me. Are you, James? He was awfully nice, and it seemed
so rude – you know – pretending not to know where you
were, and all that.'

'Don't worry, Pussy,' he said, with no detectable effort. 'No
problem. But tell me, what day was this? Did he say, for
example, that he'd still be around when I got back?'

'Oh, he didn't mention that.'

'I see.' He waited, hoping she would remember, this time,
to answer his question. To ask it again would be to sound
urgent and might possibly arouse her suspicions.

But there was some kind of a disturbance at the other end
of the phone, and after a few moments of wondering if it was
a technical problem or just Philippa, she came back on the
line, giggling and full of apologies and some involved history
to do with the girls and a new kitten. In normal circumstances
James's patience would have given way ten minutes before.
Marjorie, if she had been party to this conversation, would
have disbelieved her own ears. But the one talent that James
really possessed was a strong instinctive connection with the
human element in his own surroundings. He could use that in
any way he chose at any time, and he used it now for
patience: to sit out the gap between Philippa's capacity for
concentration and what he needed to know.

'I think it was the day before yesterday,' she said eventually, 'because . . .' and then stopped herself. She decided not to mention Lady Celia's visit just now. Later. 'No,' she corrected herself, 'it was – that's right – Tuesday.'

With the time difference, a day and a half.

'When will you be home, darling?'

'I might try to get a flight tomorrow or the next day. But, failing that, I'll be on the one I booked. I'll let you know if there's a change.'

'Oh.' There was a pause. 'I miss you, darling,' she said. She meant it. Even independently of James and her feelings for him, those words would always contain for Philippa a poignancy of their own. If she said them out loud to the cat, they would bring real tears to her eyes.

'I miss you too, darling,' he said. 'What would you like to do when I get back?'

For a moment she had his full attention once more. Which was just as well, because he would never hear her voice again.

When he was eventually able to put down the phone, James stood up and walked rapidly over to the window. The movement was nothing to do with wanting to see out, but the surplus energy of his mind attempting to spring free from the trap suddenly set in his path. To avoid Henry Allanport, he could either fly back to Bermuda immediately or he could move to another hotel for a day or two: somewhere inconspicuous where no one would find him. He decided on the first option and rang down to the desk. But every flight for the next two days was either booked or via London. He would have flown to Marbella and put the question, in spite of misgivings, before Dick Trene. But he had called in at Marbella on the way out, and Dick was no longer a friend. And when he remonstrated with himself and told himself that he could handle Henry Allanport and talk him round, he remembered that moment in London. At times in his career he had crossed swords with people and felt anxious about the next meeting, but basically he had always known that he would win. Now he had only to remember his last encounter with Henry Allanport to be certain that he could not risk another.

By his watch it was just approaching half-past eleven. It

was a risk, but he began packing. He rang the desk. He ordered a morning call for six a.m., and a car. He rang the home number of the K.S. rep and told him that as there were no more meetings he would be out of touch for the following two days, and would ring before leaving the country. And he rang Kulwar Chali.

Kulwar Chali, of strange parentage that made an Englishman mentally spell his name with an R and an E, had hooked himself on to the fringes of Ross-Gilbert's attention during the negotiations and entertainments of the last seven days. He was a small, insinuating, man who worked as an official 'fixer' for important guests, always in cheap clothes and always on the scrounge. James searched in the pockets of yesterday's suit for the card he knew he had put there. When he dialled the number, it sounded as if he had got through to an electricity terminal. Chali, in his breezeblock house, with the whining fridge and untamed electric-light bulbs whitening the faces of his friends and family, took the phone off its shrieking cradle only after a full minute of procrastination. But he was delighted with Ross-Gilbert's commission, which allowed him at least three different rake-offs: his own time, a percentage from the hotel, and money for discretion.

The following morning, he rose very early and made the journey into the centre of town by taxi along the concrete-lined highways with the frequent hoardings pasted with massive portraits of the head of state. At the Mediteran, he waited until Mr Ross-Gilbert came down and the luggage was loaded into his car. Then he got into the front passenger seat and gave discreet directions to the driver. In this way James Ross-Gilbert disappeared from the Mediteran and no one knew the obscure unlisted one-time hotel that, tottering on the brink of collapse in the last remaining old section of the city, later that morning took him in.

On the same day, Mal Harris and Celia Merrin arrived in Baghdad, but by the time they reached the Mediteran, Ross-Gilbert had already gone.

Chapter
45

'Ross-Gilbert has disappeared.'

'How do you mean? You're speaking from Baghdad, aren't you?'

'Yes,' Mal Harris said. 'I'm speaking from the Hotel Mediteran in Baghdad, and you're in London answering the phone in my office, and it's nice weather, but Ross-Gilbert has disappeared. He left his hotel in Baghdad at six a.m. this morning, just ten hours before our plane arrived, giving no forwarding details to his contacts in K.S. or here, and simply disappeared. He hasn't flown anywhere – his name's not on any flight-list, except the one we know about in two days' time to Miami. Give me the name of some contacts in Baghdad, if you can, and I'll see if I can find him before he gets killed.'

After a pause, the reply came back: 'You know that Lord Allanport was reported on flight twenty-thirty?'

Mal Harris was about to reply, but there was some confusion at the other end, and his contact in London said, 'Hold on. Hold on.'

At that moment Celia Merrin came through the connecting door from her room. The suite they had taken in the three-quarters empty Mediteran was on the tenth floor, high above the Alphaville of concrete and tarmac that had almost completely replaced the former city of Baghdad.

Mal Harris had once walked in the ruins of Ur of the Chaldees near Basra, where cuneiform paving-stones dating from 2000 B.C. were used as pathways for the labourers. 'Slowly, slowly', the site foreman had said in English, his voice full of pride. 'We are taking away the old stones and replacing them with new ones.' They were stamping the new stones with the name of Abdul Kadr Qassim; one of the troubles about liking everything new being the difficulty of keeping up.

The line cleared again, at last, and the voice in London said, 'Lord Allanport is armed.'

'I thought he might be.'

'Well, that's confirmed. Do you want it passed on?'

Mal hesitated. Celia was just standing there with her hands in her pockets. 'No,' he said. 'Is that all?'

''Fraid not. Just a minute.'

Another wait.

'Mal,' Celia said, 'can't you put that damn thing down?'

'Be with you in a minute, Cariad,' he said. 'How about a glass of beer? That little fridge will be stuffed with them.'

The voice on the phone came back. 'The Queen's Messenger on the weekly flight out to Baghdad has been replaced by Geoffrey Buckland.'

'What? I wasn't with you then. Are you there, London? Hello. Hello!' The bloody thing went dead.

'What is it?' Celia said. 'You look as if you've had bad news.' Her manner sharpened suddenly, and she said, 'Is it Henry?'

'No. That's not it.'

She handed him a beer. 'Oh, thanks. I can do with this.' He took a great gulp. 'No. Not Henry. He's here, mind, but we already know that. Something else came up just before I got cut off. That'll be them again.' He picked up the phone as it rang. 'Mal Harris.'

'Hello!' This line doesn't seem to be working too well.'

'*Quod erat demonstrandum.*'

'What? Oh, sorry. Yes. Geoffrey Buckland, I'm afraid.'

'Well, who is he on to?'

'We have reason to think James Ross-Gilbert. A present from the DTI.'

'How do you know this?'

'Two and two.'

'If all you're doing is putting two and two together, don't scare the pants off me, Mun, with your speculations. This country's been at war, remember. There have been all sorts of interests tangled up with it, other reasons for sending official hit-men like Geoffrey Buckland. Are you sure this isn't one of them?'

'Pretty sure. There was a very high-level very private meeting immediately after the warrants on Ross-Gilbert and Trene were issued on Tuesday last. Our information is that government sources want Ross-Gilbert personally silenced before he can answer publicly to the prosecutions they themselves have been forced to issue.'

'Well, thank you for the warning,' Mal said. 'Will you ring me back with those contacts?'

'I've got them for you now.'

Mal wrote down the numbers, said goodbye, and put down the phone.

'What was all that about?' Celia said.

'They were telling me that the usual Queen's Messenger on the weekly flight out to Baghdad has been replaced by someone called Geoffrey Buckland.'

'What for?'

'The Queen's Messenger's luggage isn't searched. He carries documents, ostensibly to the embassy.'

'And?'

'This man, Geoffrey Buckland, may be mistaken for a Queen's Messenger.'

'Why would that happen?'

'Well . . . Odds and ends to do with his paperwork and appearance.'

'Mal, please . . . What is he? A hit-man or something, with a gun in his briefcase?'

'That's right,' he said. 'And once he finds Ross-Gilbert, if that's whom he's after, it will be the end of him. You wouldn't believe it, would you? I'm here to get Ross-Gilbert's signature and a modicum of information from him which will recover many millions for those poor Names who have been cheated over the years. And representatives of the two groups most likely to benefit – a government minister and your cousin – are doing everything they can to get there first and kill him.'

Celia put her glass on the table and sat down sideways on the overstuffed pale blue armchair, her long legs flung over one arm, her back colliding with the other. 'What can we do? Henry's not at the Baghdad Hotel, and apart from here, it's the only decent place to stay in. He likes comfort. The only other explanation I can think of is he must know someone in the embassy; but the duty officer said he had no news. I rang from my room while you were on to your office.'

Mal looked at his watch. 'I must call those contacts immediately. Are you all right if I just carry on?'

She nodded without saying anything. She got up and went out on the balcony. For minutes only, the concrete outlines of the city below and around remained clear. And then the sudden nightfall of the east descended. The saw-tooth edges of the concrete began to blur, and against the crude grey tarmac and mortar darkness like the dust of outer space rapidly-cast drifts of violet and blue shadow. And overhead, where not one single cloud remained to dim their brightness, burned the stars in their millions. She gave a startled jump as Mal appeared silently beside her.

'There they are, somewhere,' he said. 'Ross-Gilbert, Buckland, your cousin – each of them listening for the other; treading carefully.'

She shivered. 'Have your office given you any contacts or help at all? We need something.'

'Yes, they have.' He gave her an innocent smile and drained his glass. 'We're going to a lunch party tomorrow at a farm on the outskirts of the city. There are two old friends of mine still in Baghdad whom I used to know years ago. Businessmen. The Safwar brothers, they were called – Vincent and Cyril. You should have seen them in the old days! They used to be real tearaways, the stars of Baghdad society.'

Celia smiled at him, her pale skin and hair in the prevailing darkness the only surfaces to catch the reflected light. 'You're not getting a rise out of me, Mal!'

'Pity. But there you are.'

'Who's going to be at this lunch party that makes it worth our going?'

'Everybody, plus one particular chap called Kulwar Chali, who wouldn't go to meet us separately but who likes to mix with the Safwars and will feel safe in a crowd. I think it's our best chance of making contact. There may be other people there who can help.'

'Why not telephone tonight if you know who they are? We haven't got time to lose.'

'When I say they can help, I mean they can be persuaded to help. They won't just do it over the phone.'

'I see.' She sighed and turned round to go back into the room. The restless tension that she didn't express in words seemed to have the effect of sharpening the focus in which she herself was seen. There was an edge to her. Also, once inside the room, it was too quiet. There was no need for air-conditioning at this time of year, so the loud hum of the building gasping for breath was absent. Being a French hotel of the international sort, the Mediteran was all twentieth-century Louis Quinze and pale blue soft furnishings in roughly fifty-fifty proportions. It was not a place where some-one with any nerves at all could bear to wait for action.

'Let's go out,' Mal said. 'We can't hang around here. The doorman told me of an open-air restaurant near the middle of town by the river where they cook *qusi* and have a dancer. We'll go there for dinner, and keep our eyes open. You never know your luck.'

Chapter 46

EARLIER THAT EVENING another taxi-driver had been going round the city slowly for an hour with no special directions. It was light when they had started, and now darkness had fallen. The driver didn't mind. He merely assumed he's got an unusually conscientious tourist in the back, who wanted to scrutinise every street and boulevard and side alley, and who sat there leaning forward suddenly from time to time as if something questionable caught his eye. They had nothing in common, and neither of them looked for it, although the driver rather liked the other man. He himself was a thirty-year-old Iraqi, speaking no English and lucky to be in one piece. His father had spoken English when most Iraqis learnt some. Even now the cook at the Mediteran, whose dinner Mal and Celia had so wisely avoided, had been trained in the kitchens of the RAF.

The Englishman in the back of the taxi was Henry Allanport, and what his driver didn't realise was that he had, in previous cabs, quartered the city since midday. The intensity of his purpose insulated him from his surroundings at the same time as he scrutinised them with such unrelenting attention. His reasoning was that another Englishman must stand out pretty much as he did himself, and sooner or later he would find Ross-Gilbert. To all intents and purposes he was detached and calm, as he always was. He had merely dropped certain things: enjoyment, which had evaporated into the spacious indifference of an ascetic, and humour. Although his expression was still not heavy, that quirk of ironic humour, which had tended always to flicker in the back of his eye and gave an innate shape to his mouth, had vanished. It left something, or rather an absence of something: a positive vacuum, a black hole. If one caught his eye at a certain angle, it could communicate far more than he intended of the extent of his deadly preoccupation.

The taxi now skirted the public gardens. Every bush, flower and tree was lit, sometimes ingeniously and sometimes crudely, with decorative electric-light bulbs, and a huge electric peacock blazed over the entrance. A group of tall palm trees, lit upwards from the ground, looked like suspended fireworks, their fronds exploding against the dark night sky. The taxi cruised down three sides of the square before turning off in the direction of the river and finally arriving at a restaurant. This was Henry's destination, where a gateway of wire netting and plain rusted steel angles was disarmingly at odds with the status of this, the most fashionable place to eat in Baghdad. The tables were laid under and between the scattering of tamarisk trees typically lit with the glare and shadow of the ever-present unshaded light bulbs. Over an area of perhaps as much as an acre, at wide intervals the tables with their cloths and benches had a focal point in the blazing wood fires in the middle of the ground, over which the rice-stuffed bodies of whole sheep turned on spits. In the flickering or uneven light of fire and electricity, the waiters coming and going, their faces harsh and beaten with the iron of the desert in a way not familiar in the Lebanon, Iran or Egypt, the ubiquitous military presence, the ground dry earth and dust and stones without a blade of grass, there was something of purity – a harsh romanticism that exorcised dullness and impatience.

Henry followed a waiter to a table well to the side and under the trees. He sat down to watch and, if necessary, eat. It wasn't possible to see every table and every occupant at any one time; they were so spread out, and the light an obscuring mixture of sharpness and shadow. The sound of the music was suddenly amplified to a deafening volume and then as quickly again turned partly down. A dancer in traditional dress with bare feet and stomach stepped into the area of carpeted ground near the fires. Her toes curled upward with each step and her body undulated as she moved. Henry watched her as if she were only one in a whole group of dancers, the waiters and the other customers equally drawing his attention.

He saw Celia and Mal Harris within minutes of sitting down. Their table was near the fires. The softer but still rapacious light of the flames glowed on Celia's skin, lighting the backs of her arms and her hair. He observed her without even a momentary start. If the unexpected encounter had been intended as a test of his dislocated emotions, it would have provided a parallel to the man whose knee doesn't jerk to the doctor's hammer. She was simply there. He took no added precaution to avoid being seen by her, and showed absolutely no surprise, as if his overwhelming purpose of catching up with Ross-Gilbert had deadened every other action of the mind. Although both she and Mal Harris from time to time peered around them, he was hidden under the trees and in the sharp patchwork of shadow. He studied her. He felt his heart strain as if against a leash, but he made no move. He watched the rest of the company just as carefully.

The man he was looking for – hoping to catch – would not come. He was dining at the Ambassador's residence that night. It was not a grand occasion, but they enjoyed it. Everyone except one guest was charmed by him. When he left, there was a discussion about him. Lady Herring said, 'Thank heaven you hid that copy of *The Times*. Do you think he'd seen it?'

'Is it true? That's what I want to know!' The First Secretary was a woman, and she had sat next to James and been treated to much of his attention. James himself was driven back in the embassy car to where he was staying. It was an attention he couldn't resist, and one which was to be his undoing.

As if sensing the retirement of his prey, Henry called early for his bill, and left. Celia had turned her chair round to watch the dancing, her seated figure now wholly lit by the fires. Mal Harris was looking for a waiter in order to call for another glass of beer, and nearly caught sight of Henry as he stepped into the clearing near the gate. But the waiter's body intervened. Mal peered round him for a moment, straining his eyes towards the entrance. But made, perhaps, invisible by the darkness of his own purpose, Henry stepped outside the lighted perimeter of the restaurant and immediately disappeared into the night.

Chapter
47

EARLY ON THE following morning, the room servant at the Mediteran opened the curtains in the sitting-room which connected the bedrooms of Mal Harris and Celia Merrin. There was no call to remove yesterday's flowers, as they didn't share in any early life-cycle. He wheeled in a trolley containing breakfast, and on the table deposited the edition of *The Times* that had been referred to in the Residence the night before. Then he knocked briefly at each door, announcing breakfast, and went.

For fifteen minutes everything remained exactly as he had left it. The coffee lost some of its warmth and the toast responded as toast will to being put flat on a plate, by re-absorbing the steam trapped from its own heat and going soft. At the end of that time, Mal Harris emerged fully clothed and shaved and started on his breakfast. He picked up *The Times*, and had just come to the article on Lloyd's, when Celia opened her bedroom door.

'I only want a cup of coffee,' she said. 'Do you mind if I take it back to bed?'

'Not at all,' he said. 'Listen to this before you go.' He held up the paper. 'Article about our friend Ross-Gilbert. *"The DTI yesterday issued warrants for the arrest of former under-writer at Lloyd's, James Ross-Gilbert and his partner Richard Trene, who are accused of misappropriation of funds belonging to their syndicates. However, the extradition notice required to return Mr Ross-Gilbert from America to answer charges in Britain was opposed by Justice Pearson at the DPP on the grounds that damage threatened to the reputation of the financial institutions would exceed the benefit of the prosecution. Lewis Biggin, Labour member for Rutledge South, attacked his opinion in the House as utterly improper that an administrator of justice should allow himself to be influenced by considerations other than the rule of law. He went on to say that innocent members of the public had been defrauded, and the typical defensive posture of this government when dealing with upperclass vested interests was a disgrace."'*

'Ignorant fool!' Celia said. 'I suppose he doesn't know the difference between being a Name and being a member of the public with an insurance risk when he talks about who has been defrauded, and that's why he gets it wrong.'

'Seems like it.'

'Won't he be sick as a wet cat when he finds out! Lewis Biggin, champion of the wealthy upper classes, says the rich should be cheated and the DPP was right, after all. The poor, as previously, must be harmed only by accident, and provided it was done in an attempt to help them. Such as the 1965 Rent Act and the reorganisation of state education under Mrs Williams.' She had sat down and succeeded in buttering a bit of toast, but the long draped sleeve of her dressing-gown and her dishevelled hair got in the way.

Mal was laughing. He said, 'Do you realise it's ten o'clock?'

She took no notice. He ran the back of one finger down his cheek in a characteristic gesture, looking mildly speculative as if considering two possible solutions to one question. In fact, he was wondering how best to break it to Celia that they should set off in half an hour. The colourful squalor that was her version of undress would take some organising.

'What time are we expected at this place?' she asked.

'Well – there'll be people there from about twelve. If we turn up at half past, we'll have a better chance of making our contact, whatever it turns out to be, and leaving early.'

'I'd better get ready, then.'

'I'll be out for half an hour,' he said. 'The Shipping I.S.

watcher has come up to meet me here at the hotel. Shall I see you down in reception in forty minutes?'

She agreed, still looking disturbingly relaxed and un-energetic.

In the foyer, Mal sat down with the same copy of *The Times*, and waited. After five minutes, Matthew Cotteril came through the door. They had a cup of coffee together then he handed Mal Harris the small case he had brought and left. Mal went into the downstairs cloakroom, opened the case, put the contents, excluding the old newspapers with which the case was mainly filled, into his underarm holster, and refastened it. By the time he had handed the case over at the desk and asked them to keep it for him, Celia was just getting out of the lift, and together they went to the door and picked up the first available taxi.

It was a drive of perhaps three-quarters of an hour. The Iran–Iraq War that had laid waste the lives of so many people had had comparatively little effect on the city and the earth. In the first place, the modernisation of Baghdad had done far more to obliterate the old city, and the land itself had never recovered from the destruction of the irrigation system under the Turks. It remained bare brown dust and earth on which a cupful of water regularly sprinkled would immediately grow plants of lurid fertility. And then again, the hand that had sprinkled being laid to rest or blown to Kingdom Come, as the case might be, the earth would temporarily revert to desert. At the moment there was more desert and less culti-vation in this area and over the pleasant brown dusty earth and restful emptiness the taxi bowled along until it arrived at Ramadi.

The house stood in a large compound, the gates guarded by untidy-looking paramilitary watchmen. The servants were already tending fires of rosewood chips in the compound, circled with fish speared lengthways on twigs in the manner for the cooking of *musgoof.* There were many servants, friendly and familiar, responding with smiles to any remark the guests made in passing. In the house itself, Mal stood for a moment on the threshold of one of the large sliding windows that gave from the house into the compound, his hand on

Celia's arm, looking for the hosts, Cyril and Vincent Safwar.

They were both in the room, busy already with their guests, caught in familiar gestures of hospitality as if in all the intervening years they had done nothing else and the only change was a streak or two of white in Victor's curly black hair. They were still the same prosperous would-be sophisticates, their western clothes and expansive manners unaltered by any peripheral changes, their servants' trays as laden as ever with gin and whisky. They now greeted Mal with a double act of reminiscence and bonhomie to which later, when Celia had been dealt with, they returned to add more searching questions. They didn't seem to want to talk about themselves at all; but if Mal was around for long enough, anecdotes would crop up in the conversation about tragicomic encounters with black market trade in American arms or other forms of minor racketeering, near-misses with the military, or exceptionally prosperous deals in the city. And girls, of course.

But in fact their style, so overtly extrovert, really amounted to reserve as they brushed aside Mal's polite questions about the intervening years and, as soon as they could, got down to business. They had obviously discussed in advance what to say. Their commercial and social energy was such that they knew or could find out virtually anything that was going on, and in the last five hours they had made the necessary enquiries about Mal and Celia. At this point Cyril was called away to deal with some administrative detail of the entertainment, but Vincent knew what had been agreed and could carry on without him. He explained that Kulwar Chali was expected to arrive later. Did Mal remember him? They must have met before. He knew, apparently, where Ross-Gilbert was. In fact, he had told Victor either the Seraphin or the Royal Akbar in Shojah. Both of them were extremely ancient hotels in the last remaining old area. Chali would take Mal there. How much? Victor shook his head and swept the question of money aside. Either he'd already paid Chali or he had some outstanding deal. For now, he enjoyed the largesse of power: being influential and rich. And in the future the investment might yield a return in some British trading favour. At which point in the here and now he needed a change of theme. His eyes, always observant, had spotted someone. His ringed hand flat on Mal's shoulder, he gestured to a passing servant who turned at once and offered a loaded tray. With hospitable incitements to come and eat, promises of the excellence of the *musgoof* being prepared on the fires outside and an occasional introduction, he jostled his way through his guests to start a new enterprise.

By now there were perhaps thirty people drifting freely through the house and the compound, glasses in their hands, in the ideal temperature of the bright autumn sun. Mal looked for Celia, and saw that she was being introduced to the household pet, a pelican called Hajji. The large bird, its claws precarious but practised on the gleaming terrazza tiles of the floor, stood placidly among the guests. A tall handsome young Arab stood by Celia, persuading her to stroke the underside of the bird's beak, which was, in his opinion, the softest thing in nature. He took her hand to persuade her, thereby, under the pretext of giving her a pleasurable experience, stealing one of his own. The huge bird liked to have his empty pouch stroked. He stretched his neck forward and then took a few paces towards the door, smelling the fish. A passing servant gave him a gentle push to head him off, and he drifted away, like any other guest, looking for the next encounter.

For as long as the novelty of the place and the experience of being hungry lasted, Mal and Celia found waiting for the arrival of Kulwar Chali no problem. As the time passed when he should have appeared, the logic of continuing to wait when they now knew, essentially, in which area to find Ross-Gilbert, was wearing thin. But to act independently and pre-empt the formalities might be counter-productive as well as causing offence. They had to wait.

'I'll go back into the house,' Mal said, 'and see what Victor has to say.'

Celia walked to the compound gate and went out on to the path that led down to the banks of the Tigris. On the left, an area of perhaps five acres was criss-crossed with the mud-walled maze of *serifas*. At the opening of one of these small mud-built houses of one room in its miniature compound, a young woman stood smiling with her children. Full of eagerness to talk, she asked questions and smiled and beckoned Celia inside. In the beautiful sparse tranquillity of the place, like a figure in a dream Celia followed her into the compound and into the house itself. The woman invited her to sit on the upturned orange-box that was the only furniture, making a sweeping gesture as if to clean it first with her veil. With the flat of her hand she waved aside a thousand flies like a good hostess, but not excessively concerned. Her baby's eyes were under attack. This, too, she commented on in a mixture of sign-language and Arabic, her radiant smile bordering on laughter undiminished. She asked for nothing, but only with hungry joy and ignoring the obvious impediment of language, asked eager questions and chattered, while the older children stood holding pieces of her bright green printed veil.

Outside, by the river, in the increasingly drowsy afternoon, one man stood aimlessly where the dried earth of the path descended to the water. His sparse clothes consisted of a papyrus-coloured rough linen cloth wound round his waist, and his long brown legs had no curve at the calf muscle but only the straight hard look typical of Egyptian wall paintings. Neither he nor the woman seemed to have anything pressing to do. Apparently owning nothing, there were no duties for the woman, nothing to clean or cook. Perhaps this accounted for her air of holiday. As for the man, he merely stood. Where everyone else might be, there was no saying. Perhaps the woman's husband, and all the other dwellers of the *serifas*, worked for the Safwar brothers. Perhaps her husband, even now, was holding one of the heavy silver trays. And perhaps the hand that came forward to take a large glass of gin and tonic with ice and lemons to slake the dust of his journey belonged to Kulwar Chali?

Celia stirred to shake herself free of the warm haze and utter tranquillity of the river bank, the dreaming man, the deserted *serifas*. The smiling woman stood once more in the open air at the gap in the surrounding mud wall that enclosed her house. Her feet and those of her children, decorated with some pieces of thin gold, were dirty against the dry earth. The man standing by the Tigris moved like someone in his sleep.

The scene, so peaceful, had so lured Celia away from the tension of waiting that the deafening explosion that suddenly split the afternoon into screaming fragments hit her own body and that of the woman with an almost dizzing impact. The woman's eyes grew round with the horror as the rending crashes succeeded one another, and she clutched her veil across her mouth and gripped it with her teeth as if another's death might try to get in there.

The explosion came from the rise of ground above, where the cars and taxis were waiting for the guests outside the great Safwar compound. After the heaving thud and crash of the initial explosion, pieces of an ancient black Mercedes taxi were thrown burning into the sky, with noises of tearing and snapping. But above all there was the sound of a man screaming. The man had just arrived, and had been getting out of the car. The driver himself, with his hand on the door-handle, had been blown away, taking the door with him into the scrub fifty yards distant. But Kulwar Chali, the man himself, had had one foot in the car and one on the ground, and now he had neither, but was still screaming, with his coat on fire, dowsing himself in his own blood. Only after an interminable gap did the remainder of the car go up in flames, taking him with it.

Even Victor and Cyril couldn't revive a party after that. The explosion had killed it stone dead, along with Kulwar Chali and the driver. Mal Harris, looking for Celia before all this and not able to find her, had just been told by the guards, seconds before the explosion, that she had wandered out of the compound. A feeling of despair not unlike rage seized him. He found himself by the burning car before the last pieces of metal had landed back on the ground or the driver's body had quite settled where it fell, but the right arm moved once more, falling to a wider angle as if its owner had second thoughts of how to place himself in death. Kulwar Chali was not dead yet. There were other figures near by. When the petrol-tank exploded and put an end to the screams, Mal was still not sure whether there had been a third person involved for the dust and the smoke, but the car was now a sheet of flame. He fought his way back through the crowd of guests.

And then he saw Celia.

She was standing alone on the path beyond the compound as if she were painted against a backdrop. Everything except the brilliant blue of the unperturbed sky were shades of dun and beige and sand, and she was drawn there like a blond figure in a scene painted by Lear. He had never seen anything so beautiful in his life.

'Good God! what do you go frightening the life out of me like that for, Mun?' But he said that when he was still thirty yards away from her, and she couldn't hear. When he reached her, she was still standing completely silent without moving. 'Are you all right?' he said.

She was trying to say something spiteful to pull herself together, but gave up, and fainted.

Chapter 48

'TAKE MY CAR,' Victor Safwar said to Mal. 'The driver knows the district. If there's anything left of it when you've finished, you can send it back.'

He made a joke of it, and slapped Mal on the back, partly to make up for the fact that his brother Cyril had sat down and wept. But granted that that was over-reaction and only typical of dear old Cyril, he himself was feeling none too happy. The car explosion had been a clumsy murder. It would provide an excuse for the police to put up their rates. As far as poor Kulwar was concerned, the matter of a businessman's choice of a hotel should not have such violent repercussions, even if that man was wanted on criminal charges. Victor suspected that undisclosed and more serious aspects of the affair had been kept from him. He felt the stirrings of a sense of grievance, which could only be stifled by renewed commitment and generosity on his part, and this he was doing by offering the use of his car and driver.

Now one of the servants came urgently calling for him, and Victor was glad to have to go. He just shook hands once more, and accepted thanks, with his eyes on the police jeep pulling into the compound, and a last-minute smile for Celia.

'All right, we'd better go,' Mal said. 'No time to lose. How are you feeling?'

She stood up. He put his hand through her arm and they

went out to the compound, but were stopped at the gate. Two guards with properly loaded rifles had replaced the earlier men. A random barrier seemed to have come down on the departing guests. Those who were already outside the compound were free to leave. If Celia hadn't fainted, Mal would have already been back in the outskirts of Baghdad by now, as no doubt was the driver of the taxi he had hired in the first place. But Victor, spotting their problem as he orchestrated the breaking up of his party and the reception of the police, rapidly gave the guard his personal guarantee that Mr Harris had nothing to do with the disturbance – plus a twenty-dinar note – and they were free to leave.

'Do we know where we are going?' Celia asked.

'The area of Shojah. But it's a small area with only two options: the Seraphin and the Akbar.'

It wouldn't take them long to get there. Mal looked at his watch and saw that it was twenty to five: half an hour, perhaps less. The assumption that Kulwar Chali had been killed because he was coming to guide him and Celia to Ross-Gilbert cast doubts on their own safety, which he hadn't yet had time to calculate. Celia was silent. He looked anxiously at her out of the corner of his eye.

She said, without turning to look at him, 'Cut it out, Mal. I'm coming as well, and that's the end of it.' A look of complete innocence washed over his face. 'I know you were thinking of it,' she carried on, 'and if you've got any idea of calling at the Mediteran en route on some pretext and dumping me, forget it.'

He said, after a pause, 'Look here, Cariad, you don't have to come. There's no inherent virtue, you know, in actually witnessing the squalor of violence. It looks to me as if that ham-fisted beginner Richard Trene is using his vast wealth to stay in the game, judging by the fiasco of that exploding taxi. What has that got to do with you?'

'Everything.'

'Henry, you mean?'

She didn't answer. Only she knew that under the surface of her skin the pulses were still trembling with revulsion, and even in the car she could smell the reek of burning blood like a sensual nightmare. But neither was she coming all this distance to fade at the last moment. Mal's loyalties were first to the interests of his employees, and only she had come to take care of Henry.

'What can you do, that I can't?' he pleaded. 'I'll look after Henry.'

'Oh, shut up, Mal!' she eventually snapped. 'I'm sorry I fainted. But that's the only concession you're getting.'

Chapter
49

OPPOSITE THE SERAPHIN HOTEL on the other side of the road, a line of equally ancient wood and plaster houses were coated with the same greyish mud dust. The area was old only in the sense that, as it stood or half fell down, it represented continuity, ancient buildings being repaired or replaced in patches and in familiar ways. In the wide gaps between the buildings on the side opposite the Seraphin, one caught glimpses of the Tigris, the banks littered with rubbish. In the thick ooze of its shallows a certain amount of incredible washing went on.

The Seraphin itself was decorated with the gap-toothed remains of elaborate wood carvings, and along the length of its first floor there stretched a wooden balcony. It was on to this that James Ross-Gilbert stepped now and looked briefly about him. This, he thought, was to be his last night before returning to Miami in the morning, and every minute dragged. By his watch it was ten past five. At seven thirty he would eat once more in what he considered was the disgusting dining-room below anaesthetising the bacteria in the food with whisky poured out of a Johnny Walker bottle but made up north in Babylon. Ross-Gilbert was no skilled traveller. The only version of practical geography he knew was a chain of de luxe hotels, and for this late encounter with the real thing he had only loathing. He loathed the *qusi* that tasted the way sheep are only meant to smell, and he equally loathed the sweet mint tea, and the filthy river, and the raffish squalor of the streets.

He stared now with unromantic resentment at a man who went by below him on the opposite side of the road, his bare feet moving gracefully on the dried hard mud. He wore only a dusty loincloth but carried, looped on one finger, a pair of fish tied through their mouths with grass. He passed a man half-hidden under the chassis of a dismantled taxi. Another, sitting on the steps of what was meant to be a shop, constantly touched his face with the characteristically eastern hand movement of rigid knuckles and long fingernails, his robes gathered under him. It was not a wealthy district. James felt humiliated in having to be there, but it wouldn't happen again. It had been a mistake not to accept Dick Trene's offer to get rid of Allanport, and if it resulted in this sort of ridiculous situation, he would have to reconsider.

Ross-Gilbert did not look at the windows opposite on a level with his own. A fair number of them were hung with scraps of lace, occasionally a rickety shutter left half across a pane. And behind one was a man who was watching out for him, and having marked his appearance on the balcony, turned and disappeared.

Ross-Gilbert himself half-turned, and was about to go back into his room when he saw something, and froze. A different sort of man was coming down the street. He had rounded the corner a short distance away and was already nearly under the window. But if he had been a hundred yards distant, James would still have recognised Henry Allanport. In the tired and filthy scenario, he appeared like a vengeful breath of fresh air. James stepped back, but one half of the french windows had closed behind him and blocked his retreat. Henry was making for the Seraphin, but now he stopped as if a supernatural awareness drew his attention, and he looked up. James, who had no choice, met his gaze. He just stood there, drawing on the accumulated courage of all his past triumphs. But it might be like trying to warm a house with a stock of dried ferns, that made an impressive show but wouldn't last. He had a respite of only seconds as Henry, having so much at his leisure and so inflexibly, marked him, and disappeared under the balcony to

enter the building and mount the stairs. Looking for escape
on either side, James saw none. There was no point in himself,
an inexpert climber, scrambling over the barriers that kept
the sections of the balcony private to each room. Turning his
attention inwards, his bedroom door had no key. The bathroom, such as it was, was outside. His heart beat with a vile
tearing rhythm, and muscles on hs face that had been slack
from fears of calculated detachment pricked under the
scourge of fear.

The door opened, and Henry came in. James saw at once
that he was changed. For an instant the realisation gave him
a surge of hope, but then he also saw that it was not in his
own favour. This change, whatever it was, had burned the
oxygen away from the empty spaces that exist in some men's
spirits and make them easy company. Henry, who had been
an excellent example of just such a man, was no more. He
stood now, having closed the door behind him.

James said, 'What is all this nonsense, Henry?' He managed
to put into the question just the right tone of stricture. 'What
are you doing here?' You could have sworn that he was in a
position to make his objections very uncomfortable for someone unless listened to. A slight quirk to the corner of Henry's
mouth registered his appreciation. 'Well?'

'I intend to kill you.'

'This can't be simply because you hold me responsible for
losses on the Merchaum syndicates!'

'A negligible matter!'

'No!' James corrected him, like a responsible man at a
board meeting picking up on an important point, 'It's very
serious.'

Henry smiled, but not in such a way as to give confidence.
'You stole it,' he said. 'James Ross-Gilbert.'

The pronouncing of the name at the end of the sentence
gave James a shock to hear. A simple matter, it conveyed a
depth of hatred too cool to be unsettled.

Henry said nothing more. He carried a small plastic bag
printed with the label of a Miami store, and he had taken the
gun out of it before James had had time to move. Holding it
level, he stepped over to one side. His hand was steady. His

eyelids drooped very slightly, as they always did, but their expression was no longer affectionately mocking.

James tried another tack. He said, 'Don't you want to understand why I did it?'

'No,' Henry said, and raised the gun and fired.

There was no silencer on the gun, and if it had fired properly, it would have made a noise to bring everyone running. As it was, there was a sharp crack, but not the explosive overtone of a true shot. Furious incredulity replaced Ross-Gilbert's other emotions, and he took a heavy step forward, knocking over the small table that had been in front of him.

'Don't move,' Henry said. His voice, cold and sharp, was just as commanding as James could be. 'Accidental,' he said. He pronounced the word with frigid calm. 'That was just your luck. My father's gun always did have one defective chamber.'

'Lord Allanport, I'm sorry . . .'

'And I apologise for the misfire,' he said calmly.

But as he flexed his arm again to press the trigger, the door behind him opened, and Mal's voice said, 'Lord Allanport, give me just five minutes. Ross-Gilbert, get away from the window.' Henry saw relief flood the face of his enemy. Mal said urgently, 'Lord Allanport, for the sake of the other Names, please wait. I have papers here for him to sign which will release millions of pounds back into the Names' accounts.'

Henry, who had not taken his eyes off Rose-Gilbert at the initial interruption, now, without lowering his gun or actually turning aside, acknowledged Mal Harris, and in doing so caught sight of Celia. An ambiguous expression fleetingly crossed his face, but he said nothing. Mal Harris, who hadn't completed the movement of actually coming into the room, now did so with the measured care of a cat stepping over a game of chess in progress. He kept his eyes on the two men, and with a gesture, brought Celia into the room behind him and closed the door.

'Thank heaven you've come,' Ross-Gilbert said with fulsome relief. 'This man's completely mad.'

'Stay where you are.'

'I'm not moving,' James said, just an undertone of patronising reassurance conveying the message that he knew how to make allowances for a sick man. But he stayed where he was.

Mal Harris glanced through the window. He saw the curtain opposite hooked back in the building where, for a split second, he thought he had caught sight of Geoffrey Buckland as he passed going up the stairs. Now that he saw the window, he knew for certain that he was there.

'Let me explain myself.' Mal spoke hurriedly, but like a man pressed for business. 'You don't know me, Mr Ross-Gilbert. My name's Mal Harris. My firm, Shipping Investigation Securities, has been hired by a Lloyd's agency to track down stolen funds from the Merchaum syndicate accounts, and return them.'

Ross-Gilbert stared at him with lordly disdain. 'What have these baseless accusations to do with me?'

'I want your signature on these documents, and the pass names for the fund in Luxembourg and the Isle of Man.'

'Certainly not.'

'Otherwise, I'm afraid I can do nothing to assist you with Lord Allanport.'

'What do you mean?'

'What I say.'

Ross-Gilbert's eyes went to the gun and back to Mal Harris. 'I refuse absolutely. I won't bargain.'

Celia, who had so far stood silently on the other side of the door from her cousin, looked at the man who had so proudly run his yacht into the harbour at Monte Carlo. 'I must say,' she suddenly exclaimed, 'if it's not exactly guts you've got, it's some other part of the anatomy nobody's quite got round to naming yet.'

Perhaps, even on the edge of the grave, James could induce some woman to throw a flower in after him.

'I have ten release documents here, and the two certificates,' Mal Harris continued. He walked to the table that had been knocked over and set it upright. He put the papers on it and took out his pen.

Ross-Gilbert picked one up in his hand and then another. 'Why should I take responsibility for these losses?' he said. 'You're asking me to impoverish myself to cover for others.'

Even here, in a run-down Iraqi hotel scheduled for demo-
lition and before such an audience, he could still tilt the truth
with disconcerting skill, and he could still want to do it. Into
the minds of both Celia and Henry a minute seed of doubt
fell. But an expression of such cold-blooded ferocity came on
to Mal Harris's face that James checked himself.

'You stole this money,' he heard him say quietly. 'Not a
penny of it is yours. You're not being asked to cover for the
mistakes of others.'

'That depends on how you see it. Lloyd's business is very
complex.'

'You are a liar,' Mal Harris said, 'and I am very well
acquainted with Lloyd's business. I can assure anyone who
cares to ask that you are a liar and a thief, and each of these
papers represents money you have misappropriated. I'll have
them back, or I'll leave you to Lord Allanport.' He held out
his pen.

James said, 'I resent that.'

No one moved or answered. His face stern, his mouth
turned down at the corners, his bearing judicial and indomitable, James eventually took the pen. He pulled up a chair
and sat to bring himself on a level with the low table. But
again he turned over some papers and slammed them down
with decided anger. 'Outrageous! I'll be left without a penny.
You've even got the deeds here of my house in London!'

'I don't owe you any explanation, Mr Ross-Gilbert. Sign.
And if my reasoning doesn't appeal to you, try the fact that
otherwise Lord Allanport will shoot – this time, to kill.'

Ross-Gilbert took the pen. For all his arrogant language,
he looked sick. He glanced aside into Henry's face. 'You'll
keep him off?' He bent down. It took him some time.

When he had finished, Mal said, 'The pass names.'

He half straightened up, thinking, pushing the straight lock
of hair back in a gesture that anyone who had worked with
him would have recognised. Then he wrote them down.

'Now move back, Lord Allanport.' While Mal was bent
down, he had taken his own gun from its holster. 'Please.'

Henry didn't move, but neither could he shoot. Keeping his
gun on him, Mal glanced around the room to make sure that

Celia was still out of the line of the window, then said, 'Walk into the middle of the room, Mr Ross-Gilbert.'

Ross-Gilbert obeyed, not knowing why he was being asked to move. In complying with Mal Harris's order, he must have thought he had something yet to gain. He moved into the middle of the room, keeping his eyes on Henry Allanport, until he stood where he was told, with his back in front of the window. Across the street, Geoffrey Buckland got him in the telescopic sight, and tensed his finger on the trigger. For two and a half seconds Ross-Gilbert lived, a poor man. For two and a half seconds he knew he hadn't come out ahead in the end. For an instant he wondered what the hell he was going to do about Philippa. And then, from across the street, there came what he was waiting for. The sharply muffled sound of a bullet from a rifle with an eighteen-inch silencer snapped into his back and carried him a yard forward across the floor before he dropped. A second bullet after he had fallen whined over his body into the door.

Mal put away his gun and picked up the sheaf of papers. He kicked the shutter across the window, then went over to Henry Allanport, and said, gently, holding up the papers, 'That was worth getting, wasn't it?'

Henry looked at him like a man still in a dream. He said, 'Yes.'

'You can put away your gun, then.'

'Who shot him?'

'Gentleman from London. He was in the house across the street with a rifle and telescopic sight. Someone else wanted Ross-Gilbert just as badly as you, it seems. It's just as well to have let them do it.'

'Another Name?'

Mal shook his head. 'No.'

'Then he's got him,' he said with a distasteful glance down at the dead man. 'Come on, Celia, let's go home.'

He put his arm over her shoulder, not looking closely at her for the moment or seeing how she felt.

She said, 'Mal.'

He looked up, but shook his head. 'No, Cariad. Forget it now.'

For a moment he saw a remembered image, like a beautiful watercolour of a girl standing near the banks of the Tigris. And then the invisible hand of Fate turned the page.